MW00943359

A Bit of Colored Ribbon: A Novel of the Civil War

By
Craig S. Whitmore

"A soldier will fight long and hard for a bit of colored ribbon."
Napoleon Bonaparte

This book is dedicated to the National Underground
Railroad Freedom Center – Cincinnati, Ohio
And to the legacy of hundreds of anonymous freedom
workers of the Underground Railroad

To the Reader

This is a work of fiction. Actual historic characters are introduced only to interact with the fictional characters and help them tell their story. In this sequel to *The Last Roar* I have explored once again the chronicle of the fictional Armstrong family. After serving with Oliver Hazard Perry in the *Battle of Lake Erie* during the *War of 1812*, George Armstrong realized his dream of settling and forming his own business as a builder in Ashtabula, Ohio. His long-time friendship with Daniel Dobbins of Erie, Pennsylvania, allied him to Dobbins' clandestine work with the anti-slavery movement of the Underground Railroad. His passion for the cause of freedom gained him the respect of many sympathetic supporters, not just in the Society of Friends, but also among others who vocally opposed the institution. The yearning for his children and their children to always act on the side of peace and justice was the legacy he left them. When the institution of slavery finally became intolerable to George's son Seth and grandson Marcus, the two inevitably followed their father and grandfather's example and began their illegal work as secret conductors on the Underground Railroad. Not long after, Marcus' sister near Columbus, Ohio, enlisted in the cause of freedom as a station master.

It is in his capacity as conductor that Marcus encounters Nat, an escaped slave from Alabama. The cruel conditions and treatment make escape or death Nat's only two options against a lifetime of servitude. But this is more than a slave escape story. It is a story of sacrifice, of striving to realize a man's potential, of lives placed on the front lines in wars against oppression and prejudice.

At the beginning of the Civil War, slaves who escaped or were freed by invading Union armies tried in vain to join the Northern army to fight for the cause. Because of the inherent prejudice born of over a century of slavery, even the North turned down these men of color as soldiers. However, they were initially allowed to follow along on campaigns with some armies. Called contraband of war, these former slaves served in whatever capacity their experience had given them, often as cooks, launderers, mule drivers, and even as personal servants to some white officers. They knew full well that to be captured by a rebel soldier meant instant death or a return to slavery, yet many freely chose to serve, awaiting the day they too could wear the federal uniform.

In telling this story, I have rendered some dialect as close to the patterns of the educated and of the uneducated persons of this period for the purpose of showing how language separated classes of people, whether they were white or black, wealthy or poor, urban or backwoods. The language has a distinct rhythm of its own. In no way is the intent to diminish the character of any one class of people, rather it is to reflect on how language restricted people to their own societies while excluding others from crossing societal barriers, how language is power, and the usage of the language is in itself a kind of freedom.

I am indebted to the outstanding work of the *Slave Narrative Collection*, recordings made by the *Federal Writers' Project* in 1936, and sponsored by *The Library of Congress*. The painstaking written transcription of the *Slave Narrative Collection* that rendered into print the recorded dialects peculiar to those former slaves provided me with invaluable research in recreating the speech patterns of that society. Though Nat is a fictional character of the author's imagination, he is, in fact, a composite of several former slaves whose varied stories were transcribed in true dialect in the *Collection*. It was in the language of their recollections that Nat's story was conceived.   – CSW.

Thanks to the many who aided in research for the writing
of this narrative.

Ashtabula Maritime Museum – Ashtabula, Ohio
The Bierbower Home – Maysville, Kentucky
Chickamauga and Chattanooga National Military Park
Fort Oglethorpe, Georgia
Federal Writers' Project – The Library of Congress
Haines House – Alliance, Ohio
Harriet Beecher Stowe Slavery to Freedom Museum
Washington, Kentucky
The John Rankin House – Ripley, Ohio
Joy Melcher – Civilwarlady.com
Kent Dorr – Sons of Union Veterans of the Civil War
Ohio Department
Lee White – Chickamauga and Chattanooga
National Military Park
National Underground Railroad Freedom Center
Cincinnati, Ohio
Oberlin College – Oberlin, Ohio
The Ohio Historical Society – Columbus, Ohio
Salem Historical Society – Salem, Ohio
Shiloh National Military Park – Shiloh, Tennessee
The Spread Eagle Tavern – Hanoverton, Ohio
Stones River National Battlefield
Murfreesboro, Tennessee
U.S. Grant Birthplace Historical Site – Point Pleasant, Ohio
The 73rd Ohio Volunteer Infantry Regiment Band
John M. Huffman, Jr., Director
Editorial assistance:
Kathy Mackey Willis – Cleveland, Ohio; Michael T. Rodgers
– Beaumont, Texas; Brandon Babin – Ashland, Ohio
Research assistance:
Eric P. Mayer – Ashland, Ohio

Part One

Part Two

Chapter One

Ashbie Farm, Cypress Grove – Between Stevenson
and Huntsville, Alabama
Autumn 1860

Samuel slammed the pitchfork into the pile of hay.
He jumped down from the wagon, cautiously peered out the barn door. Master John Ashbie still lounged on the porch swing of the big house, intently reading the newspaper, as was his afternoon custom. Nat pulled on the last nail, separating the shoe from the hoof, flung it angrily into the wooden box. Samuel stepped toward Nat, determined.

"I's gwanna do it. 'n you cain't stop me no mattuh how ha'd you tries."

Nat pointed the pincer handle at Samuel's face, gesturing, a low passionate voice. "You know dey cotches you up, you's gwan be whipped till de blood run agin. Marse John have 'em beat us all too if dey t'ink we know'd 'bout it and don't tell. T'ink what you's doin' to *us*!"

"I t'ink what I's doin' to *me* if'n I's to stay. Dat's what I be t'inkin' on!"

Frustrated, Nat tossed the pincers aside. "Aw, Samuel! Samuel, you jes' gwan bring trouble. An' how you's gwan make it, huh? You fool, dey kill you!"

"No, suh. Marse John won' kill me. I's too val'ble. He need all de field hands he kin git. Killin' one jes' make mo' wo'k for de res' dat's left. Den he nevuh git de fields ha'vested. Oh, he may git me a whippin', but he not gwanna kill me."

"If'n you know you's gwan get a whippin' den what you gwan chance it fo'? Samuel, you be t'inkin' about sum'uns else fo' change!"

"Tryin' and gittin' beat cain't be any mo' bad den bein' stuck he'e."

"Yes it can! I seed it 'afo'e. Looka he'e, Samuel, sometime de Lawd let you stays stuck so's you kin he'p dem what's left. So's you can be watchin' out fo' each othuh."

"Nat, don' you wanna be free?"

"Sho' do. But I don' wants to run from de hounds neithe'. I seed how dey tear up dat man dat be hidin' in de corn crib las' fall. You 'members dat?"

"I does. Warn't much left o' him atter dey done gnawin' on him. Marse John say he deserve it. I disremembers anybody ever deserve dat kin' a' killin'."

"Dey be t'inkin' *you* deserves dat kin'a killin', fool!" Nat held firmly to Samuel's elbow, his fingers digging deep into the muscle. Samuel glared deeply into the brown eyes. Nat saw the anger, the defiance. He let loose his grip and waited. Samuel shook his arm, rubbed the soreness.

"I gots to go."

"I know," Nat said quietly. "I knows I cain't stops you. Lawd knows I wanna. But not now, Samuel. At leas' wait til de dark o' de moon."

"Awright, den," he said firmly. "I waits. Dat be only fo' days, and den I follows de Drinkin' Gourd. Nat, you come wid me. We be he'pin' each othuh'. You and me, we lose dem hounds and have a good ol' time. Ain't nobody better'n you in de woods. And when we gets to de Nort', we's freemen. Den we see 'bout buyin' Semalina and Maggie and some o' de ot'ers and bringin' dem up nort' too."

Nat thought long, shook his head. "We ain't got dat kin' o' money."

"No, not yet. But I hears dat you can makes money and den de ab'litionists he'ps you buys families."

"Samuel, I don't rightly know where Maggie is anymo'. She sold off somewhe'es in Geo'gia now. I likes to see her, I likes to buy her, but it ain't no use. I don' even know where to look."

"But Nat, de ab'litionist people, dey kin fin' 'em. I knows dat. I talks to a field hand las' mont' when we was loadin' dat wagons for Marse John. He say dat a man pertendin' to be one o' de pattyrollers stopped him in de fields and as' him directions. Den he say kinda quiet-like dat he ain't no pattyroller, but he a ab'litionist. An' den he tells him all 'bout 'scapin' and dat he kin he'p him."

Nat thought on this, didn't like the sounds of it. Too good to be true, he thought. "Black man shouldn't be trustin' dem white folk like dat. You know dey been doin' dat 'round Marse William's place, you know, ove' t' de Richardson's? I hear dey do de same t'ing and some o' de slaves runs out to join 'em. What do you t'ink dey find out, boy?"

Samuel stared long into Nat's eyes. "I don' know. You tells me, Nat."

"Dey find out de man is a *real* pattyroller, and he cotches dem po' niggas up and he takes 'em back to Marse William for de reward money. Den Marse William has all fo' o' dem staked out in de barn, naked as dey was borned, an' dey all be whipped wit' de rawhide 'til dey nea'ly dead." He paused for emphasis, leaned forward into Samuel's face. "*Dat's* what dem fake ab'litionists du to you too, boy. Now you be meditatin' on dat while you gets back to work. I gots to get dis here horse shoed for Marse John. He ain't nevuh had cause to whup me, and I ain't 'bout to give him none neithuh', ain't dat right, Dan'l?" He patted the horse's rump and pushed him aside to lift his hind leg. "An' you git dat pitchfork and you gets dat wagon unloaded, boy."

"Yeh, you jus' wants to stay here so's you kin go to courtin' over on de Richardson's place. I knows dat. I ain't stupid. I knows what you been doin' on dem errands," Samuel laughed loudly and stuck the pitchfork deep into the mound of hay on the wagon, swung it hard around and flung the hay into the corner of the barn.

3

Nat held the horse's hoof between his knees, bent over, grabbed up the tool. "You jes' keeps jawin', Samuel. Dat's what you's good at." Nat chuckled quietly and grasped the pincers, pulled the nail. "And Dan'l, you jes' keeps holdin' dat leg still. Cause dat's what you's good at."

+ + + + +

Nat could count every day he had been there on the farm, every day since the speculators had brought him here and sold him to John Ashbie. Ten years, three months, and nine days he had worked on *Cypress Grove,* the Ashbie farm of nearly a thousand acres and nearly a hundred slaves. It didn't take John Ashbie long to recognize that even as a child Nat had a way with the animals. In two short weeks he had him tending the few cows he owned, then in a few months' time, helping Big Jim the blacksmith in the stables. Big Jim took Nat on as his apprentice, had him pulling at the bellows on iron-makin' days. He recognized his ability with the horses, and soon had Nat training as a farrier. For Nat, it was a dream come true. He was out of the fields and into Ashbie's good graces. John Ashbie, of course, never once allowed him to forget that he was his property, but if he was to make the most out of a situation, it was by using this opportunity served to him on a plate. And he relished it.

Once Big Jim had trained him to the master's liking, Ashbie permitted Nat to travel with a pass to neighboring farms and plantations, hired out to equestrian duties for two dollars a day, half of which belonged to Ashbie. Yet he didn't mind much. None of the other field hands earned any money, except for the young girls who occasionally hired out for fifty cents to neighboring plantations and farms on special wash days before some big event. Today was just such an occasion.

Nat received permission to drive half a dozen of the girls to the Richardson place.

The four days had already passed and Nat still refused to discuss any plan with Samuel about escaping his bondage and trying for the North, abolitionist or no. When Nat had finished harnessing the wagon, he led the horse out of the barn to load up the girls, and he noticed a black foot dangling from under the wagon bed, near the back axle. John Ashbie waited at the big house with travel passes for Nat and the six girls, and Nat immediately recognized the danger. If Samuel was found under the wagon, he would not get off of suspicion too. This would kill any trust Ashbie had in him, if Ashbie didn't kill Nat with the whip first. He patted Daniel on the rump and walked to the big house, leaving the wagon and its stowaway in the shade of a large white oak tree.

He spoke low, "Marse John, will you be a-comin' wit' us today?" He tossed his head to the side, indicating the wagon and its secret rider.

"Not today," Ashbie said, missing the signal. "Why?"

"I's jus' wonderin' if'n mebbe you be watchin' Dan'l there." He repeated the same flick of the head toward the wagon. "I shoed him 'tuther day and he look like he feel a might po'ly."

Ashbie still missed the hint. "He looks fine to me, Nat. You done good work on him."

"Thank ya' Marse John, only if'n he was to t'row a shoe or some'n 'cause o' de weight he pullin' I jes' wants—"

"Nat, now what you bellyachin' about? I said there was nothin' wrong with him and there's an end to it," he said annoyed. "And he ain't pullin' that much weight with you and these here gals. Now y'all go on and get aboard there. The Richardsons will be expecting you, and I want no dilly-dallying."

Nat closed in on Ashbie, leaned his head so his lips nearly touched his master's neck and spoke in a whisper, "I calculate somet'in wrong wit' de way dat dere wagon is pullin' and I jes' wants you to t'row your eye over it and be sure." He stepped back, respectfully kept his head lowered, waited for the words to take effect. After a beat, he looked Ashbie in the eye as an equal, winked, nodded his head slightly and tossed it in the general direction of the oak tree. "Please, Marse John." His eyes pleaded.

Ashbie squinted his eyes toward the wagon, looked long and hard, looked back at Nat and smiled, nodding, spoke loudly, "I believe I'll have a look at Dan'l there just once before you leave, Nat. Want to make sure you did your work on him properly. A beast without good shoes ain't worth a damn for workin'."

"Yessuh, Marse John. Dat's what I a'ways say. You's needs good shoes to work in. I hope I done him good." And he quickly shuffled along behind him on the carriageway.

Ashbie walked in long quick strides to the wagon. "Oh, I'm sure you did, Nat. Lemme just inspect the wagon first. Make sure you've fixed them axles good. Don't want them breaking down on the road."

At the word axles, another foot appeared and in an instant Samuel had rolled out of hiding and ran like a jumped rabbit for the slave quarters. Ashbie roared with laughter, "No, I guess you have the wagon all set the way it should be, Nat."

Nat grinned, "Yessuh, sho'ly do now. Well, I gets de gals here and we be getting' to de Richardson's. Don't want nobody to slow us down, ya know?"

"Yes, you get goin' now, Nat. No moon tonight, and it will be black as pitch. You be back before sundown 'cause you know the patrollers will be out on the roads lookin' for the likes o' y'all."

"Yessuh, Marse John. I be getting' back 'afo'e sundown. Don't you be worryin' yo'self." Nat climbed into the wagon seat, the girls all sitting in the back of the wagon on the clean hay he had spread for them.

"And Nat, I trust you, so you be comin' back with all the heads you took with you. I will take care of Samuel fer ya'."

"Thank ya', Marse John. And please don't go too hard on him. He jes' a young buck what wanna see de Richardson place, I guess. He be awright."

"Never you mind about Samuel. Now you git on goin'."

Nat thoroughly enjoyed the short drive to *Belle Vista*, the Richardson's plantation. The country road stretched for nearly three miles, passing two deep woods, occasionally bordered by split rail fences, occasionally by stone walls piled high to keep cattle from crossing out onto the road, and subsequently into a neighbor's butchering shack and smokehouse. On either side of the road stretched the fields. Near the road, cotton, mostly harvested, bore the few white tell-tale tufts among spindly dark sienna stalks. They quivered in the crisp morning air. A haze rested along the valley floor, and the sunlight filtering through the trees bathed the limbs in a smoky sheen. And out there in the distance Nat heard the singing:

Go down, Moses
Way down in Egypt la-and
Tell ol'
Pharaoh,
Let my people go.

He listened to the girls behind him humming softly, sweet harmonies joining in a counterpoint with the slaves' melody out on the field. The songs never changed from one farm to another, one plantation to the next. All of the field hands knew the same songs. Few could read, and none could read well, at least none that he knew. Yet they all knew the same songs, as though some Methodist hymnal had circulated from place to place, and all had memorized it. But these tunes were all originals, composed through the bitterness and through the longing and learned by rote through repeated singing, sharing their burden in song. Through the grey-white haze of the morning light he saw the dark figures coming through the fog, descending en masse on the remaining acres of cotton. And he thanked God on the spot that he was out of the fields, that he was driving a wagon, that he was as close to free as he might ever be. He was livin' the life.

Then reality returned. The approach of several horses drowned out the singing, and he looked behind, then ahead. No horses seen, but he could hear them, and they were coming hard at the gallop. The girls in the back of the wagon dropped their voices low, then silenced and listened. Behind them. No, they were in front, thundering out of the haze. The dark figures pressed on, charging directly toward Nat and his companions, and Daniel pinned his ears back, stomped at the ground, lifting his fore hooves up and landing heavily.

"Easy now, Dan'l. Don' you be carryin' on like dat," Nat spoke softly, gently. He tugged tightly on the reins, holding Daniel, who spooked and began to raise up again. The five horsemen rode in and immediately reigned in their horses, encircling the wagon, one large gloved hand grabbing hold of Daniel's harness cheek piece. Daniel jerked his head, nearly pulling the man from his saddle.

"Easy, Dan'l, dey don' mean you no harm. Mo'nin' gentlemen!"

"Gentlemen? Did you hear that Zeb? He called us gentlemen! We ain't no gentlemen! And you ain't our equal that you can be addressin' us as equals neither!"

"No suh, Boss, we ain't equal, dat's de God's trut'. No suh, I mean we ain't nevuh gwan be equal. No suh."

"Shut yer black face!" said the man called Zeb, whom Nat immediately guessed was the leader.

"Yass'm."

"Ya' got yer papers with ya'?" growled Zeb.

"Sho' do." Nat scrambled to pull the mass of papers from the leather pouch on his seat. He thrust them out to the man who studied them for a moment, went through each paper, scanned over them, counted the papers, counted heads of the girls in the back.

"Richardson's, huh?"

"Yassuh, Richardson's am de place we gwine to. *Belle Vista* am de place, suh. Have to get dese gals here for wash day, don'cha know. Marse William, he sho' like to see dem clo'se shine all 'bout. Umm, hmm."

"Well, boy, y'all kin git on down the road and be quick about it. No dilly-dallyin'!"

"Yassum, boss. No dillyin' and no dallyin'." He put the wad of passes back into his leather pouch. "C'mon now, Dan'l, move dem feet."

Nat shook the harness reins and the horse lurched forward, sending the girls sprawling in the hay. The five riders delighted in that spectacle and laughed heartily as they rode on past. The catcalls and epithets came thick and Nat leaned back to the girls, keeping his eyes fixed on the road ahead, spoke over his shoulder.

"You's jes' never mind dem boys. Dey ain't gwanna harm y'all. Dey jes' be sportin' witchya. You straighten you's frocks now, and get youselfs fancied up a' best you can now 'afo'e we gets to de Richardsons. Won't be fittin' fo' you'ns all to be dirtified when we gets to de wash stands."

"Alright, Nat. You jus' keeps dat horse and yo' eyes on de road and we get all fixed up," Izzy called.

Izzy was a bright-eyed, bubbly young light brown girl of about fifteen. She didn't exactly know how old. She loved to tease Nat, played up to him, trying to get him to court her, heartily disappointed that he had not. She had only worked on the farm for a year, but she had moved rapidly to make an impression. Nat played along, but his mind was set elsewhere and he couldn't allow himself to give in to her advances. It had been two years since Maggie had been sold off when she was yet fifteen, and he had learned a hard lesson. Never get too excited about someone who might be gone tomorrow— or even before the end of the day. One heartbreak was enough for a lifetime.

Then there was Emma. His heart pounded when he thought of her at the Richardson plantation. He looked forward to every opportunity to spend some time talking with her, or rather listening. She too could be gone at any time, yet she had gained favor with William Richardson's wife, Annabelle, and had become her personal servant. No more field work for her. She was twenty-two, two years older than Nat, and seemed to enjoy his company, at least that part she could share when he came to do errands on the farm. He didn't know how she dressed when he wasn't there, but she always looked sparkling on his visits, sometimes sporting a bit of colored ribbon in her hair, matching her dress. He had images of her getting ready just for him, hoped that it was so. And he especially loved her way of talking. She had a genteel quality in her voice, something that was unheard of in the coarse field hands. He felt uncomfortable, tongue-tied when she would give him a dipper of water, or when she would ask him to help her to carry an armload of firewood on his errand days. When he worked in the barn on the Richardson's horses, Emma would find a reason to come to the barn to check his progress, bring him a drink, and then linger. She could talk about anything in a gentle easy manner, and he felt awkwardly inferior to her. He would answer her questions, self-consciously attempting to make conversation with her, and he just knew she secretly snickered at his ways. Yet he always returned. And so here he was again, driving Daniel on, past the cotton fields, past the rows of massive Spanish moss-adorned white oaks lining the road – oaks that had been growing there since before the white men forced out the former masters, the Creek, the Chickasaw and the Cherokee, and settled their lands. Nat thought, how much longer until the white oak outlasted the white masters? The sun had in due course burned off the morning haze, and the morning's early fall colors were vibrant, complemented by the chorus of mockingbird and catbird calls from their colorful perches. Nat slowed Daniel to a walk and he immersed himself in the richness of the countryside. This was the section of the ride he relished, and he couldn't get enough of it, its sights, its sounds, its smells. He approached the turn onto the lane, and the big house in the distance loomed large in front of them. Izzy stood up, leaned onto the bench beside Nat. She rested her head close to his.

"Dat sho' am one fine big house, Nat. Don'cha jes' wanna own one o' dem big houses o' yo' own some day?"

"No sense in t'inkin' on dat, girl. Dat never gwine happen dis side o' de Pearly Gates. And dat jes' de way it is."

"Shaw! Yo' head ain't got no dream, fool. You jes' ben' down to de massa an' let him step all over ya' and den, atter dat, you's layin' down and he do it some mo'. Dat's what I be seein'. I's gwanna live in de North one day, and I's gwanna git me a big house fo' my own."

"Now, how you gwine to do dat, when you stuck away down here in Alabama? Izzy, you ain't never gwan live in de North."

"Kin so! I kin run. Samuel, he gwanna run sometimes and I's gwan run wit' him." She placed her lips close to his ear and kissed his neck playfully. "Unless you's wantin' to run wit' me."

Nat gently brushed her head away. "Well, you be t'inkin' on dat whilst you doin' de wash fo' de white folk today. Den you tell me how it is, cause it ain't gwanna happen. Now y'all jes' sits back in de wagon 'n you jes' waits 'til I gits Dan'l all tied up."

William Richardson and his large toothy grin appeared at the steps of the massive porch, thumbs tucked under his gold-trimmed lavender waistcoat lapels, stood under the high roof where the giant Doric columns framed him, making him an insignificant ornament to decorate the mansion. It didn't escape Nat's attention. We all small in de scheme o' t'ings, he thought. He smiled broadly in return and strolled to the front walkway. "Marse William, it am so good to see you ag'in."

Richardson stepped lively down the treads, almost skipping to the horse rail in front of the house. "Well, it's good to have you back here, Nat. I've been looking forward to you bringing the girls over today. I have some shoes needing replaced on my bays out there in the barn, as soon as you get some refreshment and get an apron on."

"Yassuh, Marse William, I be gittin' to it right off."

"Time enough for that later. You come on up to the house first and say hello to the missus," he gushed. "And I 'spect you want to say hello to Emma too."

"Oh, I don' wanna take her 'way from de housewo'k. I be awright in de barn right off."

Richardson clapped him on the shoulder, which was his way with nearly everyone, white or black. "Nonsense, boy. You will sit here for a moment and visit."

"Yass'm Marse William. If you's sayin' so."

"I say so," he chortled. "Dear!" he called loudly. "Belle! Nat's here with the wash gals!"

"I'm right here, William. No need to shout," the voice chided from inside the door.

Annabelle Richardson seemed permanently dressed for high society, except high society rarely set foot on her porch step. It occurred to Nat that she always appeared to be waiting for someone – a high official, a member of the ladies' society, an admirer. Someone who would come calling and ask her opinion on matters of the day: whether secession would actually come to Alabama, would there be a war, how did she view the future of the economy with the diminishing number of slave holders in the state, what was her estimation of the latest fashion designs, anything at all where she could share her educated opinions. Annabelle Richardson's *Belle Vista* plantation was known throughout the county as a place of temperance and fair treatment. Most blamed the perceived laziness of their own slaves on that cursed easy-handed administration of the blacks belonging to Annabelle Richardson. It put too many ideas into the thick skulls of those slaves all about Madison County. It was common knowledge among some circles that the slaves all desired her government, and they would readily leave their masters to work at *Belle Vista*.

Behind their feathered fans, the ladies begrudgingly prated on her "puttin' on airs" and prattled on her over-dressing for any occasion. Today was no exception. She stepped onto the porch, toting a dark blue-and-turquoise spotted peacock feather muff, opal and pink barbs contrasting against the blue eyes of the feathers. She left one hand tucked inside the muff while the other white-lace gloved hand remained free to greet guests. Nat sniffed, subtly shook his head, muttered, "It ain' *dat* cold out."

She rushed down the steps to meet him. "Nat, it is good to see you ag'in. How's Mr. Ashbie and all the children?"

13

Annabelle practically gushed over Nat and held out her gloved hand to him as though he had come courting her. Nat took her gloved hand by the fingertips and shook it gently, politely. He was not about to kiss it, glove or no.

"Oh, dey be fine, Miss Annabelle. Dey be doin' jes' fine," he said bowing awkwardly.

"Well, I suspect they will be wanting to buy more of our horses soon, hmm?" she asked, blithely withdrawing the gloved hand.

"Oh, I don' rightly know, Miss Annabelle. Dey not be sayin' anyt'ing in dem regards to me. I 'spect dey call on you iffen dat be de case. But I never hear'd no case 'bout it one way or t'other. 'Sides, I got too many hosses to tend to awreddy."

"Well, I just *know* Mr. Ashbie will look for the fastest horses he can get from any farm for breeding, and of course for racing. And he will have *you* secretly looking over our stock while you are here for us," she tittered gaily. "Now, don't deny it, Nat. I know John Ashbie *pretty* well. And speakin' of breedin' stock, I will call Emma for you."

"Annabelle!" William cut her off.

"I'm sorry, Nat, but William doesn't like me to meddle in affairs of the heart at all," she said with a cursory laugh.

"Annabelle, it is not affairs of the heart when you talk about breeding *people*!"

"Oh, William, Nat knows I didn't mean anything by it, don't you, Nat?" and she stepped back into the house, called, "Emma!"

"It's awright, Marse William. She don't mean nothin' by it. She jes' sportin' wit' me, dat's all."

"Still, it's not fittin' to talk like that. Next thing she'll be sayin' it in front of Jeff Davis himself when he comes to call."

"Senator Davis comin' here, Marse William?"

14

"Oh, I expect so, Nat. But some say he will be *President* Davis soon as he gets here," Richardson said.

"*President* Davis?" Nat asked. "Shooo-eee! *President* Davis! Dat's sump'in!"

"There's been much talk. Don't know how much truth there is in that though…."

"Emma!" Annabelle's voice shouted inside the house again.

"Well, Marse William, I bes' be gittin' to de barn and git to doin' dem bays you wanted done. Now you girls gwan git outta de wagon and see Tildy or Missus Annabelle about de wash. An' you be gittin' to it right off!"

"Emma will be right here, Nat."

"It's awright Marse William. I kin see her some ot'er time. I gots my work to do, and dem hosses ain't gwan shoe demselves."

Nat pulled some of the hay from the wagon and dropped it in a heap in front of Daniel, who nosed it, snorted and began to nibble. He walked to the barn and grabbed a leather apron from the peg inside the door, and soon the barn was ringing with the sound of iron, hammer and anvil. Nat already had the forge fire roaring and two front hooves shoed before Emma finally appeared at the door, a pail of water and dipper in hand. She stood a long time at the door, stepped in and leaned against a large support beam, waiting for him to notice. He turned his back to her, positioned himself in the back of the stall, keeping the animal between him and his visitor.

"Good day to you, Nat." He pretended not to hear her, lifted a crème colored Morgan's hind hoof and began to remove the nails. "I said, good day to you, Nat," Emma repeated. She stood for a moment and set the pail down at the door.

"Oh. Good day to you Miss Emma," he said at last.

15

"I expect you'll be needin' some water, Nat."

"Yass'm, sho'ly do," he said.

"Was your journey pleasant this morning? Any trouble getting here?"

"Pleasant enough. Got stopped by dem pattyrollers, but dey don' trouble us none." He pulled a single nail from the hoof and the shoe dropped with a metallic clunk onto the wooden flooring.

"Patrollers."

"W'atchyou say?"

"Patrollers. Not pattyrollers. They patrol the roads and byways, so they called patrollers, Nat."

"*Patrollers*," he repeated.

"That's right. The new girls you brought to do Missus Annabelle's wash are good workers. Tildy had them started right off, and they haven't let up yet. I believe the missus will have them back again." She watched him quietly. Then, "Nat, they said the patrollers tried to give you trouble, but you handled them. Is that how it is?"

"No, Miss Emma, dey don't give us no mo' trouble den de worl' usually bring us." He pulled a newly shaped shoe from its water bath, hung it on a nail beside him in the stall, grasped a rasp and worked the hoof.

She stepped into the stall, glanced discreetly at the barn door, quieted her voice. "They say you turned in one of the field hands for tryin' to escape before you came here today. That true?"

"I jes' let Marse John know dat we got us a stowaway 'afo' we be sta'tin' off. If he try to run off and he get cotched up by dem pattyrollers—uh, patrollers—den we all be in fo' a heap o' trouble. I don' cotton to gittin' de whippin' cause some young fool try to up and run off. So, I 'spect I saved him a hidin' and me a hidin' too."

"He just wants to be free like the rest of us."

Nat paused with the rasp in his hand. He studied Emma for the first time since she had entered. She always looked happy in her work, never seemed to be in any trouble with the Richardsons. And here she was – talking freedom.

"I don' want no runnin' off. Where would dis niggah go? Marse John am good to me, and I do de wo'k I s'posed to do. I make de bes' of it. I don't want no freedom."

"Well, I do, Nat."

"Dat's fine fo' you, Miss Emma, but I don' wants *no* troubles. I gots plenty to do on de fa'm fo' Marse John. An' I gits plenty o' eats too, a place to lay dis head at night— No, I's doin' jes' fine."

He took up another shoe with the fire tongs and thrust it into the fire. He pulled on the bellows, a blast of air blowing the fire, sending the sparks dancing up into the vent. Emma straightened the front of her apron, a bright emerald green cloth that contrasted with the daffodil yellow of her dress and the matching yellow ribbon in her hair. She took up the bucket and dipper and stepped toward Nat who pulled again on the bellows, and the fire once again roared to life.

"You finish with that mare yet, Nat?" Richardson stood at the barn door, hands on his hips, casting a long look at the two of them.

The startled words tumbled from him. "Yass'm, Marse William, I's jes' finishin' dis hoss and I's gwan to do dat ot'her mare out in de pasture, soon as I kin git 'er moved back in here. Gots de nex' shoe heatin' up fo' it. I- I- git to her de very next one." He had no idea how long Richardson had stood there, but the stance indicated it was long enough.

"Emma, did you get Nat his drink of water?"

"Yes, Master William. He got it," she lied. "I'll be heading back up to the house for the missus right away."

"She sent me to fetch you, and I expect I didn't interrupt anything important, did I?"

"No, Master William, nothing important. Good day to you, Nat," she nodded.

Nat grabbed the bridle and he led the mare back into its own stall, spoke quietly, down to his own shoes, "Good day, Miss Emma."

By late afternoon, five horses were shoed, the wash finished and hung out to dry and Nat had pulled up the wagon with his passengers ready to make the return trip to *Cypress Grove*. Nat turned Daniel toward the lane, and as they passed a wide-trunked white oak tree, he looked back to see William Richardson out beside the house, hands still on his hips, his head nodding in animated conversation, facing Emma, who stood with her arms hanging loosely to her side and her head in like manner, drooping, her chin resting on her chest.

Chapter Two
Cypress Grove

Past the cotton fields Daniel plodded along wearily. The melodic harmony of the adult Negro voices wafted a hymn like a sweet breeze from the fields. The young ones toted the picked cotton, small bags hanging low from their shoulders, slapping at their ankles as they labored to the clearing to dump them onto an open wagon. One bone-thin man, much in years, stood straight up, rested his hands on his back at the waist, bent far backward as if to touch his gray head to the ground, and then he straightened, rolled his shoulders forward and back. He looked to the road and stared curiously at Nat who tipped the brim of his hat, the man nodding in return. Then stooping over, he picked and dropped the small tufts from the bolls into the large bag slung around his shoulder. His husky baritone now trumpeted the melodious question, and the slaves answered in chorus. And once again, Nat felt thankful to be here, riding in this wagon, driving this slow plodding horse back to the farm, carrying these six young girls in the back under his protection.

The afternoon's daylight lay exhausted on the cedar and oak treetops, reposing to stretch out its weary form at the dusk. Nat turned Daniel down the ornamented lane, Spanish moss weeping from the Sweetgum and Live Oak limbs. On toward the big house the horse trudged, the young girls riding in the back, quietly reclining as they approached the barn. A crowd of field hands had assembled around the front yard of the big house, congregating between the house and the barn, and as he drew near, Nat sensed some calamitous event had just raised its vile head. He heard the low moaning of the women, the men in animated muffled conversations. Nat pulled the wagon up near a group of slaves.

"Marcella, what be all dis moanin' an' groanin' about? Somebody done took sick?"

"Oh, Nat, dat overseer from de Perkins farm, dat Jonah, he done whipped Samuel til he nearly dead!"

Nat stood quickly, looked around for Samuel, saw the faces of the slaves looking up at him, imploring. The girls in the back of the wagon leapt from the wagon, shaking the loose straw from their cotton dresses, rushing through the throng. Izzy quickly straightened her dress, looked back over her shoulder at Nat, seethed through clenched teeth, "You see how *bowin' down to de massuh*, he'p you out? Didn' he'p Samuel none, did it?" She ran for the barn.

Nat felt the breath sucked out of him, punched from his lungs by Marse John's unseen fist. He said he would take care of Samuel, said he would... what was it he said? Don't worry about Samuel? He never actually *promised* Nat anything. Betrayal. The master had betrayed *him*. But then, Nat had betrayed *Samuel*. He tried to reconcile it to himself. At least he had protected the other slaves who would've been held to reckon for Samuel's escape. He had protected the girls in the wagon, those who would surely feel the wrath of punishment. He had protected himself. The worst kind fool is the fool who deceives himself. Had he turned in Samuel only to protect himself? Well, it was Samuel's fault for trying to run. And what had he tried to run from? All the Negroes were treated well by Master John Ashbie. Floggings were rare on the plantation, had been for over a year since John Ashbie had last called in Jonah Kenton to administer justice. Kenton had nearly killed a black woman for an offense against a white woman at the market in Huntsville, left her naked back scarred for the rest of her life. And then he sold her. From that day on, Ashbie's justice was administered instead by sales. If slaves didn't do as ordered, he sold them to the speculators as soon they came calling at the farm. He didn't need any dissension on his plantation, and he removed the troublemakers before trouble could breed uprisings. Nat considered him a fair man, as masters go. There were a lot worse, and he had occasion to witness them. But here was the proof, at least to the other field hands, that Marse John Ashbie was no better than any of the other whites who owned them until they died. Nat could not comprehend Marse John Ashbie being so wicked as this. There must be some mistake. This made no sense.

Nat walked past the gathering of slaves, followed Izzy to the barn, elbowed his way past the slaves standing in the doorway like so many head of sheep awaiting the market. On the floor of the barn stretched Samuel, his spread-eagled arms and legs knotted to four heavy stakes pounded into the dirt floor. His head lay contorted to the side, dust and sweat forming a yellow paste on his face and hair. The wrists and ankles raw as stewing meat where the leather ropes cut in. Blood lay on either side of the carcass, mixed into the dust, creating deep red-brown clay. And there lay his back, flayed open and covered with flies landing to feast on his misery. He was motionless. Izzy ran to the body, dropped to her knees and cradled Samuel's head, and she wept "He's still alive," she said simply.

Nat's eyes welled up in tears, and he looked at Big Jim who stood against a support beam resting his head back against the beam, tear-filled eyes blankly staring into the future, hands clasped in prayer. Nat had no words of comfort, no words of explanation, turned from the spectacle and walked decisively, directly for the big house. Swiftly he passed through the crowd which parted for him like so many dry fallen leaves scattering in a wind. Out of respect and to demonstrate subservience, no slave ever walked up onto the master's porch unless called for. Nat was different. He had Ashbie's blessing and respect, could approach the master at any time, though always with proper docile respect. Nat purposed to use his familiarity to approach the master. He knocked on the door, took a deferential step back, head down.

"What you want, boy?" a voice sounded from the porch around the side of the house. Nat looked around the corner. On the porch swing, a rifled musket laying on his lap, sat Jonah Kenton, his bullwhip coiled and resting on the swing beside him. Several drops of blood had dripped from its tip and puddled on the white-washed wooden floor.

"Just to see Marse John, boss," Nat said, his head looking down at the puddle.

"What you wanna see *him* fer?"

His eyes remained fixed on the puddle. "Nothin' really dat impo'tant, boss. Only to lets Marse John knowed I be back wit dem girls from de Richardson's."

"Who is it?" Ashbie's voice yelled from the door.

Nat recoiled. "Jes' me, Marse John. Is Nat."

"Oh, c'mon over here Nat," Ashbie called as if nothing in the world was amiss. "You can help me with this situation, Nat."

"I do my bes' Marse John."

"I guess you know we had to punish Samuel for trying to disgrace us that way," he said coolly.

"Marse John, I feel po'ly 'bout Samuel. It be my fault he layin' in dere bleedin'. I's tryin' to figures how to live wit' myself. I didn't mean fo' him to be kilt. I jes' wants him to not gets us all in trouble. Marse, John, I's real sorry."

Ashbie clapped Nat on the shoulder. "It's OK, boy. You did the right thing by yer master. I am indebted to you."

"But Marse John, suh, he jes' a boy. He didn' know no better. I didn' mean fo' him to be whipped to death."

John Ashbie stood facing Nat, his hand still resting on Nat's shoulder. "Of course, you didn't Nat. I didn't either. And

I told Mr. Squires and Mr. Perkins so when they sent Mr. Kenton here. He just let the punishment go too far. I will have a word with him tomorrow."

"Yas'm Marse John, only right now he here on de po'ch 'round de corner," he said tossing his head in a nod to the side of the house.

"I said, 'tomorrow,' Nat," he said gently. "I will take care of it tomorrow. Now you had a purty big day what with gettin' to the Richardson's and back. I 'spect they were happy with y'all and I will get a good report?"

"Oh, indeed, yas'm Marse John. Marse William, he be happy wit' de blacksmit'in' I's done fo' him, and Missy Annabelle, she be pleased wit' de washer gals too. Yas'm, we done good wo'k for dem Richardsons. An'—an' fo' you, massuh. You's needn't fear dem complainin' bouts us. No suh."

"Well, 'spect that's about right, Nat. An' don't you worry. We'll take care of Samuel. He'll be all right in a day or two. We'll get some poultices on him, and he'll be right as rain in no time. Can't be losin' another good set of hands out in the fields," he smiled. "Now you get on home to your cabin and get some sleep. I need to talk to you in the morning about what kind o' horses Richardson has that we might be able to buy from him," he said with a wink.

So, here it was at last. Nat was expected to reconnoiter the stock and see what Richardson owned so he could advise Marse John for a potential purchase offer. His blacksmithing was only a ruse. If John Ashbie had any standing in Nat's sight, it had just suffered a blow nearly as fatal as the flogging of Samuel.

"Yessuh, Marse John. We be talkin' 'bout dem *hosses* in de mo'nin'. I be gettin' on back to de cabin and get some vittles. I's sho' hungry."

"Yes, Nat, you do that. Get something to eat and get some sleep. Good night, Nat."

"Night, Marse John."

He stepped off the porch, paused on the bottom step, felt the staring of Jonah Kenton piercing through the back of his coat, felt the eyes whipping his back too. His back tingled in pain as he started on the path for the slave quarters. Took a dozen steps, stopped, deep in thought, looked up at the stars, sought out the familiar constellations. There above the slave quarters was the North Star, the constellation Big Dipper. The Drinking Gourd, Samuel had called it. It looked to Nat much bigger, clearer, closer than he had ever noticed before. He wiped his sleeve against his eyes and abruptly turned from the path, walked directly for the barn where the crowd had begun to dwindle. Izzy sat on the barn floor, wiping the dirt and sweat from Samuel's motionless head with her apron while he moaned quietly. Nat walked in the dim lantern light to the figures, snapped out a Barlow knife from his trousers' pocket and at once cut through the leather bindings at Samuel's ankles, sliced through the leather restraining his wrists. Izzy looked at him fearfully. "Did de massuh say you kin be doin' dat?"

"I don' rightly care. He be gwan' home to get some doctorin' now."

Nat picked up the weakened form, the bloodied back resting on his cradling arms, and Samuel let out a painful gasp.

"Is awright now, Samuel. You be gwan' home now," he said and carried the boy in his arms like a sacrificial offering from the altar of the barn floor through the group of onlookers. He steadily walked north toward the slave quarters, several women forming a processional behind, while on the porch John Ashbie silently stood beside Jonah Kenton and watched Nat conducting the forms into the darkness.

24

Chapter Three
Ashtabula, Ohio   November 1860

"Where is he? In the parlor?" The short, pudgy, wax-faced man in the tight-fitted black suit stood at the door, his scuffed black beaver fur top hat cradled stiffly in his arm. Marcus Armstrong greeted the stranger, but his attention was drawn instead to the short, bony man obediently trailing him, hardened, dark eyes that searched his face. The scraggly, long chin whiskers showed brown tobacco stains, and crumbs of God-knows-what clung like yuletide ornaments. Specks of mud stippled the wool great coat's bottom fringe, the boots covered with a thin layer of mud and snow. Marcus was instantly repulsed.

"Ah – y-yes," Marcus stammered awkwardly. "Uhh – he is in the front parlor here. Please come in." He stepped aside and swung the door open for the two mourners to enter, watching the men as curious insects.

"Seth," the first said stiffly, still gripping the top hat, "I offer you my deepest sympathies on the passing of your father. George was a credit to the community."

Seth Armstrong stood erect and extended his hand, which the first accepted formally. The bony bearded man merely nodded his head to Seth. Seth ignored the slight. "Thank you, Mr. Harvey. Marcus, this is Mr. Albert Harvey, a business acquaintance of your grandfather's. It does me good to see so many of you come to pay your respects. Father was most definitely respected, and he will be missed."

Jude Simon stood casually behind Harvey, surveying the room, his arms crossed on his chest just below the scraggly, stained beard. His searching eyes hungrily seized on the blaze in the hearth, and he walked to it, stomped his feet noisily in front, loose snow falling from his trouser legs, held his hands out over the fire, rubbed them together, and once again toasted them. Marcus continued to size him up. The man wasn't here to pay his respects, couldn't be. He might have been more genial. There was a message in his demeanor, a sinister purpose perhaps.

Albert Harvey's pudgy blush-cheeks oozed arrogance. He appeared to have been poured into the ill-fitting suit, the button holes stretching open on his waistcoat. Marcus was repelled by his pretentiousness.

"Yes, I'm sure many will miss him – probably more than would say it publicly."

Marcus stepped past Simon and into the exchange, "What is your meaning, Mr. Harvey?"

"Marcus," Seth interrupted.

"No. It's perfectly all right, Seth. What my meaning is – since you asked, Marcus – is that your grandfather is noted for having illegally aided escaped Negro slaves when they reached the town. No, don't try to deny it. It is most common knowledge. And now that he has passed, rest his soul, there are many who will no longer partake of his services. Still, all in all he was a good man, did much good for the community even though he chose to flaunt the law of the land."

"My father," said Seth firmly, "chose to flaunt 'the law of the land,' as you say, because of his convictions. He believed this Fugitive Slave Law to be unjust and morally wrong. You *are* aware that he could not go against his Quaker convictions? I applaud him for it, and though he will be missed, I am quite sure it will not end with him."

Albert Harvey smirked at Seth, stepped heavily past him, and approached the wooden coffin resting on the long dining table. Black crepe cloth hung in swags, rented for the purpose, surrounding the coffin. A folded tattered American flag lay on an end table at the foot of the coffin. Jude Simon reached to feel the flag material. "How appropriate," Harvey muttered. "Dressed in his favorite color, black."

"Please leave that flag alone, mister!" Marcus spoke a low directive to Simon. "That is my grandfather's and the family will keep it with *our* family."

"Oh, yes," said Harvey, "we must give the flag its due respect, Jude. This is the famous battle flag your father kept from the fleet that sailed under Captain Perry in the last war with England? We have heard so much talk about it. A lot of family pride rests there. Let's see, now. Which ship was he on?"

"He sailed on the *Lawrence* and then the *Niagara*, but the flag is not from the battle. It is from the funeral of the officers on the island. It covered Lt. John Brooks when father helped row his body ashore in the funeral procession. He kept it both as a memento and as a reminder of his stance against wars," said Seth.

"Yes, he was a pacifist, wasn't he? Well, I trust his teaching wasn't wasted on his children and grandchildren," said Harvey.

"Mr. Harvey, if war comes, you can be sure we will follow our convictions. And if you are here to pay your respects to my family, you are welcome, but as it appears you are here for another purpose, I must ask you to state your business or be moving along."

"My business, Mr. Armstrong, is this. Many influential people know your father aided those who hid runaway slaves here in Ashtabula. It is also known he was recruited by Daniel Dobbins of Erie many years ago to steal other people's property. And it is also known that he had aided William Hubbard in doing the same. Now we must let *you* know, that since his death, there will be those who will be watching you and your son, as you, uh, take up the family business, shall we say?"

"Mr. Harvey, my father's life-long friend passed nearly five years ago and we have had no contact with the family in

27

Erie. As far as Mr. Hubbard, you are misinformed. My father was, until last month, involved in building. Mr. Hubbard's lumber yard and warehouse did business with my father. You should know that. You too have done business with the Hubbards, and even with Mr. Hulbert."

"Most assuredly not the *same* clandestine business of your father. Everyone knows that William Hubbard's brothers founded the *Sentinel* and that your father subscribed to its abolitionist sympathies."

Marcus interrupted, "As you say, Mr. Harvey, my grandfather's sympathies are common knowledge."

Jude interjected, "He was also a friend of Alexander King. And King was bosomed friends with John Brown. And you all know what happened to both of them."

Marcus' face was red. "John Brown has been dead for a year, mister, and my grandfather was a carpenter who also made cabinets. Mr. King sold him cabinet hardware! And there is no crime, federal or otherwise in that! With Mr. Lincoln's election, I expect the common knowledge of *your* pro-slavery sympathies will soon garner much more open scorn than you are feeling now!"

"Unless someone kills the son of a bitch first," Simon glared.

Seth stepped between his son and Harvey, whose gloved hands had clenched repeatedly into fists at his sides. He spoke quietly, yet firmly. "Mr. Harvey, since I did not seek this dialogue with you, and shortly you will prove an unfortunate embarrassment to yourself when the *invited* mourners arrive, I suggest you finish your respects for my father and be on your way. Good day."

A light knock at the door, and Marcus turned to greet two women wholly outfitted in mourning black standing at the door. They bustled in, the cold air following them, and snowflakes resting on their shoulders and bonnets.

Recognizing the women, Albert Harvey pulled his short frame up stoutly, tugged down at the front of his black wool great coat, attempting to close the gaping button holes at his stomach. He failed. He looked one last time deeply into Seth's eyes, began to speak, paused, then, "My respects to your mother," he said with a slight stiff bow from his considerable waist and turned abruptly for the door, Jude Simon on his heels like a malnourished obedient pup.

Catherine Hubbard watched the two men silently until the door shut behind them. She rolled her eyes to the heavens, shook her head in revulsion, turned to Seth. "We've come to see your father and give our respects to Polly," she said gently. "Is she inside?"

"Yes, Mrs. Hubbard, she is in the bedroom at the top of the stairs. She will be pleased to see you."

The two women stepped into the parlor, stood before the body of George Armstrong, silently, prayerfully, dabbing at their eyes with black kerchiefs. Then they pulled from their muffs and tenderly laid red and white ribbons across his folded hands. Curious sentiment, Marcus thought. He looked for meaning from his father. Seth shrugged, beckoned him closer as the women turned and climbed the stairs, their black silk dresses rustling against each baluster.

"We will soon be watched," Seth spoke low. "You will have to take delivery of the freight immediately."

"But, Grandfather's funeral?"

"Immediately after that. There can be no delay. The package of lumber must be delivered to the warehouse with all possible speed. I will let William know when you leave. He will be at the graveside, I trust, and we may make the arrangements at that time. Remember, you must leave immediately afterward. It will be a more difficult road to New Lisbon in the snow, so haste is essential. You will meet a station master there by the name of Mr. Anderson. He is a

Friend and will give you guidance to the next station. Now, the packet ship to carry the lumber to Canada will sail on the twelfth, so no delays. Ice is already forming and this will be our last delivery for the winter."

"And *those* men?" Marcus asked.

"They will be watching me, son. They may suspect you, but I trust they'll be too busy shadowing me here than following you for a delivery of lumber. There is much more freight at the Hubbard's barn and at Mr. Hulbert's cellar. We will keep them busy following us, so you will have little to fear. Still, beware that someone else may be in their service. Just keep your wits about you, and employ a sharp eye for anything unusual on your return. More directions will follow. You must time your return to be mid-day, not night time. They always look more for night activity, so suspicion will be minimal in daylight. Marcus, your grandfather would be proud of you."

"I wish I had helped with the cause earlier, Father," Marcus said.

"Better late than never," he smiled. "He always said your studies in Oberlin would come to fruition. Besides, your sister has shouldered the burden for the cause without complaint. She has done what you couldn't while your studies continued."

"Yes, but Martha has carried my burden far too long. I will long regret that I had not done more. When I learned of the arrest of those Oberlin men, John Copeland and the others, that affair taught me more than all of the class studies did."

"Still, you had to choose your own mind." Seth grasped his shoulders, "Martha will be happy that you have joined us. Your mother would've been proud of you, and I am glad to have your assistance, Son. I may have not expressed it rightly before, but I am equally pleased you didn't join your friend at Harper's Ferry. Well intentioned, yet a foolish move. There is more we can accomplish without violence than with it. Your grandfather would agree with me. You're here alive, and you're of more use to me than you would've been standing on a scaffold beside Brown."

Marcus turned away from his father, paused to look on his grandfather's face silently, turned back. "But John Copeland didn't just talk abolition, he died for it!"

"Marcus, martyrdom only shows the intensity of their beliefs, not the correctness of them. Yes, those men with Brown brought much good to the cause, but then they threw it away on a desperate act. There are causes worth dying for, but none worth killing for. Murder is still murder, and it can't be justified. My father – your grandpa George – felt that belief deeply, and that belief lies in there with him. There are ways to fight back against the disease of slavery, but the murders done by John Brown and his clan were not the way to fight."

He looked over his back to the window in the door, nodded to the door. Marcus turned, opened it to a small gathering of seven Negro mourners who shook the snow from their clothes on the porch and stepped into the hall, quietly greeting Seth. He watched them slowly, reverently shuffle into the parlor and surround the coffin, each placing a left hand on the coffin, the right to their own heart, then spontaneously begin to sing a quiet hymn. Yes, his grandfather had truly been a blessing to the community, he thought.

Chapter Four
Hanoverton, Ohio December 1860

Marcus shivered and pulled his collar up higher, nervously waiting on the hard wooden seat. Light snow collected on the horses, and it erupted in puffs of white with each swat of their tails. The wood beams piled high on the wagon tied triple around with heavy rope left no chance of a sudden shift to crush the cargo. Mr. Anderson had been inside the Spread Eagle Tavern for nearly twenty minutes talking to the US Marshal and two unseemly-looking deputies. To Marcus, nothing seemed amiss or the men would have come out to search his load of wood once more before giving him passage north. Marshals and other law officers customarily did not stop and search any wagons carrying goods, and Marcus wanted an opportunity to challenge them on an illegal search. He thought that he understood his professor at Oberlin well enough, yet his confidence wavered in challenging the law in this village. He might quote the Bill of Rights to the men, but then he might only call attention to himself and consequently to his cargo. And in the village, he didn't know who was friend and who was foe. A college educated young man driving a lumber wagon team would certainly invite the curious. Be patient. Wait. Moreover, don't self-righteously wave about any educational credentials. And trust Mr. Anderson. He listened intently, could hear no movement, no signs of life from the pile of wood beams behind him. He wanted to get down and check, but checked his own movement instead just as the tavern door swung open in the alley by the stable entrance, revealing Mr. Anderson pulling on his coat.

"Thank you, gentlemen, and when I am back in town for business, the next round is on me."

The marshal laughed loudly and held the mug high as a toast, the two deputies in concert calling their thanks, and

Anderson climbed into the seat beside Marcus, elbowed him hard.

"Git-up there!" Marcus called and the horses lurched forward on the brick and stone street, moving slowly past the brick businesses and on down toward the church.

"Just doin' his duty is what the man said. He wasn't about to search us again, but they did get word that a runaway was sighted south o' here and up 'n disappeared," a smile on his face.

"They suspect us?" Marcus asked.

"They suspect everyone when there's a profit to be made. I think he's willin' to turn his head this way or that, dependin' on who has the bigger wallet. Doesn't matter, he let us go and that's good enough."

"I haven't checked the load too often, Mr. Anderson, but I hope it is still all right. Didn't seem to move much while we were stopped."

"What, that load of lumber? Oh, it's quite safe, I assure you," said Anderson. "I expect the way they packed it in, every beam and splinter is warm and snug for a safe travel."

At the corner, Marcus turned the team down the hill toward the remnants of the Erie Canal, a massive transportation ditch now obsolete – gift of the railroads. He looked behind them, back up the hill, up at the brick house on the corner, a lighted lantern glowing softly in the window, the window of an upstairs room which had no door. "Clever," he chuckled to himself, and reined in the horses, pulled hard on the wagon's brake, as the team struggled down the steep hill toward the Canal Street. They passed the merchant buildings in the dark, and soon turned north. The team clopped on, a soft cadence beating on the packed snow, no words exchanged between Marcus, Anderson, or the load of lumber, nothing that could betray their intentions.

Later in the evening they saw the glow from the houses of Salem. As they approached the town, Anderson silently indicated their destination, a side street, darker than the main street, but for amber colored light seeping from some closed shutters. Marcus drove the team onto the side street, pulled into a barn, the doors standing open with two lighted signal lanterns placed on a pickle barrel on the right side, and one lighted lantern on a nail keg to the left.

The barn door closed, the ropes loosened, three heavy timbers pulled from the end of the load, and two well-worn shoes appeared as the figure squirmed out feet first. Anderson grabbed the shoes and pulled while Marcus held a lantern. A young, thin black boy of about sixteen years of age slid off the wagon and stretched his arms high overhead and bent down to touch his toes. His threadbare jacket exposed his elbows through two perfectly placed holes.

"Wait here," Anderson said, and he disappeared through the barn doors and into the night.

The boy stretched, looked out into the black night, his breath puffed white against the dim lantern glow, tried to focus his eyes on the blackness, then looked back in at Marcus.

"I's Samuel. Who you?"

"Marcus."

"Dis still be Ohio?"

"It is," said Marcus. "For a couple more days, you're still in Ohio."

"When we's goin' git to freedom in Canada?"

"Soon," said Marcus. "It will be all arranged. Be patient."

"I guess I kin wait fo' a bit mo'. I's mo' close den I ever thought I's gwan git."

"Well, we're not out of the woods yet, but we soon will be."

"Woods? What woods you talkin' 'bout. Dey ain't no woods here, onliest thing I see in de dark is dem big houses outside."

"Just an expression. It means we are still in danger until you're safely on the boat out of the harbor."

"What boat? What ha'bor?"

"Can't tell you that, Samuel. The less you know, the less you can tell if we all get caught. Just know we are headed for bigger water than you've ever seen, I reckon."

"Any mo' comin' dis way too?"

"Maybe, Samuel. But you don't need to know that either. Just be patient."

"It be hard fo' nigga to trus' white men. So, I jes natural curious."

"I can imagine. But you *can* trust us. We all are putting our lives out there to get you safely out of the country, and we *will* do it." Marcus dimmed the lantern, and in the amber glow he saw the scars on the boy's neck and face. They were older scars, he thought, but in this faint light they looked wickedly repulsive. Samuel saw the tears in his gaze, put his hand to his neck, rubbed it gently as if to soothe it. "Bullw'ip did dat," he said simply. "Won' never happen ag'in, dough."

Marcus dragged his coat sleeve quickly across his eyes. "Not as long as I am here it won't," he said.

The heavy barn door opened slowly, and Anderson stepped inside. "Put this hat on your head, boy. And take this coat and button up. Now follow me, and walk straight up just like you belong here."

The three picked their way in the dark up a side street, a long climb from the railroad line below. A large stone and brick house loomed above them just as a sliver of moonlight peered from behind a cloud. It cast enough light for the three to see the approach to the porch. A door opened to a warm, inviting parlor, a fire crackling in the hearth. No words exchanged, Anderson nudged the hesitant Samuel into the room, and the door closed tightly, leaving Marcus and Anderson out in the cold. They quietly stepped down, walked half slipping on the snow-dusted street, and soon were safely inside the barn. Anderson began to unharness the horse team, and Marcus silently joined in. The horses, brushed out, blankets placed upon their backs, busily fed on their oats while the men, dragging their own woolen blankets, climbed into the hay mow, and wordlessly burrowed in for the night. Outside, the silver-blue tinted trees stood mute, not a breath of wind to rustle their naked, snow-laden branches, and the snow fell more steadily. Soon it covered the shoulders and rabbit fur trimmed slouch hat of a shadowy figure sitting on the porch steps of a neighboring house. A match was struck, and from a short bent Billiard pipe the smoke rose into the frosty night.

+ + + + +

At Ashtabula Harbor, Seth Armstrong met William Hubbard at the top of the hill where a broad winding path descended to the Hubbard warehouse alongside the harbor entrance. The bitter cold wind and the hardened white edges of the harbor's waters below foretold the coming ice on the lake. It was up here they could converse freely without threat of snooping eyes and ears. The blustery gusts and the slapping waves against the jetty muffled their words.

"Should be later this morning or very early afternoon," Armstrong said.

"He must unload the lumber at the warehouse and then return the wagon and package to my house. The barn will be ready for him to stable the team and leave the wagon. Catherine will have the blankets ready for any of God's creatures in need of warmth. When he leaves the wagon –

and any of its contents – in the barn, then he may retire. I will handle all transactions from there."

"I have seen a couple of men loitering about the waterfront."

Hubbard looked down to the waterfront, saw no one there. "Was Jude Simon with them?"

"I haven't seen him since the funeral, why?"

"He is the one I would want to watch carefully. The others might be spies for Harvey, but Simon is another kettle of fish entirely. He is the braggart cut-throat that most men should despise. That man reeks of violence, and would slit a throat for a mere slight. Anyway, I think Marcus will be safe and under no suspicion when he returns with the load of lumber. Simon would not dare try anything around here. Many would help him off to the gallows if they had a just reason."

"Still, I hope my son takes no foolish chances, Mr. Hubbard."

"You've raised a good lad, Seth, and a young man of intelligence. He's clean as a hound's tooth, and he keeps his wits about him. He will do you proud, and, I dare say, the cause as well."

"Yet I worry. I will feel much better when he pulls in with the wagon."

"Worry no more, Seth. Isn't that his wagon?

Down Walnut Street came the wagon of lumber, Marcus at the reins, huddled under his coat and a wool blanket along his shoulders. Steam rose from the backs of the team of horses, twin clouds snorted from their nostrils, and they pulled heavily through the ruts in the snow covered street. The men trudged through the drifts and met Marcus at the crossroads.

""I am glad you are back, son," said Seth. " I trust your journey was uneventful?"

"Nothing to speak of, Father. Good to be here finally and we are all mighty hungry."

"Well, you may drive the team on down to the warehouse where my workers will help to unload your goods. You may bring the wagon back to my barn with any packages you may have brought for my wife and me."

"I will do that at once."

The wagon lurched forward and soon Marcus had turned the cargo down the main street and to the waterfront. He pulled the wagon inside the warehouse and several of Hubbard's men rushed to pull the logs and beams from the wagon, stacking them on a growing pile destined for shipment. Marcus helped Samuel out from the wood pile. He stood upright, stretched and immediately climbed back into a small box built into the tailgate of the wagon. Marcus smiled, closed the door and slipped a padlock on the lid. The wood unloaded, he drove the empty wagon back up the street to the heights above, turned onto Walnut Street and on toward the Hubbard house. The barn doors stood open and Marcus drove the team inside. Barn doors fastened, he unlocked the padlock and out sprang Samuel, grinning a wide smile. "I's free!" he exclaimed.

"Not yet, but very soon," said Marcus. He saw Samuel's face abruptly change. "Don't worry, we will get you free, and you will celebrate Christmas in Canada. Now, you wrap yourself in these blankets and get in that hayloft up yonder. I have to unharness the team here and feed them. They call this 'Mrs. Hubbard's cupboard,' and for good reason. She will be out with victuals for you soon. Just keep quiet and Mr. Hubbard will let you know what happens next."

Samuel climbed up the wooden ladder and stretched out in the straw, pulling two woolen blankets over himself. He looked long at Marcus, and that infectious gap-toothed smile caused Marcus to laugh. "You keep grinning like a Cheshire cat, Samuel. You're going to grin even more when they get you across that lake out there."

Chapter Five

Belle Vista, the Richardson Farm   January 20, 1861

The Christmas season had passed all too quickly for the slaves. The change in John Ashbie's demeanor toward them had now altered their living conditions for the worse. Samuel's flight last month had put the surrounding plantations on notice. The whites were all nervous. Masters and their overseers scrutinized the slaves' comings and goings, they frequently revoked their travel passes, and as words of freedom wafted through the farms, the overseers grew even bigger ears. Growing season had ended, and idle hands and minds could dream up all sorts of mischief, so vigilance was high. Abraham Lincoln at last took the oath of office, and the talk of secession, which had spread about on every wind that blew out of the Carolinas had reached Mississippi and Louisiana, and now Alabama. Annabelle Richardson had begun posturing herself on the probability that Jefferson Davis might finally be recommended to lead the secessionist states. She would at long last rub elbows with the highest office in the land. Alabama's vote had passed, and Virginia Clay and her husband Clermont would soon return from Washington to assume duties in the new independent state government. Annabelle practically salivated at the possibility that her friendship with the Clays might be rewarded. She began using her slaves to prepare the plantation's grounds for what she anticipated would be the idyllic destination for the political elite. Everything needing cleaned and polished had been re-cleaned and re-polished for the pretentiousness befitting the occasions. She avowed that her slaves would make her the admired model of all Southern belles. But even in Alabama's northernmost county, slave holders like John Ashbie recognized that slavery was a dying institution, and the inevitable would finally overtake them – that the risk of a war would indeed be a major risk – quite possibly the ruin of their livelihood. Yet, to a man, they all chose to hold on as long as possible, long enough for one more profitable year of planting and harvest. Then they would think on emancipation. Or maybe the next year. Or the next. War would skyrocket prices and the possibility of growing a quick fortune guided their decisions.

Talk of war now dominated most conversations, black or white. And the cautiously attentive slave could glean much useful information. Those who had secretly learned to read stole glimpses of the newspapers whenever they cleared the masters' homes of trash. Many a newspaper found its way from the burn pile to the slave quarters before the flames consumed the objects of their curiosities. And those who readily digested the news, before committing it to the flames, freely shared the knowledge with their fellow sufferers at home and about the county. The news spread from farm to farm like a pestilence, and the whites attempted to eradicate the disease before it infected their own world.

It was under this risk of discovery that Emma continued to meet Nat. Since the episode of the whipping, Nat had only ventured to the Richardson plantation three times. John Ashbie still could not convince Master William Richardson to part with any of his horses, no matter what proposition he laid before him. Yet each of those three times the master dispatched Nat to work for Richardson, he sent him with another offer. Nat knew the answer after the first trip, so he quit asking Richardson. He chose to always bring back to Marse John the same *no* answer and just let it stand. He cherished his few moments with Emma and used the time to listen to her talk, even though it always got around to a discussion of running for the North and freedom.

41

"Nat, I have seen the abolitionists," she murmured as he bent over the fire, turning the white hot metal with the tongs. He pulled at the bellows, and two long bursts of air flared the flames, scattering sparks up into the chimney vent. "You hear me, Nat?"

"I done hea' ya' Emma." He pulled angrily at the bellows again, a low roar sounding in the flames.

"He said I can leave anytime. They have people what will guide me north and I need to just fix a time. I'm gonna be free, Nat."

Nat refused to look up, turned the metal again and drew out a misshapen horseshoe, laid it on the anvil and clutched the hammer. The ringing broke the quiet, startled Emma, who looked around, expecting searching eyes and ears. Between the harsh resounding clangs, she spoke. "I want you to come too. Do you hear me Nat? I want you to run with me. We can get away. Nat? The abolitionists will take two, I just know they will."

"Uh, huh," he said, and brought the hammer down with three final clangs, sank the iron shoe deep into the slack tub, the bubbling hiss punctuating his affirmation.

"I brought you water."

"I's seed it, Emma."

"Saw it..."

"I's saw it, Emma."

"Well, if you get thirsty enough, you'll want it. So, I'll just leave it here by the door." She set the pail of water and dipper on a keg of nails inside the barn doors and turned quickly. Nat listened for the rustling of the taffeta dress and hoop skirt.

"She sho' do dress up right smart, don' she, Queenie?" he muttered to the black Tennessee Walker. The horse looked at him, looked to the door, snorted and pawed the dirt. He finished pounding out the shoe, sunk it again into the slack tub, the hiss and steam rising from the water. Nat nailed on the finished shoe and walked Queenie back to her stall. The fire in the forge quenched, Nat retrieved the water pail, pulled on his heavy greatcoat and went to the big house. Annabelle Richardson greeted him at the back porch.

"I come to give dis here pail back to Emma."

"Thank you, Nat. Just set it there on the porch and I'll have Emma fetch it in."

"Yas'm Mizz Richardson." Nat looked around toward the windows, leaned back to see around the corner of the house.

"Was there something else you'd be wanting, Nat?" Annabelle Richardson asked with an air of satisfaction.

"No, ma'am. Well, nothin' particular. Only iffen I could sees Emma jus' a wee bit, a'fo'e I git on back to Massa Ashbie's..."

"Nat, you sweet on that girl?"

"Oh, I don' rightly know, Mizz Richardson. I jes' wants to sees her fo' a bit. Iffen you's to let me...."

"Nat, no use in getting all bothered about Emma. She isn't going to be here much longer." She watched Nat's eyes, let the effect sink in.

"She be gittin' married off?"

"Maybe. She didn't tell you? Well, that was unkind of her!"

"She be sayin' she be leavin' soon..."

"She did? Well, sure if she isn't. No, she's not getting married. Mr. Richardson has been offered good money for her, and she will be leaving here once the man comes by with the payment. But I don't know how she knew she was leaving soon."

Nat grasped that he had given away too much. "Oh, I 'spect de way folks talk, chillen and sech, she be hearin' from dem little 'uns."

43

Annabelle watched Nat carefully, searching for any hint of deceit. "No one was told, Nat."

"Well, sommuns musta tol' sommuns. Dat's how I sees it."

Annabelle Richardson remained cautious. "You may see her on the front porch, but I caution you not to say a word about her movin' on. I might have to report it to Mr. Ashbie."

Turning an imaginary key at his lips, "No'm, I's gwan keep de lock on my mout'."

Nat's heart was heavy, and he walked around to the front of the big house, stood off the porch steps, looked up at the giant Doric columns, held his hat before him with both hands. Soon the front door opened, and Emma stepped out, saw Nat, a sudden smile breaking into a wide grin. She stepped further onto the edge of the porch, looked down at Nat. He felt a large soft lump in his throat, wanted to speak, tears forming. He saw Annabelle Richardson at the window inside.

"Miss Emma," he said quietly, looking down at his hat, folding its brim, nervously curling it with his fingers. "Miss Emma..."

"You can jus' call me Emma, Nat. You know that."

"Please step down," he said quietly. "An' don' be lookin' back at de house."

Her smile disappeared. She read the trouble in his face even as he stared down at the lowest step. She walked down the eight large steps, and Nat could hear the dress rustling, saw her feet near his, spoke in a near whisper.

"I's gwan say goodbye, Miss Emma."

"You're *going* to say goodbye," she corrected.

"I's gwan say goodbye," he repeated. Then in a whisper, still to his feet, "You's gwan be sol' off."

"Wha-?"

"Don' say nuthin'. Jes' be quiet. Missy say you gwan be sol' soon," he repeated in a whisper. "When you gwan run?"

"Emma!" Annabelle Richardson's voice called from the house.

"Coming, Mrs. Richardson!" she called gaily. "Soon!" she whispered to Nat, and she took his hands in hers, pressed them tightly to her breast. Their eyes met, the worried determination marked on her face. "Soon," she said firmly. She reached up quickly, and pulled at the bright yellow ribbon from in her hair. It came out in a long strand across her face, and she quickly, secretly crumpled it and pushed it into his hands.

Emma turned from Nat, abruptly changed into her broad smile and skipped up the steps in an exaggerated cheerful run to her mistress. Nat watched her go, hands still crumpling his hat at his waist, and still holding the bunched up yellow ribbon. He wanted to say more, couldn't find the words, the soft lump in his throat curbing his voice. He hoped he had said enough.

With the sun sinking before him, his drive back to the Ashbie farm was a more chilling trip this time. The warmth of Emma's embrace wasn't with him this time. In fact there was nothing at all to feel warm about this time, not even the bright yellow ribbon safely tucked away in his pocket. Deep inside, he felt his attitude change. Before, he would've never entertained the thought. But this time he too was willing to join the ranks of Samuel; Emma; Isaac, who ran from the Townsend farm; the Burns twins who had attended the Methodist Episcopal church in Huntsville; all those slaves who desired freedom enough to attempt escape just as soon as an opportunity presented itself.

"Whoa, Dan'l," he pulled on the reins as the three men at the end of the Richardson farm lane blocked his way.

"You John Ashbie's Nat?"

"Yas'm, I's Nat."

"You got yer papers on ya, Nat?'

"Yas'm. Sho'ly do." And he produced the well-worn travel papers from his coat pocket. The men all wore heavy oil-cloth coats, collars pulled up against the evening air, but he recognized two of these as the same patrollers who frequented the roads, referring to themselves as "home guard" now that talk of an imminent war was on everyone's lips. They took it upon themselves to enforce the laws the local sheriffs didn't. He waited patiently while they attempted to read them in the dimming light.

"I guess these are reg'lar 'nuff, Zeb.

"Where ya' bound for, boy?" Zeb asked.

"Backs to Massa John Ashbie's place, boss. Gots ta git dis hoss back fo' he gits too col' and den gits sick. Massa don' truck wit' no sick hosses."

"Mebbe we want to see how fast that horse o' your'n kin run, Whadda ya' think, Calvin?" he took out a long barreled revolver and waved it toward the road. "Now, you git that horse o' your'n on over there and jes' wait 'til I say to go."

"But, boss, Massa John don't like ol' Dan'l to be run. See, he ain't a trotting hoss. He a field hoss, and he jes' good fo' pullin'. Now you takes dat bay o' his'n, why he gwan beat any hoss in de county, and dats a fac'. Why I seen him git…"

"Boy, you just don' know when ta' shet up, do ya'?" He pointed the pistol at Daniel's hind quarters and cocked the hammer. The sound of a horse riding at a full gallop cut through the quiet, and all heads turned. John Ashbie appeared on the road, riding hard toward the men. Nat sighed softly and lowered his head, smiling. Zeb holstered his pistol and turned to face Ashbie.

"Evenin' Mr. Ashbie. Good evening for a ride, isn't it?"

"Only if you *have* to ride. Nat, how's come you are still here? I wanted you home long ago, and Mrs. Ashbie made me saddle up and come get you."

Nat saw an opportunity. "Well," he drawled out, "you knows me Massa, I gits to jawin' wit' ever'body and den I doesn't see de time pass. I guess I has to be mo' keerful, I guess dat's what I has to do."

"Well, you leave these men be and get Daniel moving now. It will be sundown soon. Gentlemen, a pleasant evening to you all."

The patrollers smugly reined their horses around and turned on up the road passing the Richardson's lane and on in the direction of New Market. John Ashbie led the way, and Nat drove Daniel on, ever watchful over his back to see that the patrollers weren't in pursuit. Ashbie glanced back, reined in his horse, and pulled alongside of Nat's wagon.

"T'ank ya' Marse John."

"Nat, don't you be worryin' 'bout those ol' boys. They aren't going to fuss with you as long as I'm here."

"I sho'ly 'preciate dat, Massa John. I sho'ly do. I don' know what I done to make dem wanna stop me. I's not late, is I?"

"No. But I did see them ride past the house, and thought they'd be coming this way. They are getting a bit more power hungry as home guard and they take the law into their own hands. I suspected they might be up to some mischief, so I decided to ride on out to see what become of my wagon and Daniel."

"Yas'm, they wanna skeer ol' Dan'l into runnin' off, but you's jes comin' along in de nick o' time."

"Nat, there's going to be a war soon, sure as I'm sitting here riding this mare. I don't expect we will do very well in it. Senator Davis is going to be our new president. The president of our confederacy. He's going to go to Montgomery. That's where our capital will be."

"Yas'm." Nat watched Ashbie, who seemed a bit more agitated than ever.

"Nat, do you know what that means?"

"No suh, I sho'ly don't."

"It means Alabama will have a big fat target pinned on us. Them Yankees will eventually come down here, and there will be fightin'."

"Oh, Massah, dey ain' gwan come all de way down to 'Bama. Dey ain't nothin' down here fo' dem but suga' and cot'n and 'bacca. Dat's 'bout de way I sees it."

"Nat, they will come for the spoils eventually. Now I got a job for you, and I have been thinking on it for a long while, and that's another reason I wanted to talk with you. I am going to have you make a funeral."

"Who passed, Massa?"

"Nobody died, Nat. I want it to look like somebody did. I have a wooden coffin, 'bout sized for a little pickaninny child, and it is going to have some of our valuables in it. The folks around here will be watching us to see what we do with our things, and I want to be ready. Nat, when did Noah build his ark?"

"Jes' afo' de rains come, I hears. Why?"

"Just before the rain, Nat. Not after. Before."

"An' you be t'inking it gwan rain real ha'd, Massa John?"

"Real hard, Nat. So, you're going to go have yourself a funeral with that coffin that you and I are going to load onto the wagon. Then you draw me a map of where that coffin is buried."

"Massa, I's cain't read, so I's cain't write neither."

"No need to write, Nat. You just draw me pictures on a napkin or a handkerchief I'm going to give you. Then you give me the map when you come back. What's in that coffin will be safe until we beat them Yankees – or until they beat us. Either way this family will survive to start all over again. You have always served me well, Nat, and I trust you to do this."

Nat saw the intense look. It wasn't a look of love or trust, as he thought of love or trust. It was a look of command, a look of control. At once a glimmer of light flashed in the back of his mind, and Nat saw the new day dawning for just that instant. He had a purpose.

"T'ank ya' Massa. I's gwan do it jes' like you done tol' me. You kin trus' yo' Nat. When you wants me to do dis buryin'?"

"I will let you know soon enough. No one is to go with you, and no one is to know about it, especially that no account overseer Kenton, nor any of the patrollers. This will be done between you and me. Not even Mrs. Ashbie is to know, understand? I will let you know when to do it, Nat. But it will be very soon." He slapped Daniel's rump and the horse started, lurching the wagon forward and onto the lane to the big house at the Ashbie farm, John Ashbie riding on ahead at a gallop.

Soon. That was what Emma had said. He felt for the piece of ribbon balled up in his pocket. Soon she was going to break for freedom. Soon she would head north. She would need money. He would need money. And now Master John Ashbie had just laid before him the plan to give it to him. He only hoped it would be soon enough.

Chapter Six
Cypress Grove   February, 1861

Nat maneuvered the wagon back into the yard where the light snow had melted on the warm ground, turning the lane and carriage circle before the house into a slick, muddy quagmire. He drove the team of horses on and pulled directly into the barn. John Ashbie stepped down from the porch of the big house, strode slowly toward the barn, oblivious of the mud. Nat saw him come, pulled the shovel from the back of the wagon, stood it in the corner just as Ashbie entered.

"Ah, Marse John, I's back."

"I can see *that*, Nat. Have you got anything for me?"

"No."

His voice rose. "Nat?"

"Oh, yas'm Marse John, I fo'gets dat I has you han'ka chief dat I borried. I sho'ly 'preciate dat, Massa."

"Well, you could keep it, he said boldly, a cover for his real intent, "but I will need it myself. I will get you one to replace it. Of course I will have to wash this one good."

"Oh, yassuh Marse John, only jes look at dat purty drawin' on it fust."

"Oh, I will Nat. And I thank you for doing your duty for me. I'll have that pen and ink bottle now too. Tomorrow, I need you to go to William Richardson's. He will have some work for you on two horses I am thinkin' on buying from him. You can have the rest of today off after you take care of the horses and wagon in here."

"Oh, I does 'preciate it so. I's sho in need of it Marse John. I's gwan git right to dese here hosses."

"Well, see that you do, Nat. You're a good worker, Nat. I've told everyone so, and Richardson knows your worth. You do me a great credit, Nat."

"Yassuh, Marse John, I knows it. Dat's why I keeps on keepin' on."

Ashbie took the handkerchief, smiled looking at the black ink drawing, pocketed the pen and ink bottle, and walked back to the house. Nat unharnessed the horses, led Daniel and Meshach to their stalls.

"You sho' am de bigges' fool I sees here in a eternity!" The woman's voice startled him, and Nat looked around, saw nothing in the darkened corners. "Up here, Nat Ashbie," the voice called again. Nat looked up into the hay loft, saw Izzy's dark eyes.

"W'atchoo doin' up dere, gal, a skeerin' folk like dat?"

Izzy leaned over the edge of the loft, her simple dress enticingly open at the top. "You sho' ain't skeered o' me, is ya'?"

"Dat all depend, girl. Why is you hidin' in de loft like dat?"

"To put de fear o' God in you, Nat Ashbie."

"I ain't Nat Ashbie! I's jes' Nat. Plain ol' Nat."

"You's Nat Ashbie, jes' like I's Izzabella Ashbie, and jes' like Big Jim was Big Jim Ashbie. We all belong Marse Ashbie, 'ceptin' fo' Samuel. He ain't no Ashbie anymo'. He a free man. And you's needin' some skeerin'. You's t'inkin' yo' massa love you like his only chil' de way he hab you runnin' his errands. We all seen you take dat coffin off fo' buryin'."

"I does like I's tol', same as you. So don' be puttin' on airs wit' me."

Izzy pulled herself up, crawled to the ladder and climbed down to Nat. "Sump'in special in dat coffin, ain't dere, *Nat Ashbie*?"

"I done tol' you befo' dat I's jes' Nat. I don' belong to no one. When I's free, den I chooses my own name."

"Well, dat ain' gwan happen anytime soon, Nat. You's ain' gwanna be free, not de way I's hearin' it."

"You's got sumpin' to say, gal, den you jes' loosen dat tongue and be sayin' it."

"Dat's why I stay here, fool. To let you *know* you's a big fool. You's done buried dat coffin somewheres fo' Marse Ashbie, and you be t'inkin' you's maybe gwan git a reward from de massa. De only reward you's gwan git is to be sol' to de spec'lators."

Nat looked long and hard into Izzy's eyes, looked for deceit, a cruel joke perhaps. She leaned against him, looked up, pressed harder against him, wrapped her arms around his waist. The tears formed in her eyes.

"Izzy, you's bes' not be lyin' to me."

"Swears on de Good Book, Nat," she sobbed. "Mart'a hears de massa and missus when she up at de kitchen bakin' de bread. She say dat de spec'lators wants to buy you from Marse Ashbie. And he say he ain' gwan sell Nat. Den de spec'lator say he gives fifteen hun'erd dollah in gold fo' you to go. Den massa say to missus, 'we kin use de money if de war come.'"

Nat pulled away from Izzy, rested himself on the tongue of the wagon, trying to take in this news. He looked up into her eyes, a questioning look.

"Swears ta' God, Nat."

He thought long, looked around the barn for anyone within hearing. "You alone, Izzy?"

She shook her head. "I was tol' ta come here alone and wait fo' you so's you'd know befo' night time, in case you's wantin' to be doin' anyt'ing 'bout it right off." She watched him intently. "If'n you do, you's takin' me wit' you, ain't you Nat?"

Nat stood up at last, paced the floor silently, looked out at the afternoon sun, then nodded his head in a silent affirmation to an unasked question in his own mind, turned back. "Izzy, I needs ya' to do somet'in crazy fo' me. Kin you gits to de big house befo' I has to leave tomorra' and gets me dat bottle o' ink and dat writin' pen from Massa's desk?"

"You cants write, Nat."

"I said it's crazy. Kin ya' git it?"

"No, but I kin git Mart'a to git it when she goes to bakin' in de summer kitchen early mo'nin'. She kin git into de big house den."

"Awright den. You be gittin' Martha to git it out and git it to me. Don' let nobody see you'ns o' you's gwan git de skin whipped of'en yo back, sho as you standin' dere!"

"W'atch you gwan do with dat ink, Nat?"

"Dat's a secret dat bes' be kep' by jes' one. You jes be gittin' it."

"When you's gwan ta' run, Nat? I ain't foolin' -- dey's gwan sell you to de spec'lator, sho' as you's standin' dere!"

"Dey ain't gwanna sell me. I has it all added up in my head, and dey ain't gwanna sell me."

Izzy's tears streamed on her cheeks. "Den how you's gwan stop it?"

Nat stood up tall, smiled, grasped Izzy on both shoulders and looked down into her eyes. He grinned at her, held her until she smiled. "I's gwan draw a picture." And he let her go and walked through the barn door, a light spring in his step.

+ + + + +

The morning sun had just broken through the early haze as Nat finished harnessing Daniel to the cart, the steam from the horse's nostrils rising with each snort. "You's jes' as ready as I is, ain't dat right Dan'l?"

The barn door rolled open, and Martha scurried in, a shawl and blanket wrapped around her shoulders. She looked quickly back at the door, thrust out an ink bottle and pen and into Nat's open hands. She quickly turned and ran from the barn back toward the summer kitchen. Nat burrowed the instruments deep into the bag of oats and tied the burlap rope, led Daniel from the barn into the crisp bright morning. At the house, Ashbie stood with a letter in hand. Nat gulped hard, thought of the evidence of his larceny just four feet away.

"Nat, you give this to Richardson when you get to the farm. It concerns a matter of business."

"Buyin' and sellin', Massa John?"

"Buyin' and sellin', Nat. That's all business. You tell Richardson my final price is in there."

Nat tried to hide his fear. "Yas'm, Massa John, I tells him. Uh, you gots my pass fo' gittin' pas' dem patrollers, Massa?"

"Oh, yes, I'll have to write you another."

Nat panicked, thought quickly on the missing pen and ink. "Uhh -- No need fo' dat Massa. I keeps de one you gives me las' time when I buried dat coffin, if'n dat be awright." He searched through his trouser pockets, vest, coat, drew out a folded pass. "I gots it now," he grinned.

"Good boy, Nat. Well, be off with you now. And good-bye, Nat."

Nat thought he heard a tone of finality in the salutation, climbed into the buckboard seat. "Ah, Massa John, fo' I go, I 'spect you fo'gets dat clean hand kerchief you's gwan give me..."

"Yes, indeed I did. Thank you, Nat."

He pulled a clean white handkerchief from his coat pocket, held it out to Nat who leaned far from the seat, snatched at it, touched it to his nose, and stuffed it inside his vest. "Much 'bliged, Massa John, you's sho' good to me, Massa. C'mon, and git up dere, Dan'l."

The light overnight snow had coated the road, deadening all sound. Nat saw no hoof prints, no wagon wheel ruts of any kind. No trespasser or traveler who might recognize him. No patrollers to ask for any papers. No one to interrupt this insidious duty he had resolved for himself. He drove the buckboard on past the lane of William Richardson's farm, studying the road ahead. Eerily quiet. He searched the road behind, the fields, the lane once again, all directions for any person who might identify him. He was utterly alone. Three miles later, amidst the stillness only broken by the soft clop of Daniel's hooves and the creak of the buckboard's axles, he saw the neighboring lane, the one he had earlier determined would be his destination. He turned Daniel up the lane, driving him faster, leaving the main road and any chance witnesses quickly behind. Ahead he recognized the stone arched bridge over one of the small streams, a tributary that emptied into the Flint River. On a small rise a few yards to the north of the bridge stood a grove of cypress trees. Nat jumped from the buckboard and ran quickly though the snow to the grove, tied the handkerchief to a low branch and just as quickly mounted the buckboard seat and turned Daniel back to the road and down toward the Richardson farm. In a field one mile from the Richardson farm stood a singular red oak tree, its leaves stripped bare from the winter winds, one large branch broken and hanging by its wood and bark hinge to the trunk. Nat tied Daniel to a tree at the road's edge, reached under the buckboard and untied the heavy rope wrapped around the axle. Out thumped a shovel. Picking it up, he quietly mocked John Ashbie. "Should'a looked fo' runaways dis one mo' time, Massa!" He crossed the field to the lone oak tree, and there drove the blade of the shovel deep into the hardened ground.

Nat busied himself at his work, digging quickly and stopping only occasionally to search the horizon for travelers and patrollers. In a half hour he had dug up the coffin, wrapped the rope around it, and dragged it across the field to the buckboard, hefting it into the back. He covered the dirt over his excavation, tossed a few shovels of snow over the dirt, scattered his footprints with a tree branch dragged in his wake. Then he drove Daniel quickly back to the bridge. He checked for his landmark, the grove of trees on the hill, the white handkerchief on the branch, retrieved the treasure-laden coffin from the back, and dragged it to its new resting place. He pried open the lid. John Ashbie had entrusted him with valuables alright. There in the coffin lay various silver serving pieces, two heavy bags which Nat immediately discovered were filled with gold coins, three pieces of imported chinaware, and a bundle of Northern bank notes. His heartbeat raced, and he quickly closed the coffin, sealed it, and soon had it re-interred under three feet of Alabama clay. On the white handkerchief he pulled from the limb, Nat carefully drew out the map of his new burial plot with the pen and the black ink bottle from Master John Ashbie's desk, using symbols only he would understand, folded it on the wagon seat and sat down on the map with the most satisfaction he had known in many years. Then once again, Daniel made the final trip over the road of his robbery. Passing the former burial plot, Nat placed the ink bottle and pen in the crook of the tree by the road, then tossed the shovel out into the field. He had wanted to leave no evidence, yet the temptation to leave clues was too much to resist. Now, come what may, he was ready, and he looked happily toward the Richardson plantation's lane just as a light snow returned, silently, sacredly obliterating the evidence of the funeral held for Massa John Ashbie's wealth.

Chapter Seven
Belle Vista Plantation   April 1861

The weeks had passed and not once did anyone even hint that Nat would be sold. Every time he was sent to *Belle Vista*, he expected it to be his last time. At first, when he drove the buckboard past the scene of his late crime, his conscience gnawed at him. He inwardly debated the act of stealing another's wealth, the moral question of right and wrong. Ultimately, the wrong triumphed. Any regrets had now melted away with the last remnants of the winter's snow.

Today he drove past the field, finally feeling confident in its obscurity. Once the momentary anxiety had subsided that his larceny might be discovered and that he would suffer a whipping until he gave up all information, Nat now settled to work shoeing the four horses William Richardson had stabled. He stopped on occasion to look up, a habit he could not abandon, hoping to see Emma standing at the barn door, a water pail and dipper in hand for him. And each time, his hopes had fallen. It had been over a month, and no one had seen or heard from her. He missed her voice, the genteel way she had of talking – educated, not the crude tongue of the common field hands. Oh, but she was refined, and she had inspired him to rise to that level of refinement. His speech would keep him a slave even after he was free, she had said. And he had wanted to please her, to rise in her eyes. "Patrollers," he repeated half aloud, "not pattyrollers." She had been sold before she could make good on her escape to freedom, but at least she had escaped the patrollers of Madison County. The best he could hope was that she had a good master now and had a measure of respect from her new owners.

Above the clang of the hammer and anvil, above the clatter in his own mind, he heard the clamor from outside the barn. "It's war! Finally it's come!" Nat stuck his head outside the barn doors to see two men, their horses showing the steam and lather of hard riding, jumping down from the saddle and babbling on excitedly to the Richardsons who now had gathered on the front porch. The long anticipated war had finally come, and Nat couldn't make out whether there was pleasure or anxiety in the exchange. But all the whites were worked up nevertheless, and he could not imagine what implications that news might hold for him.

"Massa William," he called, running toward the commotion before the house. "Massa William!"

"What is it, Nat?"

"Massa William, did you'nse say dere's a war?"

"Yes, Nat. But it's in South Carolina, so far. The soldiers there fired all their cannon on Fort Sumter and forced the Yankees to surrender it. We are in it up to our necks, and I hope they don't get the noose around them."

"Yo' agin' de war, Massa?"

"I am, Nat. But we all got to hang together."

"Yo' sho'ly do," he said ironically. "Uhh, Massa William, I's mos'ly done wit' dem hosses now and be finishin' up real soon. Does you wan' me to stay 'round fo' any pa'ticular at all?" He hadn't seen any strangers about, and feared the inevitability of his sale still lurked somewhere. Might as well just come out and confront it. He was surprised by the answer.

"No, I think I will need you next for some work on my wagon wheels, though. But that can wait, Nat. I will send over to Mr. Ashbie when I need you next. You do good work, Nat. And Nat?"

"Yas'm, Massa William?"

"Would you like to come work for me permanent?"

Here it was at last, yet it was not at all what he expected, no rough men with dogs and chains to tie him up and haul him away, no whips in hands. Just a simple request. Curious, he thought. He guarded his words.

"Oh, I don' know. Massa John Ashbie like me purty well, and he sho' be mad if'n I's to axe him about comin' to yo' place permanent. I's jes' not wantin' to upset de hay cart, ya' know?"

"I understand, Nat. But you are here often enough and understand my horses, and you can make working wagon teams out of the worst of the lot. You have a way with them, Nat, and I will talk with Mr. Ashbie about it."

"Massa William, I's hopin' he not be gittin' it in his head dat I axe fo' you to talk to him. I wan' no troubles. Please, Massa William?" he pleaded.

"Don't you worry, Nat. It is entirely my idea."

"Yassuh, Massa William." He hesitated, finally had to say it. "Massa William, I's jes' t'inkin' dat maybe it best dat I come here long ago, not dat I wan' to be away from Massa John Ashbie, 'cause he been powerful good to me. Jes' dat I had mo' den hosses as reason to come to blacksmit' fo' ya'."

Richardson looked at him, studied his face, pulled him aside out of hearing and walked with him back to the stables. "Nat, I understand your meaning completely. I had hoped you would come here too, but Mr. Ashbie would not have it. I know you were sweet on Emma, and I am sorry I had to sell her off. But she had gotten it into her head to run, and I couldn't have that as an example here on my place. I still think if I had done the right thing and bought you from John Ashbie then she would've stayed here. But it can't be helped now. I truly am sorry for that, and so is Mrs. Richardson. Emma was the best laundress and house hand in the county, and I often said so. You know we even had her learn to read and to write so she could help the children, and be respectable when we had our many guests visit? Truly it was a shame we had to let her go. But she had made her choice."

Nat stared hard at Richardson. Choice? She never had a choice in the matter. "I's seein' what ya' mean, Massa." He understood clearly what Emma had thought. To many of the laborers, it had looked like an ideal position, but she was no better than the common field hands back on the Ashbie farm. No better than Samuel. Emma was more educated than even the Richardsons had believed. She had privately studied reading and writing on her own, and she had studied well. More than that, she had studied how to make a life, eventually as a free woman.

"But you come here to work, and maybe there is another gal I can buy for the farm that may work out for you."

"Yas'm, Massa William, mebbe dere is. Well, I's gwan get dem las' two hosses fixed up fo' you real good."

"All right, then, Nat. You do that and I'll see if cook can't rustle up some extra food to bring out to you when you're done."

"Yas'm, Massa William."

He watched Richardson, an animated conversation with the two riders. As he pulled on the bellows, the fire rising and sparks erupting, the glow heated his face which had already begun to burn with Richardson's words. Bring out some food fo' me? I's not one of yo' hosses, he thought. He tugged with renewed energy. He wouldn't wait for a sale. Over a month ago he had already hidden away his plan – in a coffin in a field only one mile away. He would buy his freedom with John Ashbie's own wealth, and then he'd use it to buy Emma from wherever she now labored. Or maybe he would just take the chance and run, and damn the patty– the patrollers.

The morning dragged on, and when he at last stepped up onto the buckboard, a roll of cornbread in his pocket, he was proud that his blacksmithing work was the best he had ever done. If this was the last time he would ever work for free for Master William Richardson, then he would make sure the Richardsons remembered him and realize what they had lost. His artisan work would remain here as a reminder, pouring salt into the wound of his disappearance. But of course salt *would* make the wound heal faster, at least that's what Jonah Kenton always insisted when he was done exacting punishment with his whip. Let's see if it done work dis time, he thought.

Daniel pulled against the muddy ruts, the road revealing tracks of many riders and wagons. The road indeed had been busy this day while Nat had worked at the Richardson farm. He inspected the lanes and fortified himself with the belief that no one these past weeks had sought out the gravesite of his treasure, that John Ashbie was none the wiser to its loss. Daniel plodded on, leaving behind the coffin's secret resting place under the grove of cypress, leaving behind the Richardson farm, and once again leaving behind his dreaded sale to the speculators. Nat drove on, comforted that the reports of his immediate exodus had been wrong.

As he drove up the lane and past the big house at the Ashbie farm, he confronted the same animated exchange as at the Richardson's. Word had come to the farm about the war. Pearl and John Ashbie tried to calm the slaves on the plantation. The war was far away, they said, and it would never affect them. Prices would soar, they said, so they could actually make money. Ashbie saw nothing but profits. Besides, he had already tasked Nat with providing for his own security, secretly stashed in a child's coffin, so the farm would just ride it out.

"Marse John," Nat called out as he reined Daniel in.

"Nat?"

"Marse John, I's done heard 'bout de war a'comin'. Heard it ober at de Massa William's place. Is we all safe here?"

61

"Not to worry, Nat. That is something for those people in South Carolina to handle. But President Davis has said we will have soldiers and militia enough to keep the Yankees out. He asked for a hundred thousand volunteers to form the army to stop them, and the papers had said he got them."

"Yas'm, I hear dat at de Richardsons' place. Uh, Massa John? Massa William say he wan' me to come work for him permanent." A flash of anger showed on John Ashbie's face which Nat read immediately. "Uh, I done tol' him dat I jes' as soon stay right where I is, and dat he kin jaw all he wan' to, but I's stayin'. An' 'asides, you don' need any o' his money. Dat's what I done tol' him, Massa."

Ashbie looked hard at Nat. "Nat, you didn't tell him anything else, did you?"

Nat caught the meaning right away. "No, suh, I tol' him jes' like I be tellin' you. I's gwan stay wit' Massa John, and dat's all dere is to it. He need me, I says. Anyways, he say he gwan talk to you'ns, but I figger I lets you get a heads up afo' he kin git here."

"You're a good boy, Nat. No, I will meet with William Richardson, but my answer is still the same."

"Yas'm dat's what I be figurin' too."

"You get Daniel taken care of and then I need you to saddle up Queenie for me. Then I want you to get that team harnessed up and driven to the field. We are behind in plowing, what with the rains and all. There's plenty of daylight left, and I need your extra hands on it."

"Yas'm I gits right to it."

Nat led Daniel into the barn, left him tied, and saddled Queenie, taking her to Ashbie. Back in the barn he sat down on a stack of feed bags, stretched his legs out, felt in his pockets for the cloth, pulled out the handkerchief with the crude map, and pulled Emma's soiled ribbon. He was never without these, and now he wrapped the yellow ribbon around

62

the folded map like a present, tied a bow in it, tucked it in his coat pocket. A gift to himself.

+ + + + +

Ashtabula, Ohio
April 1861

Marcus folded the newspaper in half, laid it on the table before him, concentrated on the words, reading aloud. *"The cannon shots fired against Fort Sumter was the yell of pirates against the Declaration of Independence; the war-cry of the North is its echo. The South, defying Christianity, clutches its victim. The North offers its wealth and blood in glad atonement for the selfishness of seventy years. The result is as sure as the throne of God...."*

"The only thing that is sure, Marcus, is that many will die in this coming war."

Marcus looked up from the newspaper. "Wendall Phillips doesn't seem to think so, Father."

"Mr. Phillips is a great man. Of that there is no doubt, but this speech of his distorts the final cost. In any place in that speech there did he say he would lead the charge into battle?"

"No, Father."

"When the North offers its blood, does he say that he too will bleed for the freedom of the slaves?"

"No, Father."

"We need men like him to be active in our abolition movement, but nowhere must I advocate for throwing lives away needlessly. Patience – and our cause – will eventually triumph."

"Father, have you read any of the news? Patience came to an end."

"And you want to run off and join the great crusade, son?"

"It's not that, Father. I didn't join with Mr. Brown or any of the others in the Virginia raid. I thought then that it was foolish, and I didn't think it was necessary. But this is different – the South has fired on us. I want to do something."

"You are. Mr. Hubbard has given you enough journeys to aide our cause and you have confounded the enemies of freedom. And you have done so brilliantly. You deserve enough accolades for that alone. There is no need to carry a gun to fight for what you believe is right."

"Father, what I see in men like you is that you want the rain, but you don't want the thunder and lightning."

"You don't have to bring the storm yourself. That's God Almighty's job. Our fight will go on from here, and you will be here on this – our own front line – every time we get a request for another delivery."

"But no one knows of it…"

"That's as it should be. Son, are you doing this for recognition? For a medal? If so, then you're laboring for the wrong reasons. It was Napoleon Bonaparte himself who once said that a soldier will fight long and hard for a bit of colored ribbon. Our ribbon – your ribbon – is the satisfaction of helping just one more slave break his chains and reach freedom."

"I want to do more."

"God in His own good time will show you what you must do. Right now, you have been shown the task at hand, driving the wagons and delivering the freight."

"And you have more freight awaiting delivery, Marcus."

The voice startled Seth, and he turned from the table. "Mr. Bartlett, come in."

"Good afternoon, Seth, Marcus. Mr. Hubbard sent me here. He said you could drive another wagon to a station for

64

us. It's not a long journey and relatively safe for you if you can do it."

"Marcus can drive for you, Simeon. When is he needed?"

"Marcus, if you can leave Saturday, you are to pick up a coffin at a Dr. Chase's office in Orwell and take it to Unionville. The cemetery across from the Unionville Tavern is your destination. When you arrive, ask the innkeeper if anyone can help you to bury a Friend. When he says no, you tell him that you will do it on your own accord, and has he a shovel? That will be the sign. The person who gives you the shovel is your contact. And Marcus, don't make the mistake of talking to the coffin," he smiled. "Here is your story: you have been hired out to transport a smallpox victim directly to the cemetery. That should keep prying eyes and crowbars away from your goods."

Chapter Eight
Unionville, Ohio

Marcus solemnly loaded the pine box onto the back of the wagon, draped the heavy black cloth over it and bid his farewells to Doctor Chase, the Reverend Stewart, and Mr. Wilson, the church sexton, assuring them of a prompt, sacred interment. And carrying their well-wishes he drove the long road from Orwell back to Unionville. The entire operation had proceeded with such deception that even he could see no conspicuous flaws in it. Yet he had that disquieting feeling that he had been observed. These men with whom he had never worked before had developed their smuggling into an art. They were Rembrandts, all of them. Still, he often looked over his shoulder. No one following him. The box in the wagon rested snugly against the side walls, roped in to prevent its shifting. Beneath the edge of the black material he could see the gap left at the head of the coffin. As long as no one asked to see the body, he could keep the air circulating until they reached the cemetery. He felt no fear for himself, only that he might blunder somehow and his cargo would suffer. In a way, he felt soldierly, standing up to an enemy that he despised, and he dreaded the possibility of failing in his duty.

At Unionville, Ohio, the tavern's business was slight. He had not known what to expect, but the lack of business would make him stand out even more. Be always vigilant, his father had told him. Keep a sharp eye out. Look for anything out of the ordinary. Everything seemed ordinary enough as he tied the horse to the rail in front of the tavern. Another black horse shared the same hitching post.

"I am looking for the proprietor," he said to a red-bearded, gruff looking fellow seated outside on a bench, whittling at a piece of pine. He turned, showing a squinting

66

set of eyes highlighted by a deep scar running from the bridge of his nose to his left cheek, an old wound, but menacing enough to cause to Marcus shudder.

"Inside," he indicated, casually aiming the large Bowie knife at the door. "Ask for Mr. Belwin." He returned to shaving slivers from the section of pine, squinting intently at his handiwork.

A short gray-haired man with overgrown side whiskers, wire-rimmed spectacles, and thick, hairy eyebrows that nearly cascaded over the top rims stood behind the tall bar, leaning heavily on his elbows and intently staring into the newspaper.

"Belwin?" Marcus asked.

"That's me," he said, raising only his eyes over the rims and nearly hiding the pupils behind the brows. Marcus was struck by the irony that this comical figure might in fact be the grave associate he required. "I am in need of someone here to help me bury a Friend who succumbed to smallpox in Orwell. Dr. Chase has hired me to bring the poor soul here, and I need to get help with the Christian rites for her."

Belwin looked past Marcus and out through the window to the wagon. "Who are you?"

"Name is Marcus Armstrong. The deceased is a Mrs. Whitcomb from near Orwell."

"And who is that outside at the wagon?"

Marcus whirled around, saw a man standing at the foot of his wagon, peering intently at the coffin. His eyes widened. "I need your help now!" he whispered quickly.

Belwin grabbed a shovel from behind the bar and crossed to the door. "Follow me, Marcus," he said. "Isaiah," he called, "it's good you are here! I have a smallpox victim that needs to be buried immediately over in the cemetery. Can you assist this man and me?"

Isaiah, a wiry, lanky young man of about twenty years, who bore a deep scar from his lower lip to below his chin, looked up as though he had been caught pickpocketing. "Uhh... smallpox, ya' say? Uhh... can't just now. Would like t' help, but I have uhh... errands t' finish. Wish I could. Smallpox, huh? Sorry, but some other time." And he quickly untied his horse from the hitching post and rode off on the aforementioned errands.

Belwin chuckled quietly, spoke to the whittler on the porch. "Peter, are you ready?"

Peter smiled, the gruff exterior melting away with a subtle humor Marcus had missed. "Now I am," he said, and he spat a large brown stream into the spittoon at his feet, and dragged his stained coat sleeve across his red chin whiskers. He retrieved a short handled shovel from beneath the porch steps and tossed it, clattering into the back of the wagon. The three climbed into the wagon and Marcus turned the temporary hearse across the road to the cemetery. Up a narrow path they plodded, the two accomplices sitting with the full dignity of the occasion, and Marcus, holding the reins, regarding them in utmost admiration.

Between two sugar maple trees, the wagon halted, and immediately the men jumped down, drew the coffin from the wagon and gently placed it on the ground. Peter scanned across the cemetery, down one side of the road and up the other, then promptly pried at the pine box with the shovel. The nails screeched, the wood creaked, and the cover gave way, yielding up a disheveled young black woman clutching a woolen blanket. She squinted, focused her eyes in the bright daylight, then smiled broadly, her white teeth gleaming, yet not uttering a sound. She stiffly rose from the coffin, and the men helped her out of her refuge. "Stay low," Mr. Belwin said to her firmly.

As she crouched on a stump, they took the shovels and pried at the thick white limestone slab covering the shallow gravesite. Sliding the heavy stone aside exposed wooden cross-tie steps descending into the dark. Peter produced a short candle stub from his coat pocket and handed it to the woman.

"Light this from the matchbox lying on the steps. Then use the light to follow the tunnel to its end. Wait there and I will help you."

The woman looked down into the blackened grave, the smile fading and fear in her eyes. "It's all right," said Belwin. "You have come this far, and we are not going to let you get caught now."

She attempted a smile, mumbled something which Marcus could not understand, and cautiously went down the steps, retrieving the matchbox. The last he saw of her, she was huddled over the steps attempting to strike the match as they slid the massive limestone slab over her grave.

The men quickly broke down the coffin and lay the boards in the back of the wagon, covering them with the black tarpaulin. "Will she be safe?" asked Marcus.

Belwin wiped his hands on his trousers, cheerily slapped Marcus on the back. "Don't you worry about her. Your task is done. That tunnel will lead under the road and into the cellar of the tavern. She will have food and safe haven there, and then we will move her on to the next station." Marcus stared down at the grave he had just covered, deep in thought. "Marcus? Marcus! Your task is done. Thank you."

Marcus looked down once again, then halfheartedly climbed onto the wagon, reluctantly turned the horse toward the road. From deep inside, he couldn't let her go. He wanted to see her safely out of the country, but to leave her with someone he didn't know troubled him. As he drove away, he looked back to see the two men digging at the earth near two maple trees which had grown so close together they had fused into one large trunk, reaching high over the cemetery. The men were digging a new grave, or the semblance of one for anyone looking for the turned earth of the smallpox victim's final rest. His strong admiration for the conductors was tempered by his reluctance to release his charge to someone else. He wrestled the inner frustration. It was his duty to finish the task. And as he grudgingly drove the wagon on the pike back toward Ashtabula, he considered how he might fulfill his duties more to his complete satisfaction.

+ + + + +

Ashtabula, Ohio

William Hubbard stood on the front porch, hands grasping his coat lapels, a strikingly self-satisfied looking figure. He nodded to acquaintances clattering by in their carriages. It was a gloriously vivid spring afternoon with yellow daffodils speckling the spacious side yard of the Hubbard house. Lake Erie was calm today, and soon another merchant ship would carry his cargo across to Canada. Marcus drove by and called his greeting.

"Did your journey go well?" Hubbard answered brightly.

Marcus reined in the horse. "It did. I will return your wagon to the barn now, if you wish."

"Splendid. Come around after, and we'll talk. I may need your services for another delivery soon, and we should discuss it. By the way, did you happen to meet up with Jude Simon on your journey?"

Marcus looked about. "No. Why? Is there anything amiss?"

"Put away the wagon and horse and we will discuss it."

Marcus finished his work and met Hubbard in the front parlor, extolling the work of the abolitionists who had assisted him in the escape of the woman. "I'm more and more amazed at the risks they all take, but I'm equally amazed with how

70

efficient they are. They had the whole operation planned out before I arrived and had a yarn to spin to justify every move they made. I've never seen anything like it."

"As long as one creature remains in servitude, you will see more than just that. John Price's rescue that you witnessed at Oberlin should have convinced you that we will go to any length to free brethren in bondage. Your father and grandfather had expected you would be a part of our crusade, and you do credit to them both."

"Mr. Hubbard, when do you know you have done enough?"

"Enough?"

"When I carried that poor woman in her coffin to freedom, I felt I was doing something worthwhile. Then I had to leave her with the station masters at Unionville. I know they'll conduct her on until she reaches Canada, but I still had trouble letting go. How do you know when your task has ended?"

"For me it ends when they are safely aboard the ship and onto Lake Erie. I am the last stop on the railroad."

"But I am only a conductor, Mr. Hubbard. I can take them just as far as the next station. How do I let go?"

"I see. What did your grandfather tell you?

"He never discussed it with me – with father perhaps, but not me. I don't know."

"It's trust, Marcus. We all have our jobs to do. Think of a pocket watch. The spring is wound and it drives the watch. But inside are many wheels and cogs, each doing its job. Not one wheel is more important than one lever. The clock face is not more important than the spring. The case is no more important than the hands. All must work together to tell the time correctly. And when you realize you are just one piece in the process, you'll find your burden will be lighter. You can

71

only control what is in your care. Leave the rest up to Providence."

"Easily said, not so easily done."

"It is for me. Complete your duty as it is assigned to you, and let the rest take care of itself. We must only address what's in our immediate safekeeping – which is why I asked about Simon. Did you see him anywhere?"

"No. I would have noticed that."

"He left shortly after you did, and the committee thought he may have followed you. You saw no one at Orwell or at Unionville?"

"A man about my age was snooping around the wagon while I was in the tavern at Unionville, but he soon left when the tavern keeper mentioned smallpox. Never saw a trace after that. If he was still suspicious he might have had someone else watch the cemetery, but no one was there. Of that, I am sure."

"Jude Simon has been busy tracking any of our movements. Thus far no one has been reported or the marshals would have moved to arrest any of the Friends."

"The men at Unionville knew the young man snooping around the wagon, but he scared off easily with the threat of smallpox. Doubtful Simon was linked to him, or he wouldn't have fallen for the ruse."

"Still, Simon knows of the young boy Samuel. He confronted your father about him. Of course, your father denied everything, but you are implicated and he will watch you closely."

"Samuel is free, isn't he?"

"As free as you and me and living in Canada now."

"Then that's all that matters. I can take care of myself."

"When will you return to Oberlin College, Marcus?"

"I don't think that I will, Mr. Hubbard."

"Does your father agree with that?"

"He doesn't know. I told him I was leaving school only to help with grandfather's affairs and that I would stay through the summer."

"He suspects, Marcus. He said you have even spoken of joining the Union Army. He believes you have a future in studying the law, yet he is concerned that you would throw it all away."

"No one has refused my help so far. In fact, you all have sent me on more missions than I had ever thought I would see. Father never…."

"Your father is happy for your help, and he wanted to give you a part in the Railroad. But that was only while you are here, and to keep you busy until you return to Oberlin. Seeing the movement firsthand is an education in itself, and I believe it will help you. You will be more valuable by completing your law studies and attacking this slavery pestilence in the courts. Come with me, I want you to see something."

Hubbard took a lamp from the mantle, lit it and led Marcus to the cellar door, descending the darkened steps. Another door opened and inside the dimly lit area sat perhaps a dozen glistening black bodies, looking uneasily at the two of them. "This is Marcus," he addressed the group. "He is one of us, one of our conductors. Tonight he will lead you to your next rendezvous." Marcus looked at the dread, the uncertainty in each black face, and he felt sickened. Hubbard laid his arm across Marcus' shoulder. "This is why you must complete your studies in the law. This war the rebels started will come to an end. I have no fear of the final outcome. But then we will need good men in the courts, men who will defend these people when they are finally free. Marcus, you must be one of those men."

Chapter Nine
Alliance, Ohio   June 1861

On April 19, after the surrender of Fort Sumter, President Lincoln requested an army of 75,000 men be raised from the remaining Union states to suppress the rebellion. The northern states answered with over 100,000 men and the training began in earnest. Ohio's enthusiasm for the Union produced nearly 23,000 men eagerly volunteering for the three-month enlistment. Training camps had begun to build in Ohio: Camp Dennison near Cincinnati, Camp Chase near Columbus, Camp Buckingham near Mansfield, and dozens of others soon springing up like spring morels. The end of June had arrived and Marcus saw his opportunities dwindling. Soon the original enlistments would end and the Ohio boys would return. His fight had remained on the front lines of Ohio, conducting escaping slaves by way of his wagon teams. By his careful count, he figured he had transported nineteen more passengers as hidden cargo since the young black woman in the coffin. In his wagon under loads of lumber, or crammed into the clandestine cutaway box under his driver's seat, or even in his least favorite conveyance, the coffin, he had carried the unfortunate fugitives to freedom. Though his deliveries came to the Hubbard house in Ashtabula, he knew of others in Elyria, and still others in Sandusky, through the Bass Islands, and Cleveland. Few would admit openly of abetting criminal activity, yet through his father, he learned names of sympathizers who might turn a blind eye to his activities. His passage on the Warren-Ashtabula turnpike became a familiar spectacle, and many Friends began to recognize him on sight, offering him food and drink as he passed. It was precisely because of that familiarity that Hubbard and others insisted on revising his routes and sending him to other areas of the state. His father dispatched him south on errands to Limaville, to Marlboro, to Salem, and finally to Alliance to meet J. Ridgeway Haines.

Sharing the same Quaker beliefs as Marcus' grandfather, the Haines family was none too secretive about its abolitionist sympathies. The Western Anti-Slavery Society, with its headquarters in Salem, had openly held two of its meetings at the Haines house and its 120 acre farm in Alliance. Two years earlier, Seth Armstrong had attended one of these with his father, George, and was immediately welcomed. Seth had continued to keep abreast of the society's activities, and he ultimately wrote a letter of introduction for Marcus, directing him on his most recent errand to meet with the Haines family. Ridgeway and Sarah Haines' son John liked Marcus immediately and they soon became fast friends. In the Haines house front parlor they sat over a luncheon.

"Father says that you studied at Oberlin?" asked Tump, as John was known in the village.

"I did," said Marcus, "and am still studying there. I came home to assist father when grandpa died and I have stayed on, but will return in the fall. I suppose I am destined to pursue the Law."

"Did you know Charles Langston?"

"I knew of him. I was in Oberlin when he was finally released from jail. I have never met him, but have seen him. It was a very brave affair. I doubt that I would've been so brave."

"Why do you say that?" Tump asked.

Marcus thought for a moment, formed the words. "I believe in total emancipation, freedom for the slaves. And the work I do now isn't much, but father says it helps. But if it came to going to jail for those beliefs, I would have to think hard on it."

"Those Wellington rescuers were released through the use of the law, and through plenty of pressure in the courts.

In thinking on the whole affair, I don't believe that they were really in any danger."

"Well, Tump, I was there, and it looked to me like they were in grave danger. It was about to become violent, and I knew I couldn't join in with them. Earlier, I had thought of joining with John Brown's son and helping free the slaves, but father advised me against it."

"Luckily so," John said.

"I wasn't convinced that his resolve for violence was necessary either. Anyway, I am here now and willing to secret away anyone who is escaping. I want to do something grand." He saw Tump's look. "Oh, it's not that I want any special recognition...."

Tump studied him for a moment. "You wish to remain anonymous, yet you want to do something grand. You're a curious fellow, if I may say so."

Marcus smiled self-consciously, "I expect I am."

"Taking a stand for what you believe, by its very nature, makes a wreck of anonymity. I guess when it all whittles away, your motives are the only thing that is important, don't you think?"

"I guess so."

"None of us does this for the honors, Marcus. We do it because of conviction. At least that's what I have been taught since I was old enough to understand. Many a night I have sat in this house on that staircase over there, cradling a musket, just in case slave catchers tried to break through that door," he said, nodding toward the parlor's archway. "I don't expect any reward for it – just doing what's required."

"Have you thought about joining in with the volunteers?"

"What, the army?" Tump asked.

Marcus nodded.

"Well, I suppose I have. Senator Sherman has called for volunteers to enlist for more than the original three month enlistment. A friend from near here, George Harlan, is planning to enlist, as well as many boys from the neighboring farms. I suppose if I can stay away from home for the two years they are requiring, I will make a good soldier. What about you?"

"I don't know that I would make a very good soldier at all. I have thought on it. Father of course would speak out against it, and my grandfather would have also. I just want to be doing something more, now that we're at war with the rebels."

"Well, until that day comes, if ever, we are to be about the business of transporting. And so, Father and I would like you to accompany me on an errand. We need to pick up a load of the first cutting hay to take to the Dickinsons in Randolph. I would appreciate your company."

"Hay?" Marcus said studying his face.

"Hay," he said, showing a subtle smile.

+ + + + +

The wagon harnessed, and the hay loaded, the two men drove the road through the village, passing the photography studio of Emmor Crew on Main Street. A small display of his work adorned the front window of his gallery, beckoning the adventurous patriots to come join them in the noble cause. Boys dressed in Union uniforms stood before a backdrop of American flags, artillery pieces, or army tents, resting their hands on the same ornate Gothic chair, sometimes displaying a proud swagger in the pose, and more often unconsciously revealing a timorous, bewildered look. Before the studio stood a short, bony man with hardened, dark eyes and scraggly, long chin whiskers with brown tobacco stains. He glared long and hard at Marcus as the wagon passed by.

"You know him?" Tump asked.

"Why?"

"He seems to know you."

"I saw him in Ashtabula a few times. He was at my grandfather's house during his wake. Jude something...."

"Simon. Jude Simon. He's a bounty hunter. His business is slave catching," Tump said simply.

"You know him too?"

"I have seen him in Salem before. We were at Mr. Hise's home for a meeting of the Society and he was hanging about, seeking an advantage. Mr. Hise had him escorted off the property, but he was seen about Salem at various times. He made no secret of his business of apprehending runaways."

"That's a bit dangerous for him, isn't it?"

"No Marcus, it isn't. You see, he has the *law* on his side."

Soon they turned onto Iowa Avenue and followed the road out of town, riding parallel to the Cleveland and Wellsville Railroad line, on toward Limaville and to Randolph. Beyond the town, they heard a rider quickly approaching from behind. Marcus looked back. "Simon," he said. Jude Simon reined in his horse beside the men. "Watchya got in the hay, Armstrong?" he snarled.

"Do you always begin greetings this way?" Marcus quipped.

"I'll have a look at that hay you're carryin'."

"Looking for anything in particular, Mr. Simon?" Tump asked. "Or are you just hungry?"

The boys burst out laughing at the butt of the joke. Simon quickly snatched the pitchfork from the pegs on the wagon's back, flipped it in the air, and caught the shaft like a pike pole, drew it back to throw it. The two cowered. "That is not your pitchfork! Leave it alone!" Tump yelled.

"Gladly," Simon snarled, and he violently threw the pitchfork deep into the mound of hay. Immediately, the frustration flashed across his face and his cheeks reddened.

"Are you quite finished? We have to be about our business, and I assume you need to be about yours?" Tump said.

"All right then, but you two are up to something. I've been watching you."

Tump shook the reins and the horses lurched forward. "Well, don't strain your eyesight, mister. You might miss something really worth watching," Marcus called, and the wagon rattled on down the road, leaving their laughter floating on a cloud of settling dust for the breeze to swoop up and carry back to perch on the coat and tobacco stained beard of Jude Simon.

+ + + + +

The hay was quickly unloaded in the Dickinson barn, and a receipt given to Mrs. Dickinson. On the back, Ridgewood Haines had written three letters: *URR*. Mrs. Dickinson read it, smiled. "Come this way." And she hurried across the yard to the house, pulled on the outside cellar door and called in, "Quickly." An older, skeletal, gray bearded black man, wearing torn pantaloons and a burlap sack as a waist-length shirt, tied about the middle with a cotton rope, appeared in the doorway and smiled broadly showing a nearly cavernous mouth of neglected teeth.

Tump slipped a board from the box on the back of the wagon and a false panel dropped open, revealing a hidden compartment. "You will be safe in here. Now quickly get in!" The poor creature hesitated, looked at Marcus who nodded his head in agreement, flashed him a quick smile, and held out his hand. Marcus helped the man into the box which had no holes for air and looked very much like a part of the wagon. "Slide that board under your head aside." A gaping hole appeared, big enough for the man to hang his entire head through if he wished. "Lay quietly and we will soon be home," Tump said, and he slid the panel into place, slipping the board into its grooved channel, securing the box.

The dusty road was an easy ride back to Alliance, and the sun had just touched the tops of the fields sending a red-orange glare across the stubble as the wagon drove into the village. Down Market Street they drove the team and up the winding lane to the barn. Inside the barn Marcus released the board and the panel fell off of the wagon, causing the pitchfork to clatter on the gravel. "What is your name?" he asked the slave as he helped him out. The man groaned a little and stretched his hands high overhead.

"Lawda mussey. Dat feel good," he said. "Name is Elijah, suh."

"Well, Elijah," said Tump, "let's get you into the house for a proper bed."

The men crossed behind the house and slipped into the side kitchen. Sarah Haines greeted them at the door. "Welcome," she said. "I have food prepared and will bring it up shortly. John, take this man up."

They led the man up a narrow, steep staircase which ended at a wall. Two doorways flanked either side of the stairs, and they stopped between them. Tump pulled out a Barlow knife, pried at the wall panel, and it popped loose. Marcus set the panel aside revealing a door only four feet high. Tump knocked three times slowly and then twice in quick succession. A latch sounded and the door swung in to an attic room directly above the kitchen. It was dimly lit by two lanterns that revealed two black faces peering out at them. The man and woman stepped back, Tump stooped low, and he led the new arrival into the room. Marcus waited on his hands and knees, his head thrust inside the room. Six pallets, thin mattresses lying on each, lined the walls around the room with a white chamber pot thrust back into the corner behind the door. A nail keg and two chairs occupied the middle of the room, flanking a small round side table, set with stoneware and spoons and knives. "This is Elijah," he said to the couple. "Mother will bring food up shortly. Have a restful night, and one of the family will see you tomorrow morning. Good night."

"Bless you," Elijah said, and he grabbed Tump's hand, awkwardly pumping it up and down in an act of uninhibited thanksgiving.

Marcus self-consciously backed out of the room, standing up in the hallway. Tump closed the door, leaving the panel free for his mother to enter. That possessive feeling welled up again, a nervous fear of the unknown, and Marcus stopped at the bottom of the stairs, immovable, staring blankly. He wanted to go back up.

"Marcus? What is it?" Tump asked.

"Is there anything else I can do?"

"Yes, there is." It was Ridgewood Haines' voice from the parlor. "You can get some rest. You two have had a long day, Marcus, and you will return to Ashtabula in the morning. Your work here is done."

"Maybe there is something I..."

"Marcus. You have done enough. We will take over from here. Your father will have more for you to do, I am sure. Goodnight."

As he lay down in his bedroom, the restlessness kept him tossing fitfully. Mr. Hubbard was right, of course. He needed to let go and trust the others. "Your work here is done." The voice repeated it like an echo until he drifted away.

Chapter Ten
Cypress Grove Plantation   July 1861

Plantation owners, disheartened by reports of minor defeats at the muzzle of the invading Union army, finally received encouraging news of a major Confederate victory for their forces at Manassas Junction, Virginia. The Union army had been turned back and forced to retreat from their attack on Bull Run Creek, running in panic until they reached the safety of Washington City. The newspaper reports cheered the success, the "great skedaddle" they called it. Inwardly disheartened, the slaves remained outwardly indifferent to all news of the war. Self-preservation governed all behavior. The Ashbie slaves performed their best to maintain the status quo, patiently awaiting their ultimate delivery. Nat continued to complete his farrier duties at John Ashbie's behest to an ever widening clientele in the area, and had now become renowned for his abilities. The money he received, always demanded in gold, promptly alighted in Ashbie's coffers, a portion of which was secretly entrusted to Nat to deposit in the security of the rude coffin in the distant field. Of course, Nat obeyed to the letter his instructions and periodically visited the grave to inter the newly acquired gold. Ashbie calculated himself to become a wealthy man after the war, and he encouraged Nat's help with bold promises of future rewards. But those who assumed Nat had settled into the comfortable role of the dutiful servant were ignorant of the aching for freedom he felt on every journey, all while talking his way past patrollers and scoundrels who safely waited out the war as home guards. His most recent work assignment had taken him to a short three days' stay at a Huntsville plantation, and upon his safe return he happily welcomed the sight of the grand house of Belle Vista.

"Massa John," he said, "You wants me to take dis pay to de field agin?" He held out the bag of gold coins to Ashbie, who clutched at it a little more protectively than usual.

"No, Nat. I think mebbe I'll just keep it here this time. We may have need of more money on hand soon. There's talk of shortages coming, and it's best to be prepared. I have to feed the family, you know."

"Yas'm, dat's right, Massa John. You gots to eat."

"Of course, after the war, we'll survive with what you and I have buried. I'm pleased that you and I have prepared for that."

"Yessuh, I al'ays say, you's bes' be prepared."

"Exactly," Ashbie said, and then lowering his voice, speaking firmly, "And that's why I need to put away as much money as I can now. And you are going to help me with that."

A subconscious worry came over him, and he looked around for eavesdroppers. "How kin I he'p?" Nat asked cautiously.

"Next week, a man from Huntsville will be here. He wants to hire you out for a few days. He has many horses, and says the government wants to buy them for the Confederate cavalry. So he has asked me to hire you out and to have you stay with him for a few days, getting them shoed and groomed to sell. And Nat, he is willing to pay," he said with a sly grin.

Nat returned the grin. "Oh, I see, Marse John. We'se gwanna be even richer." And he giggled an arrogant laugh, his pure white teeth displayed broadly.

Ashbie smiled meaningfully. "Oh, yes, Nat. *Much* richer. Now you get that wagon put away, and come up to the big house after you've eaten. We'll have all the details then."

"Yas'm, Marse John."

At the slave quarters, the talk was low, rumors mixed with fact dripped like honey, and the slaves zealously spread both.

Work in the fields had stopped unusually early, even for a Saturday night, and the small community of workers had combined their cooking to make a gathering meal, usually only reserved for weddings and the few allowed holidays. Talk of the war, of the victories and defeats, punctuated the meal. Then the topic turned to what would become of the farm. The Ashbies were going to face hard times just like all the neighboring farms. How would the slaves survive when the Yankee soldiers arrived, as most assumed they would? Mrs. Annabelle had worried aloud to Martha that they would have to collect on all debts owed to them and save the farm. But that wasn't enough; Big Jim had been sold off along with two young girls while Nat was away. Everyone was expendable when money was in need.

"Mebbe I kin he'p wit' keepin' you'ns all here. Massa say he done hired me out to Huntsville fo' a few days nex' week. I makes enough money fo' him dat we kin outlas' de war."

William, one of the younger field hands, slapped down his hoecake on his plate. "And what gwan happen to us if'n de Yankees win, huh? Dat money do no good to us."

"You t'ink dey gwanna win, Nat?" asked Marcella.

"Don' rightly know. If'n we win, t'ings go on like befo'. If'n de Yankees win, some say we be freed. Eit'er way, we gwan need money to lib here."

"You ever t'ink 'bout keepin' any o' dat money, Nat?"

Nat grinned. "Oh yas'm, Martha, I sholey do. But I ain't doin' not'in' to make Massa John mad enough to sell me off. I be makin' him piles o' money and he be lookin' out fo' us, so dat atter de war, we be keepin' de farm goin' wit' what I done brung in."

"You t'ink he be keepin' dat promise, Nat?"

"I don' hab no reason to mind anyt'ing else. Him and me, we be partners, in a way."

The slaves stopped eating, a vacuous silence filled the room. They all stared at Nat like he had cursed in a church meeting. Nat thought about the coffin he had already moved, visualized it in the field near the cypress tree, thought about how John Ashbie had no idea where the treasure had been secretly laid to rest. And he considered now that he really had no notion of just how he could make good on helping the others. It was himself or them now, and he stopped short of spilling the entire secret. He felt into his pocket, fingered the crude map he had drawn, tied with Emma's ribbon. Nat looked at the silent group, one by one. "You's t'inkin' I's wrong. But I tells ya' dat Marse John Ashbie and me, we's done worked out a plan. I cain't tell ya' all about it, but I knows dat I kin lib like a king some day."

"It be takin' a heap a money to lib like a king, Nat.," said William.

"A heap o' money I gots," he blurted out, realized he had said too much, and stared at the table and the meager food on his plate.

The others broke out in raucous laughter, slapped him on the shoulders and back. "Sho' you do, Nat. Sho' you do." More laughter.

They hadn't believed him. It was just as well. When he returned from Huntsville next week, he would take half of his payment and make a short detour to stop at the gravesite, bury it there in the coffin, and return the rest to John Ashbie with the lie that this horse breeder would send him the rest. In the meantime he would plan his run carefully, secret away what clothing and food he would need, and pay his respects to the gravesite one last time. Then he'd make for the north with as much of his treasure as he could carry.

+ + + + +

85

In May, the Kentucky convention began which would settle the question of secession for all time. Kentucky eventually would vote to stay with the Union, though the split votes were an indication of the deep rift in the populace. Slavery, an important element in the economy, would remain in Kentucky, but cotton was not king to them, and neither was the King Cotton mentality. Now even fewer slaves worked the farms and plantations in the northern counties. Though Kentuckians saw the future of slavery dying before their eyes, many older generational families determined to hold out until ultimately compelled to do so by the Union they supported. The southern counties continued to embrace the Old South mindset. Kentucky would remain a buffer to an all-out invasion by the Union Army into the Deep South, playing to both sides. The Ohio River was a natural border to hinder any invasion, and to hinder any slaves attempting to gain freedom by way of Ohio.

The last day of July 1861 came, and with it came Nat's excitement of stowing away more money for his own escape to freedom. He could not even hint to his closest friends of his plan to buy some of them out of their bondage. When they would get word of his flight, they might take heart in his determination to free them too, but for now, they must remain where they were. He was on edge all morning until finally the wagon arrived with the man from Huntsville. Nat finished packing a cloth bag with his leather apron and some clothing to take with him to Huntsville. For safe keeping, under his bed in the slave quarters he stashed another bag with the rest of his scrounged clothing – warm clothing he would eventually need in the North this coming winter.

"Nat! Marse John say de man from Huntsville here to take you to work. Ya' bes' be a-comin' now."

"I be along directly," he said and gave one last look about the place. Confident he had everything ready for an immediate escape upon his return, Nat closed the door to his quarters, a small shed that he was privileged to share with no one since Big Jim's sale. His plan was set, his goal straight forward in his own mind. Within a week of his return, he would strike out for freedom.

The wagon at the big house was an unusual sight. Not built for a lengthy journey in comfort, but for hauling agriculture, feedbags and the like, it sat waiting, two men resting on the wagon's bench. A shiny coated black mare hitched to the front railing pawed at the ground. Master John Ashbie stood on the front porch of the estate between the imposing Doric columns, shaking hands with a tall, mustached, gaunt man sporting an exceedingly tall stovepipe hat, long mustard-seed colored coat, and moss green trousers with black pinstripes, an amusing figure to Nat's thinking. So this skeletal scarecrow is who he would be working for in Huntsville. Well then, if it brought more income he could liberate from Marse John, he could tolerate the humorous figure for a week. Nat tossed the clothing bag onto the wagon, stood dutifully by its side and awaited John Ashbie's blessing. Annabelle Ashbie stepped onto the porch and looked in his direction. Nat put his fingers to his hat brim to tip it, but Annabelle jerked her head around and retreated into the house. Missy Annabelle sho' do carry on so, he thought. He slid up onto the wagon, his feet dangling over the back, looked to John Ashbie, smiled and waved. Ashbie lifted his hand to wave, clenched it into a fist and dropped it to his side. He looked down to the porch floor and turned inside. Nat watched the snub, and in that angry moment he vowed he would keep *all* of the money he would earn in Huntsville and never return to Belle Vista until he would ride his own elegant horse in as a free man.

The scarecrow figure rode ahead on the shiny black horse, his colorful clothing shining like a beacon even in the daylight. At the end of the lane, with Belle Vista far behind them, the wagon stopped, and in an instant the two men in the wagon seat had jumped down, circled either side of the wagon and grabbed Nat's arms. The skeletal rider, galloped up to him, drew a pistol and pointed it into Nat's face.

"You jes' behave yourself, boy, and no harm will come."

The two riders clamped on leg irons and chain. One arm was shackled to the side of the wagon, and in short order Nat was secured for his journey. The confusion and anger rose together.

"I's not gwanna run, boss. Marse John and me, we have a agreement dat I neber run but do de wo'k I's hired out fo'. You don' needs to chain me while we's gwan to Huntsville. I hab wo'k dere to do fo' you'ns."

"You ain't going to Huntsville, boy. I paid good money for you, and you are going where I say you're going. First we got to pick up a couple more, and then we'll be moving on."

Nat couldn't believe it. He fought back the anger, the tears. "Marse John done sell me?"

"That's right. And you should fetch a pretty good price for me when we get to where we're headed."

"And where dat be?"

"Kentucky."

Chapter Eleven
Old Washington, Kentucky   August 1861

The wagon bumped and creaked on the dirt road, climbing yet another steep hill, the team of horses straining to pull the wagon. As it finally reached the crest and picked up speed, from his perch on the wagon seat, Nat saw there to the right, up on that even higher hill, the big house. Displaying four massive white porch columns, the whitewashed brick mansion rose above the highest elevation of the entire farm, standing sentinel over the whole of the Marshalls' kingdom. It consumed nearly 1500 acres and stretched to the left of the road as far as Nat could see, on down the hill, down to the Ohio River somewhere in the distance out of his sight. The young slave boy, Jacob Marshall, handled the reins skillfully, and slowly tugged at them as they approached the Marshall's lane. The white overseer rode on ahead toward the mansion.

"Mus' be a heap o' field hands here to be wo'kin' dis farm," Nat said quietly.

"Not so much. Marse Marshall, he good to us. He hire out de field hands fo' de tobacco and de corn. We here is mos'ly workers fo' de big house, fetchin' and gittin' and such. He git us plenty to eat, and he say we be gittin' freedom when we wo'k our time in."

Nat looked hard at Jacob, studied the pleasant, hopeful naiveté of his face. "An' how long ya'll be wo'king for de Marshalls?"

Jacob let the reins slack in his hand and rubbed his chin, looking heavenward as if reading the answer on some vapor in the cloudless sky. "I 'spect about ten year now."

"Uh, huh," he said sarcastically. "Freedom be jus 'round de corner, ain't it?" Nat looked down at his manacled ankles, looked up at Jacob, now shaking the reins to speed up the horses, then shook his head in disgust, muttered quietly to himself, "Anyways, it be jus' 'round *my* corner."

The wagon turned up the lane which sliced a gentle curve through the rolling field, heavily green with wide tobacco leaves and golden-tasseled cornstalks. Out in the middle of the field to the right sat a whitewashed house-like building with two chimneys rising above the low roof peaks. Jacob was correct. No slaves were about, at least none Nat could see in the fields surrounding the big house. They slowly passed to the right of the house where the overseer who had purchased Nat at the sale in town dismounted from his horse and went to the massive rear porch, reporting to Martin Marshall. Nat noticed three slaves behind the big house chopping wood, stopping long enough to inspect him before bringing the axe down again with a cracking thump on a chunk of maple. A thin pretty black woman appeared at the back door, curtseying to the two white men as she passed by them, carrying a load of various color dresses in her arms. He knew her immediately – Emma.

Jacob stopped the wagon behind the big house and climbed down from the driver's bench, pulled the reins to a hitching post and quickly had them knotted. Nat sat still awaiting orders, surveying his new situation and lightly rubbing the chafe on his chained ankles. Across the yard on the opposite side of the big house stood the summer kitchen, a light wisp of smoke rising from the small chimney, carrying the aroma of cooking pork. Nat's mouth fairly watered with each deep breath. Beyond the summer kitchen about 30 yards distant stood the slave quarters, a tolerably small two story brick house with two chimneys poking through the peak at either end of the roof. Nat noted that the brick matched the big house, yet the wide whitewashed double barn door implied a sharing of the quarters with the animals or at least with a buggy or carriage of some sort. Emma disappeared into

90

the slave quarters, glancing back just for an instant. Nat absorbed the whole of the farm and buildings, memorizing every detail, creating a mental map of the place. The high roof, the top floor's two windows facing the back yard, the uneven brick pattern that started straight and level at each corner, then meandered like a river current along the center of the back wall, the roof of the porch supported firmly by six narrow columns. The open yard, bisected by a brick path, led from the porch toward the back of the yard, up a small rise, passing by a thirty-foot bald cypress and a smaller oak tree towering above a small family cemetery. He focused on the few headstones. "Dey born here, dey live here, dey die here. Hmmpf! Not gwan be my restin' place," he muttered quietly to himself.

"What you say, dere, niggah?" asked Jacob.

"I say, it be a nice, pleasant place," Nat smiled.

"Sho' is."

A voice sounded behind him. "Your name Nat?"

Nat turned to face an older gray-haired man, of about 60 years. "Yassuh, it is."

"My name is Martin Marshall. I am your new master now, Nat."

"Yassuh, Massa Marshall."

Marshall looked him up and down as if inspecting a prize stallion, bent down and unlocked the ankle chains. "You look fit enough. I always trust my overseer, Mister Kelly, to pick the best at the auction. I think you'll do. I am told your trade is to work with horses."

"Yassuh, Marse Marshall. I guess I be 'bout de best blacksmith in Alabama." And he stood grinning foolishly at Marshall. Then after a beat, "Leastways, while I be dere. Uh – at least dat what my ol massuh, Marse John tol' me – a-an' 'bout ebryone else what come to de plantation. But I 'spect dey's gooduns here'bouts too. Best dey is in Kaintucky."

91

Martin Marshall sized him up and laughed at his self-effacing humor. "Well, there's good ones in Kentucky for certain, but I expect as good work from you as your old master did. You will be in charge of all my stock, and I have many good horses. I expect them groomed as needed, I expect you to see they are properly shoed at all times, and I expect you to drive teams for my wagons and to drive my carriage when called upon. If you can't handle it, I will have to get someone who can."

"Oh, I sho'ly can, Marse Marshall. You jes' gib me dem reins and I do de res' fo' you."

"Very good, Nat. You go on now, and find yourself a place in the quarters over yonder," he said pointing out the small brick building. "Ask for Emma. "

"Yas'm I will, and t'ank ya'."

"Another word, Nat. I run a fair place. I use no whips here, and will not allow anyone else to use them. I expect a full day's work. You will not want for food nor clothing, and you have all Sundays off and half Saturdays. But you are still my property, and anyone who tries to run off will be caught and sold down to New Orleans. I think they will not find that situation in the Deep South as agreeable as it is here. Now, go on, Nat."

Nat didn't like threats, and he had already fixed his mind on seeking an opportunity. But first things first. Get to know the farm, the other slaves, Master Marshall, and especially the town. Then ask round for the abolitionists. He had heard they were concentrated heavier in Kentucky than they were in Alabama. Someone must know something – but how to make contact without raising suspicion?

Inside the brick building, Nat surveyed the main floor. An elegant shiny black carriage sat in the middle of the room, facing the double doors. A cot occupied the left rear corner of the room. The brick fireplace at its head made up the center third of the wall. Well, if he must stay through the winter, at least he would be warm. On the cot he dropped the bag of clothing, apparel he had so carefully packed to do his expected work in Huntsville. Most slaves sold at auction could take nothing with them but the shirts on their backs, some, not even that much. At least he had those with him. But it felt good to be finally free of the shackles he had worn from Alabama until his purchase by Marshall's overseer. He sat on the edge of the cot, trying the lumpy feel of it.

A pleasant voice from the staircase, "Does the bed suit you, Nat?"

He stood quickly. Emma descended the steps at the far end of the quarters, a rough-looking multi-colored patchwork quilt draped over her arm. She smiled that same smile he had come to anticipate at Belle Vista Plantation.

"Master Marshall says you can have this. It belonged to a no account runaway that he ended up selling off. I had to wash it yesterday for his new blacksmith, but I had no idea the blacksmith was you. I hope you like it, Nat."

The same old feelings crept up again. Here she stood, the perfect speaking house servant, assuming her duties again and unwittingly humiliating him with her words. He chose his carefully, looking down to his shoes. "It be fine, Emma. Dey both be fine. Thank you."

"I expect you will want something to eat. We eat at sundown, after I am done serving the master's house, Evangeline will bring you something. There's seven of us upstairs, one over there on the other side by the other fireplace. You and he will have to mind the fire at night in both hearths when the cold comes on." She looked out the window, searching. "Nat," she at last said quietly, "how'd you ever get sent here?"

"I 'spect I knowed too much."

Emma turned from the window, sat on the cot beside Nat. "You say what?"

"I hears ya'll gots sol' off 'cause ya'll tried to run off and dey cotched you up."

"I never did. I got sold before I *could* run. Master William and Missy Annabelle said they heard I was talkin' about running off, and they sold me to the speculator that came around about just so's I wouldn't disgrace them." She watched Nat's face which showed no emotion, yet she sensed a deep anger that was unusual for him. Usually the quiet, reserved happy worker she had often brought water to just to be near him, he now seemed nervous, expectant. "What was it that you knew too much, Nat?"

Nat hesitated, looked about the room. He was emphatic. "You keep dis secret, Emma."

"Of course, Nat."

"Befo' de war started, Massa John Ashbie done had me do a buryin'. But de onlyest t'ing I got buried was a pickaninny coffin. In it he had me puts gol' and silber and some o' his val'bles to hide from any soldiers. He say afte' de war am done, he gwan dig dat up and be a rich man to start all ober, win or lose. He gots me to put in my payments fo' de wo'k he hires me out to do. Den he has me draw a map on a hankie fo' him to hide so's he kin gets it a'ter de war."

"He a smart man, I guess."

"He not so smart, Emma. 'Cause I done takes dat chile's coffin and I digs it up and puts mo' treasures in it, den I buries in in ano'der place, and I draws a second map on a hankie he gives me. Dat one I gots right here wid me," he said, patting his coat pocket. "I 'spect he knew dat I knows too much about his grave, so he done sol' me off so's I can't get to it, or tells nobody 'bout it." Then he grinned that wide grin she liked. "But I gits de las' laugh. 'Cause I knows where dat chile's coffin am buried. And I gwan git it some day and Massa John, he done he'p me get started on my own. Eben if'n he don't know he done it."

Emma had sat on the bed, her mouth open, awestruck. "You did all that by yourself, Nat? Well, I guess you are about the smartest man I ever met." Then she wrapped her arms about him and laughed with her head on his shoulder, a feeling he enjoyed immensely. "You're sure something, Nat Ashbie."

He pushed her arms down gently, looked deeply into her eyes, spoke firmly. "I ain't no Nat Ashbie. I jus' plain Nat."

"All right, just plain Nat."

"Where do de massa say I am havin' to work? 'Cause I ain't no fieldhand."

"Look out the window. See that house out in the middle of that field, the one with two chimneys? That's the barn and the forge. You will work there."

"How much land do he say he got, Emma?"

"I don't know for sure. Some say over two hundred acres. Look over there, down the hill to the road and beyond that road, down the next hill. See down there? You can barely see it. That's the Ohio River. And way out there, that's Ohio."

"Freedom," he said.

"It is, but the slave catchers are all around here and they have no fears about going over there to Ohio and catching any runaways. The law is on their side too."

Nat looked at the land across the river, then at the distance between the slave quarters and the near bank of the Ohio River. "You hasn't give up on freedom, has you Emma?"

"I have not given up, Nat. But I'm wiser now that I got sold once. So I don't dare mention it to anybody. Even here on the farm, you don't know who you can trust."

"Cept fo' me…."

"Except for you, Nat. But if we get to the river, then we have to cross it. They say the river is deep somewheres and not so deep other wheres. You need a guide to make it."

"Wheres do I gets me a guide?"

"I expect in Maysville. It's not far from here. But in Washington, you better not ask around."

"De fustus chance I gets to go to de town, I's gwan as' fo' somebody to guide me."

"No! Don't ask. Just wait. Someone will soon come to you. Now you get washed up. I left a bucket there for you. I have to get back to the kitchen and help with fixing supper for the Marshall's." She walked to the door, slipped quietly out, then thrust her head back in. "It's good to see you again, Nat. And it's surely good to have you here."

Chapter Twelve
Oberlin, Ohio   September 1861

Fall's chill had come early to Ohio. What had amounted to only minor skirmishes between Union and Confederate forces in Missouri and Virginia, had produced varying results. None of these could warm the hearts of the Northern citizens so desperate for encouraging news, and those few Union victories that were reported could not wipe from memory the embarrassment of the Battle of Bull Run. The cry arose for larger armies to march to the killing fields. Communication or chance meetings with school chums made Marcus even more compelled to lend himself to the fight; none more convincing than when he met Adam Watling, his "pard" as he called him, while visiting in Oberlin. He and Adam had been schoolmates during the last educational year but had not kept in contact once Marcus left for his grandfather's funeral. Though they both shared fervent abolitionist sympathies, Watling had originally determined to remain in college instead of joining the crusade. Both young men had studied in Professor James Fairchild's moral philosophy and theology classes and respected his teachings, becoming close friends after their semester with him had finished. Then Marcus had left the campus for home. By chance, Marcus met Adam again at Professor Fairchild's home near Oberlin.

Fairchild poured another cup of tea. "Are you sure of your decision then, Mr. Watling?" he said.

"Thank you. Yes, as certain as I have been of anything, Professor Fairchild."

"And you say your father approves of this?"

"Yes sir. Naturally, he is reticent of his full support, and doesn't wish to alarm Mother about it, but he does believe in the cause. Most importantly, he wanted me to make up my own mind."

"So you haven't told her yet?" Marcus asked.

"Not yet, but I will when I return to Mansfield. She will likely guess as much when she sees me home from the college so soon."

Marcus privately admired his bold decision to join the Union Army, but couldn't outwardly support the choice that might put him on a front line facing hundreds of Rebel muskets. First, Tump Haines had told him he would answer the call for volunteers, and now his college friend would carry a musket too. He was angry with both of them for their rashness. Or might it be his jealousy that they would get the glory of a uniform while he worked in secret for the abolitionists?

"Don't you want to help me in the abolitionist cause? I could use another good man as a conductor."

"Marcus, we must each follow our own calling. That is what you have been called to do, and this is what I have been called to do. When Governor Dennison said a camp would be built near our farm, that's when I knew I had to join. Don't ask me how, I just knew. Besides that, you don't need me. You work well enough on your own. You have said as much today."

"I didn't mean it like that, Adam. I wasn't bragging about my work, only telling what I had been doing – trying to persuade you to join me. Have I failed?"

"Not failed, Marcus. It wasn't a test. I had already made up my mind to enlist."

"Men," Professor Fairchild interrupted, "it isn't glory you're after, are you? In either of your callings, it cannot be for personal gain, and you must be certain of it. These are dangerous times we are living in, and the reward you seek can never be an earthly one. You might expect one day to hear the Master say, 'Well done, good and faithful servant' and that will be the highest reward you can receive. But *never* let it be for personal glory."

"No sir," Marcus said.

"No sir," said Adam.

"Will you leave today, Mr. Watling?"

"I have already packed, Professor Fairchild. I leave this afternoon. On Wednesday next, I will muster in at Camp Buckingham. We will get regimental assignments then." He finished the tea in the awkward silence and rose. "I guess this is good-bye for the time being then."

Marcus had sat quietly taking in the implications of his friend's decision, and he reluctantly rose to follow Adam to the door. "Good-bye, Adam. You have been a good friend. I will remember all of the lads in our study sessions with fondness. Please write when you are able."

"We will meet again, Marcus." And he left.

"He is a brave young man," Fairchild said as they watched him go.

"Am I any less brave?" Marcus said.

"There are many kinds of bravery, Mr. Armstrong, many kinds of servants. You are another kind, no less brave. And no, I don't wish to debate that point with you. Instead, I want you to go to the Bardwell's at this address," he said, handing him an envelope. "Drive my wagon, and pay my respects to them. They will have a delivery for you to make – to Huron, I believe. They are expecting you, so you must leave now. Report to me how you get along when you return my wagon."

Marcus reluctantly acquiesced and followed Fairchild to the barn where the horse and wagon had already been prepared by his stableman. "This journey will give you more time to consider your duties. We are *all* soldiers in the Lord's army, Mr. Armstrong. Marching to different drummers perhaps, but we are *all* soldiers. Godspeed."

At the Bardwell home on the corner of East Lorain Street and Water Street, Marcus received his next instructions. Though the Bardwell home was known to be as active a station as the Haines's in Alliance or the Hubbards' in Ashtabula, curiously Marcus had no one waiting there for transportation, as in the past on his Ashtabula deliveries. Instead the Reverend John Bardwell's wife gave him specific instructions for his delivery to Station 100, Black River Village (Lorain). Oberlin was openly referred to as Station 99, and the bold behavior of the conductors defied anyone to try to stop them. Cornelia Bardwell was no exception. She charged him to openly drive along to West Marsh Swamp where "freight" delivered from Ashland, Station 97, would await him. In yet another drop-down door in the wagon, he would then secret away three souls to the banks of the Mouth of Black River for their final journey across Lake Erie. As he drove on the pike to the swamp, he remembered his grandfather had told him the story of his own escape from Canada by canoe across Lake Erie nearly fifty years earlier, about passing the Mouth of Black River, and about seeing John Reid's trading post on his way to freedom at Presque Isle. And now, he would transport escapees from the United States to their rendezvous with a canoe that would take them to freedom in Canada. He could almost hear Grandpa George laughing at the irony of it all.

At the swamp, he pulled alongside two young black men and a young, light brown complected girl crouching down in the high grass. After he looked about for anyone in the area, he quickly dismounted from the wagon, swiftly pulled a pin, dropping the back gate that concealed a long dark box built into the wagon bed.

"Quickly," he said. The first grabbed his hand and clutched it tightly. "Thank you, Massa…."

"Marcus," he corrected.

"Thank you, Massa Marcus."

"No. It's just Marcus. You men come a long way?" he asked the second man.

"We'se come all de way from Tennessee."

"Well, you don't have much further to go. Now, quickly, get in.

The first climbed in and squirmed deep inside the box, followed by the next, who said nothing but paused, squeezed his hand. The young girl, not much younger than Marcus, looked at him with tear filled eyes before sliding in. Marcus avoided the emotion he felt coming over him, instead, forcing a smile at the young woman. She looked up at him, smiling affectionately. He felt strangely drawn to her, affectionate, warm.

"Marcus," she repeated, her eyes glistening.

"That's right, it's Marcus," he smiled. "I am from Ashtabula, Ohio."

"I 'members yo' name til I's in eternity. I's Izzy. I's from Alabama."

Chapter Thirteen
Old Washington, Kentucky   October 1861

Nat stabled the horse, and ran the long path from the barn, looked immediately for Emma in the slave quarters. He couldn't contain his excitement, needed to tell her everything. In Maysville, a man had sought him out while he waited at the hitching post for Master Marshall. His news was great, and Nat had to share it or he would likely burst. He observed her through the crack in the partially open door hanging the wash out on the long rope stretched between the big house and the great pin oak in the yard.

"Hsssst!" he whispered. No response. "Hsssst! Emma!" he whispered louder, opening the door enough to betray his position.

"You finally back, Nat?" she called.

"Shhh!" He called, beckoning her, "Come here."

Inside the barn, out of hearing range he laid it all out. While he and Master Marshall picked up the feed for the horses, a freed black businessman who had stopped at the store helped him load the wagon. Marshall had gone to make his deposits at the bank, and Nat had time to hear the businessman out. He had connections in Mayfield with the Underground Railroad. He seemed trustworthy, and he detailed the route he knew, how he could get Nat and anyone else to come across the Ohio River into Ripley.

"When we git 'cross de Ohio, dere am a white man, name o' de Reverend John Rankin. Him an' a free black man name o' John Parker – he a business man – dey kin he'p any'uns dat want freedom. He say dey get us to a station 'n dey move us on to Canada."

Emma was hesitant. "Can he be trusted?"

"I done t'ought on dat. I foun' me a free man name o' de Reverend Elisha Green. He preach at de African Bet'el Bap'ist

Church in de town. He say he know de business man purty good, and he say he can be trusted. But he cain't he'p any hisself, 'cause he be watched all de time. We's got to trus' somebody some time, Emma, or we's lost. And I's willing to try."

"When did he say we can go?"

"Now. Tonight. No time to make plans, he say. De longer de wait, de more certain dat Massa Marshall will learn of it. We gots to go tonight."

"It's a long way to Maysville, Nat."

"We be takin' de buggy, Emma. You axe Missus Marshall if'n you kin go to town dis afternoon to get cloth or some such. I will drive you. Marshal trusls me 'cause he believe dat I will come right back, 'cause in daylight, ain't nobody try to run. So we jes' gets los' in de town and we hide 'til night. Den I shows you where to go. It much easier in de daytime. See, dey ain't no patrollers here. Dey got bounty hunters, de reverend say, but we will be away from dem quick."

"I have wanted my whole life to be free, Nat. And now that you say I can be free by tonight, well, it just scares me."

"Ain't skeerin' me to be free. I's so ready, dat freedom best be skeered of me."

Nat returned to the forge, drew the fire with renewed vigor and was soon beating the red hot iron horseshoe into a straight rod. He took the bend out of it first, reheated it to nearly white-hot, and then he attacked it with a determined fury, seeing in the metal every overseer whom he had ever watched lay the rod or rope or rattan to the back of his brethren. Beating, heating, beating. He fixed his mind on his impending deliverance, and now he prepared his insurance policy. On and on he used his anger, laboring until he had flattened the upper half of the horseshoe into a straight blade. All the years of pent-up hatred that he had hidden from Massa Ashbie, from Jonah Kenton, from the patrollers on the highways, from the white plantation owners, from their overseers, from the speculators, from the auctioneers – he marked each one off in his brain – releasing them in a rush of emotions and beat each of them with the iron hammer. *CLAP-CLANG, CLAP-CLANG!* Over and over. He plunged the blade into the water, the red disappeared and the steam hissed its cry of emancipation. Then he set to work with the file, grating and honing it to a razor sharp edge. In time, he sat down and began the meticulous stropping of the gladius against the wide leather straps in the harness shop. The metal whipped a constant rhythm, slapping a bright sheen onto the blade. It was proud, satisfying work that he could show to no one. Taking up one long strap of leather, he carefully wound it into a tight spiral on the upper half of the iron – the finishing touch to the handle of his masterpiece. Now let someone *just try* to lash him for running.

Nat drew a bucket of water at the well, walked to the slave quarters as Emma entered the Big House. He washed, put on a new change of clothing, dressed like it was his Sunday meeting wear. Under his trousers, he strapped to his leg a knife sheath with the end ripped open. The gladius fit tightly into it, with the blade protruding through the tip another six inches. The trousers hung loosely down to his boots concealing the bulge of the weapon on his shin. He buttoned up his best floral print shirt and tied a loose red handkerchief around his neck. Stuffed into his front pocket was Emma's yellow ribbon she had given him, wound around the treasured white handkerchief – the map of his bank statement for accounts received on behalf of Massa John Ashbie, now buried in a child's vault in a field in Alabama, the down payment for his new life as a free man.

"My lands, you are a sight! I haven't seen you that dressed up in a long while, Nat." Emma stood at the door and looked at him head to toe, and then back up. Nat could only smile sheepishly. "We best get going 'for one of these gals here tries to snatch you up."

They received their travel permits, bid their quick goodbyes to Mrs. Marshall at the drive – with the admonition to get back well before supper – and hurried off at a trot, Nat skillfully handling the reins and Emma proudly seated beside him clutching a yellow parasol. They presented the perfect picture of an afternoon day off. No one on the road gave them a second glance.

In Maysville, Emma went to the millinery shop, purchased some goods with Mrs. Marshall's Confederate currency, though both Union and Confederate were accepted in the town. Nat waited with the wagon and looked for the worker he had met. No one approached him, and he tried to hide his uneasiness lest Emma should lose faith in him and their singular purpose. He began to feel the eyes of someone staring at him, someone who knew his secret and would suddenly shout it out to the marshal or the bounty hunters. He imagined a sinister purpose in every white man or woman's smile. They all must know something. He could only brace himself for what he expected. Nat unconsciously scratched at his leg, felt the weapon hugging to his shin. He hadn't planned on how he would quickly draw it out if needed, and now it seemed cumbersome. He hunched over, a solitary black figure dressed in a floral shirt and bright red neckerchief, tried to look inconspicuous, squirmed at the absurdity of it. Guardedly, he repositioned the sheath under his trouser leg.

"Are you asleep?" Her voice startled him, and he quickly sat up. Emma stood at the wagon, an ample supply of cloth folded neatly over her arms, and waited. "Are you going to help me up?" she teased. Nat quickly jumped from the wagon seat and took the cloth in one arm and helped her step up with the other hand. "Seems a pity that Missy Marshall might never see this material. I like it ever so much," she said.

"Den you takes it wid you, Emma."

"No, Nat. I won't be stealing from her. She never harmed me, and I won't *ever* steal from her. I will leave it somewheres so someone will find it and return it to her."

"She done stole yo' freedom by keepin' you as her slave. Dat come up to stealin' in my eyes," he said.

She picked up the cloth, stroked it slightly, dropped it in the wagon. "No. It stays with the wagon."

"We needs t' see if'n some'un's about dese parts t' give us de plan. I don't see no sign o' dat free nigga' man what tol' me to come here."

"What about the Reverend Green? You said he knew whom to deal with?"

"He say he be watched all de time. I don' know dat he be he'pin' us to 'scape."

"Excuse me, sir," Emma said to a white man coming out of the railroad office. "Do you know where we can find the Reverend Green, sir? We are wanting to get married and would like to meet with the reverend."

How coolly she lied to him, a charmingly bright smile on her face, then adding a hint of coyness for effect. Nat's mouth hung open at the audacity. He swallowed hard, exchanged a look with the stranger. The man considered the two, studied them for a moment. Nat bent to rub his leg, felt the knife. The man broke out in an animated laugh.

"She shore has you all trussed up, boy. She got the claws in *you*!"

Nat grinned sheepishly, "She sho'ly do."

"Hmmmpf! Now if you two are done sportin' with me, would you kindly tell me where I can find the Reverend Green?" Emma assumed a pose of effrontery, a posture that she had gleaned from years of waiting on and observing Missy

Annabelle Richardson, and she drew herself up tall in the wagon seat, smoothed the lap of her deep blue gown with her gloved hands. She stared Nat and the white man into silence, waited, her lips pursed with mock anger. Nat fidgeted in the wagon seat, rubbed his leg again.

"Down this street, and turn left, and up the big hill. On Fourth Street you will see the Bierbower House. You can see its roof from here," he said pointing up. "The Bethel Baptist Church is right there. Reverend Green should be somewhere close by. Ask at the Bierbower House if you can't find him." He looked at the two of them again. Once again the boisterous laugh. "Good luck, boy. You got yourself a real pistol there." And still chuckling to himself, he walked away. Emma couldn't resist.

"No, sir! I got *him*!" she called. Again the boisterous laugh.

Nat shook the reins, turned the wagon and followed the instructions. At the corner, they turned to head up the tall hill to the Bierbower House. Then he saw him.

"Reverend Green!" Nat called.

The reverend turned, recognized Nat.

"Dis is Emma. We ready to run now."

"I told you, I can't help you. They watch the church all of the time. It takes careful planning."

Emma faced him, the earnest voice trembling, "Reverend, we just told a white man in town about us wanting to get married. He thinks we are coming to see you in that regard. If we leave Maysville too quickly, this might cause more suspicion, don't you think?"

Reverend Green looked about for anyone spying him out, shook his head.

"We're desperate," she said.

He thought long, silently. "All right then. Let me ride up with you."

Inside the empty church, the Reverend Green laid before them their best option. In town, near the river was a yellow painted house where they could get help. Either the businessman whom Nat had met, by name of Arnold Gragston, or John Parker would come there and see them across the river. As they were expected at the Marshal farm before sunset, it would not take long for Marshal to set the hounds on their trail. Timing was critical. The reverend excused himself to make arrangements to dispose of their wagon. Nat and Emma stretched out on the wooden bench-pews and waited in silence for Green. Within the half hour he returned. He carried food and two blankets for warmth. An abolitionist friend had taken the wagon and headed with it to Dover, also a known hotbed of abolitionist sympathies. This should force the bounty hunters into hours of searching the Dover-Minerva area for the two runaways. But now the two of them could no longer be seen together. Emma would leave immediately for the yellow house and wait there. An hour later, at sundown Nat would join her by another direction.

"Thank you, Reverend Green. I will always remember your kindness. God will reward you one day."

"Thank you, Emma, but I get rewarded daily. I bought my freedom years ago. The Lord planted my roots here so I could go no further. Now this is my field of labor, and I am quite content in the work. I need no other. Now go quickly, and God go with you."

Almost an hour had passed while Nat waited his turn. The sun had set and the orange glow of evening had faded to deep yellow when he finally ventured out. He walked down the steep hill, leaving the church and Reverend Green behind, the Bierbower House standing sentinel over him, its massive brick construction and two story white-washed front porch towering above the town. Known abolitionist sympathizers, the Bierbowers used their standing in the town to flaunt the

Fugitive Slave Law and had at times even hidden some slaves in their paid servants' quarters or under the floorboards. Nat had no need to stay long enough to be hidden. The longer he stayed in Maysville, the more chance he would be captured. He tossed a salutary wave in its general direction, just in case some other poor unfortunates may be holed up waiting an opportunity. He hoped they too could find their freedom across the Ohio.

The yellow house at the bottom of the hill had one lantern in an upstairs window, a quilt hanging inside another. In the pattern were the familiar cryptic symbols representing the dark gray of slavery, the blue of the Ohio River, and the bright yellows and greens of freedom. Nat rushed up to the door, looked around cautiously for prying eyes. He boldly knocked on the door and was greeted by a white man holding a pistol pointed directly at his chest.

Chapter Fourteen
Maysville, Kentucky

"Can't be too careful," came the voice. "Inside quickly." Nat slipped in and the man hastily closed the door behind him, holstering the pistol.

"Name is Nat. Dis be where Emma stay?"

"She's in here, Nat." The man led him into the parlor where Emma sat sipping on coffee with the air of attending a garden party.

"Hello, Nat," she greeted him casually.

"Emma, you be all right?"

"Yes, Nat. Our hosts have been very gracious. Did anyone follow you?"

"Not dat I can see in de dark, but I's purty sho' nobody done folla' me."

"Sit down, Nat. We will be leaving here very soon, once we see no one has been snooping about. Reverend Green says that one of our women disposed of your wagon for you, so that should send the hounds on the trail of another for a while. Tonight a man will take you down to the river and west along the bank to the landing. It's a bit of a walk, but it's necessary to be down river away from any encounters. A boat will be waiting and the man will take you across the Ohio to Ripley. He will lead you where you must go next. But at all hazards, do not question him. You must move rapidly and quietly to the next stop. Any delays at all will increase your chances of capture." He stopped and looked slowly at both of them. "Is any of this unclear?"

"No, suh."

"No, sir."

"Good. Now we just wait."

Leaning back on the rose colored double-ended chaise lounge, Nat fidgeted. He could find no comfortable position.

Emma sat upright, prim and perfect posture, as befitted the chaise. Nat shifted his weight forward, then tried to lean back, suddenly stood. "Does we has t' wait long?"

"Not long, Nat. Please relax and be patient."

The incessant ticking of the pendulum in the school clock on the wall marked the seconds, and with it the mounting tension.

"Nat, when you get across the Ohio, try to say as little as possible."

"Why?"

"This may sound harsh and I don't mean it so. Your talk betrays you as a field hand, as a runaway. You want to blend in as a freedman. Anything you say will let someone know who you are. It's not your fault, Nat. But if you want to stay alive until you reach safety in Canada, say little. If you are going to stay in the United States, then it is even more important to blend in."

"Like Emma?" he asked.

The man looked at her, embarrassed. "Well, yes, like Emma. She will blend in anywhere. You will have to study it."

Emma said nothing, looked self-consciously at the floor, softly cleared her throat. She sipped the last of her coffee.

The last glimmer of light had long passed when a knock came at the side door. Again their host drew his pistol and stood at the side door, opening it cautiously. In the dark a figure whispered, "They ready?"

"All right then," the host said. "Go with him, and be quiet."

Emma stopped at the door. "Thank you, sir. You will be rewarded. What is your name?"

"I have no name. Now go."

They stepped out into the night and followed the figure quickly across the main street and down a side alley to the river edge where the railroad tracks bordered the Ohio River.

Stepping carefully over the crossties, they dropped down from the railroad bed to the bank.

"Just keep moving," the figure whispered. "And stay close."

Emma's plan to dress as if for an outing hindered her running ability, and she struggled to rush along with the hoop dress gathered up about her knees and clutching the blanket the Reverend Green had given her. She tripped and went down in a heap with a low cry. Nat rushed ahead and grabbed her waist, lifting her light frame and nearly tossing her to her feet. Less than an hour later they stopped. Well outside the town's edge, they collapsed to the ground and sucked in the night air in deep gulps. Crickets and frogs sang along the bank.

"Don't they sound pretty?" Emma said quietly.

"They'll sound prettier in Ohio," said the man. "Come down this way, both of you. The boat is here."

"Don' hear no patrollers," Nat whispered.

"That's good, then. They might be miles away. Or they may be about the bank. We won't know until we get into the water. Get in."

He pulled the boat from the brush along the river edge, pushed the bow into the river and Emma stepped in. Nat pushed it clear of the bank and climbed in. The stranger pushed it into the current and locked the oars in place, beginning a steady strong pull. "Keep low, both of you."

The boat drifted down river, caught in the slow current. Their oarsman kept a steady rhythm with the oars and once they were in the middle of the river, he again spoke.

"It's safe for you to sit up now."

Emma sat upright, straightened her gown and pulled the blanket over her shoulders. Nat looked about the shoreline behind them, peering into the darkness. Not quite dark o' de moon, but dim enough, he thought.

"John Parker!" The voice carried across the water from the dark Kentucky shoreline. Then a musket shot rang out. Parker pulled heavily on the oars, quickening the pace. A trio of shots, nearly simultaneously fired, erupted and two splashes kicked the wake of the boat. Emma fell to the seat and curled up.

"Emma!" Nat cried. "You hit bad?"

"Not at all," she spluttered. "But someone ought to pay for this dress!" She pulled at the mass of ruffled material at her hip. A hole revealed where the musket ball had passed through and out, landing in the water off the bow. She lay across the bench seat and tugged the gown down tight against her body so none of it showed above the gunwale to tempt another shot. Nat curled down onto the bench seat at the stern.

"They have to reload, so we can get a few more yards and be out of their range. Just stay low," Parker said. His quickened pace carried the boat closer to the Ohio shoreline and the current continued to move them even further downriver. The combination put them out of range within a minute, as three more shots fired, splashing harmlessly behind in the vanishing wake.

A few yards from shore, Parker turned the rowboat up stream and pulled slower, letting the drift turn the vessel and drive it onto the gravel shore. Two young white men sprang from behind the trees, grabbed the bow and dragged it onto the shore. Indistinct shouting carried across the water, and they heard the sound of loud splashes. Four horsemen had ridden their animals into the river and began to cross slowly, searching for the shallows.

"Quickly, no time to waste," one of the white men said.

Nat and Emma jumped from the boat and scrambled up a path to the riverfront street where the storefronts and residences remained darkened.

113

"You for sure Mr. Parker?" Emma asked.

"I am, Emma. They will look for me, but they don't know for sure it's me. I am going home so they will come to my house to search first. You must quickly follow these two men through that woods yonder. The path there will lead straight up that hill," he said pointing. "It's called Liberty Hill and it's not easy climbing, and there are one hundred steps to your liberty. On the top of the hill you will go to that house," he said pointing. "The one with the light on up there – that is the Reverend John Rankin's home. He will take you in and hide you. Now be quick about it. You're not free yet."

"T'ank ya' Missuh, Pa'ker. We bot' be in yo' debt."

Parker took the outstretched hand, squeezed it firmly, quietly studied Nat's face as if to memorize another triumph. "Now go." And he ran down the street toward a house beside a small work building. Nat and Emma followed the two young white men up the alley, looked back to see the horsemen meandering across the river in pursuit, still looking for shallow footing for the horses. They were yet a good distance away, but as trackers, they would be relentless. At the base of the hill, the four began the climb. One hundred steep steps disappeared into the darkness. The thick brush on either side soon obscured the escapees.

"Sholy glad you got dat blue dress, Emma. Dat hide yo'self purty clever."

Emma stopped, turned aghast. "My parasol!"

"Yo' say what?"

"I lost my beautiful yellow parasol when I fell on the tracks," she moaned.

"Dat's good, Emma. Dat parasol done stand out like a candle in de dark. I gets yo' 'nother one when we's free."

Steadily they climbed, but noticeably slowing as the incline's height now began to fetter their movement. Only thirty steps, and Nat could feel his legs ache, helping Emma when she stumbled in the dark, kicking at loose stones beside the rock steps. Still they ascended the hill. "Jacob's ladder," Emma murmured quietly. They couldn't see past the high riverbank below, but the voices of their pursuers were now more distinct. Soon the hunters would be ashore, if they weren't already. How many stairs now, sixty, seventy? Nat had quit counting. His legs kept driving him ahead, half pulling Emma with him. One tedious step at a time. The two white men stayed nearly ten steps ahead of them, stopping to look back every few steps and check on the progress of their charges. Finally at the top where the scrubby brush opened to a clearing, Nat fought the urge to throw himself on the front lawn of the Rankin Home. The welcoming oil lamp placed in the left window spread its warm glow across the yard. The final steps formed a straight line to the front door, past a tall flagpole holding a lighted lantern at its top. The door opened and a gray-haired man with long neatly trimmed side-whiskers and dressed in a black suit with a white clerical collar stood at the ready, a rifle in hand.

"You've done well, boys," he said. "Please, bring our guests in."

Nat and Emma wearily ascended the last three steps and into the house. Jean Rankin caught her at the elbow and helped her onto the settee. John Rankin rested the rifle against the wall inside and bolted the door. The room was cheered by pale blue floral printed wallpaper, green ivy vines printed among the petals, small red berries accenting the vines. Nat embraced the details of this, his first room of freedom. A fire kindled in the white painted fireplace, the hearth warm with crackling logs, book-filled cases built into the walls, framing both sides of the hearth, and an oil lamp glowing from every table and from the white mantle above the fireplace. The wooden floor shone like a mirror, clean and inviting. This was a learned man's home, and Nat felt welcome here.

"Any trouble, boys?" Rankin asked of his two sons.

William stood beside the window pulling the curtain aside to peer out. "Bounty hunters," he said. "They fired at the boat. Then they came across the river on horseback, probably making their way to Mr. Parker's home first. But they will surely arrive here father."

"Then we have no time to waste. Mary, take this woman up stairs to the room. Thomas, you help this man to the summer kitchen."

With no other instructions, the girl hurried Emma up the stairs and into a room to the left. Nat saw her disappear into the room and quickly followed William out the back. The air was cold, the moon only a sliver, but the stars speckled the sky and cast a sparkling silver gleam on the dew-covered grass. Inside the summer kitchen, the darkness was oppressive. Nat groped around the room.

"What's your name?" asked William.

"I's called Nat. I cain't see nothin' in he'e."

"That's good. Means the bounty hunters can't see you either." He lifted up the flooring and an even blacker hole appeared. "Please, Nat. Get in here. Don't be afraid. This is only for a short while. When we are sure no one has followed, we will have you out of there and into a bed for the night. Just stay quiet and keep listening. You will be fine." As he closed the floor on Nat he quietly said, "We've never lost anyone yet."

Inside the hole, Nat felt for the walls, half afraid he might touch something living. Then he felt down them for the floor. It felt clean with nothing he must avoid stepping on or sitting on. A heavy cloth, feeling like a woolen blanket, and a coarse material stuffed with straw for a pillow had been prepared there. He shifted down to the blanket and lay back, resting his head on the pillow. The fatigue from the whole day finally laid its heavy hand on his neck, his shoulders, his back. The legs were knotted and cramping from the run, the crouching in the boat, the final climb, and his muscles burned. He felt for the knife on his shin, loosened the ties and drew out knife and sheath, and laid it by his head. Too tired to sleep, he lay on his back and tried to ignore the pains.

Soon he heard several horses ride past his hideout, and the shouting began. Reverend Rankin's voice boomed as though from his Presbyterian pulpit. Angry words countered, and the verbal tug-of-war echoed across the farm and into crawl space where Nat cowered. A shot rang out. Silence. A young woman's voice cut through clearly, "Next one will be at you. Now get off this land!"

More shouts, but less animated followed the warning, and the horses rode off. Nat lay quietly listening until the door opened on the summer kitchen, followed by the boot tread. The floor boards raised and a lantern shone in.

Nat squinted into the light, "Dat, you? Massa Rankin?"

"There are no masters here, Nat. It's William. Come on and get out of there. We won't have any more trouble tonight. You come inside and wash up, and get some rest."

Nat followed William into the house where John Rankin greeted him with a wash stand and water in the bedroom. Nat bathed and joined the Rankins who had brought Emma down from the hidden room upstairs. It was decided they would stay two or three days at the farm until transportation was ready. Emma would be sent north to Canada by way of Springfield, Kenton, and Sandusky, and Nat would go north to Circleville, to East Towne Street in Columbus where Fernando Kelton would secret him away toward Ashtabula and on to Canada. The two would rendezvous in Port Dover, Canada. The slave catchers would search for an escaped couple, so their escape had a greater chance of success if they split up.

The escape was well-planned with Nat and Emma giving themselves entirely into the hands of the Rankins and the dozens of other abolitionists who would conduct them from station to station, and ultimately to freedom. Nat was naturally hesitant, though he believed the Rankins were good people.

"I trust you completely, Reverend Rankin," Emma said. "I have wanted this for so long, and I am come this far, I guess I can go a bit farther in your care."

Jean Rankin sat beside her, took her hand. "It is much farther, and it won't be easy, but the thing will be accomplished. Everyone who believes in freedom for all of you will see to it.

"I's havin' trouble trustin' anyones. Dat is, 'til I gets to Massa Marshall's. And den I's findin' de people who wants to he'p me and Emma git away. But I larns long ago not to trus' too many. Dem dats wantin' de money fo' sellin' us back to slavery will do mos' anyt'ing to gits it."

"Well, Nat, I suppose that's so," Reverend Rankin said, "but we don't do business with anyone who will sell another human being back down to slavery. It is an abomination, and I will have none of it. You will be free. You can bet your life on it."

"Seems dat whats we been doin' all day."

A nervous laugh.

"Yes, I suppose you have," Jean Rankin said.

Emma had been reading an appliqué hanging in its frame on the wall close to the door. "Nat, I still believe in them and their work. Mrs. Rankin," she said pointing to the wall, "is that what you believe?"

"I sewed that a long time ago, dear. It took a very long time, I recall. And yes, I do believe it."

Emma stood up, walked close to the wall. "These are good words, Nat. They are from the *Holy Bible*, and this is what these white people who help all of us are believing. We must trust them."

She read from the framed work on the wall:

Thou shalt not deliver unto his master the servant
Which is escaped from his master unto thee.
He shall dwell with thee, even among you,
In that place which he shall choose in one of thy gates,
Where it liketh him best.
Thou shalt not oppress him. -- Deuteronomy 23:15-16

Nat closed his eyes, breathed deeply. "Amen."

Chapter Fifteen
Columbus, Ohio   Tuesday, November 1, 1861

Only a week before, the people of West Virginia had voted to create their new state, a state which had been proposed by the Second Wheeling Convention of August 20, 1861. West Virginia's delegates to the convention had seceded from the secessionist state of Virginia and adopted the new name. Ohio abolitionists living along the border of the new state saw this as a disapproval of slavery, and an endorsement of their cause. The actual truth of it was not all that transparent. Ohio, along with the Border States, contained radical elements from both persuasions. West Virginia, Kentucky, and even Ohio still harbored enough Confederate sympathizers that the danger for runaways was even more pronounced than in the Confederate states. In the secessionist states, Nat could readily assume that everyone was a threat to his freedom. Now, unless a conductor personally knew another conductor and transported him directly to that sympathetic station, an undetected bounty hunter seeking published reward money might very easily haul him back to the plantation, or worse. He still felt he could trust no one. Yet he had watched Emma put her complete trust into the Reverend Rankin's organization.

His good-bye to Emma was harder than he had ever anticipated. She had left for her Sandusky destination under the care of one of the Rankins' associates. After keeping a low profile at the Rankin farm for two days, she had left in the early morning in full confidence of the conductor's expertise. Nat had little time to say good-bye. Promises exchanged, a kiss that he had longed for, and sharing the location of the fortune in the Alabama field awaiting them both after the war and freedom – all of these intimate exchanges ran together in that brief parting. She feared for him and left him with the admonition to "...say little that will give you away." Was he that unrefined that she might never want to be with him? Was he giving away with every word spoken the telltale sign that he was not free, but still a runaway slave, the property of Marse Marshall? As he was moved from station to station, his guardians perfectly concealing his journey to Columbus, he avoided conversation with any of the conductors and station agents. He now sat waiting in the carriage before the Kelton home, a new coat complimenting his formal dress, a bold derby hat on loan from a conductor in Washington Court House completing his disguise. His thoughts of Emma now formed into a firm resolve. He would make himself worthy of Emma and worthy of his newfound freedom. He would converse on her level when next they met. No more would he be embarrassed to speak his mind. He might just stay in Ohio, blend into the population of freemen, stay closer to his buried treasure than he could ever be while hiding in Canada. During one of those cold nights when he had curled up in the hollow wall under one station's staircase, listening to the family bemoan his lack of formal education, he began to form his intention. He would not make himself a person to pity. He would make himself an educated free man. He would make Emma proud. Here on the porch he reaffirmed it.

"Nat!" the voice called. "Please come inside now."

His reverie broken, he drew himself up with a righteous dignity and strolled arrogantly up to the porch of the Kelton house. His conductor waited with Ferdinand Kelton at the door, formally introduced him, and Nat held out his hand in an exaggerated impersonal manner. But then came the verbal betrayal.

"Nat, I am Ferdinand Kelton. I am pleased to make your acquaintance."

"Dat be awright, suh. I's jes proud to meet ya." He heard his words tumble out, immediately wanted to take them back in and swallow them all. He bowed his head, took off the derby hat, held it in front of his waist, tightly gripping it with both hands, and stared at his feet.

"Likewise, Nat," Kelton said. "Please come in."

In the parlor a young attractive woman of about twenty-five stood near the fireplace, observing him. Nat felt as if he was trying to pass inspection, like the ones he saw on the slave auction block in Old Washington, Kentucky. He watched her from the corner of his eye, keeping his head bowed while she sized him up. She had curly dark brown hair, dark probing eyes that seemed to see through him, and a pursing mouth that appeared to restrain a flood of words that might gush out at any moment like a bursting levee. She wore a deep green dress with a high neck, trimmed in chestnut brown. She had a stoic elegance about her, and at once Annabelle Richardson flashed in his mind. Yet she was everything Richardson was not. There was not a trace of condescension in her manner. She was wealthy without the obligatory conceit. Emma, he thought, would have gladly served this woman. He gave her what he considered enough time to judge him, raised his head, looked her firmly in the eye and waited. Immediately she emitted a self-conscious laugh.

"I'm terribly sorry," she said. "I didn't mean to stare at you, Nat."

"But ya' did stare, Missy," he said firmly.

"Yes, I suppose I did. I am Martha Connor. My husband and I will guide you from Mr. Kelton's house when we deem it safe for you to travel. I do apologize, but I was staring at the clothing you are wearing. Are these all yours?"

"Some o' dem's give to me. But mos'ly, dey's mine. I's wore dese since I run from Kaintuck."

"Well, Nat, I think you look very smart in them, and I must say it will be easy to pass you off as our hired worker until we can get you to Granville. Yes," she said looking him over again and nodding her approval, "these will do just fine."

Nat began to relax for the first time in the week since he had left the Rankin home in Ripley. He had been shuttled from one barn to another, to a house, to a corncrib, to any hiding place his conductors had arranged for him. He took comfort only in the knowledge that he had kept moving, if only at fits and starts, mile upon mile, farther away from the Ohio River. But now, here in the Kelton house, he felt more than protected; he felt welcomed. And that night, he slept on a real bed with a real blanket for the first time in over a week, and for only the second time in his life, as far as he could remember. This is how he intended to sleep the rest of his life – once he was free.

+ + + + +

This load of lumber was his last delivery of the day, and Marcus wearily drove the wagon along the lane by the harbor's dock. He felt groggy from the day's exertions, his eyes irritated from the cold winds. The Hubbard warehouse was nearly empty, so the workers could help him easily leave the boards on the open racks just inside the door. Maybe he'd have one of the workers leave the wagon at the Hubbard barn so he could take time to stop and see Grandma Polly before his supper. Long day, he thought. And he hunched up his shoulders, stretched his arms backward, rolled his neck side to side, his neck letting out an audible crack. He felt a tight knot of muscle burning in the small of his back. He wanted to just lie down and stretch out for a few hours. Or perhaps for a week. Maybe she'll even have soup, he thought.

"Marcus, I have a telegram from your sister and brother-in-law." William Hubbard beckoned him off of the wagon, and away from the workers, read:

Freight delivery soon. Stop. Package leaving Granville tomorrow. Stop. Forward by way of N.P. Stop. Delivery to Alliance. Stop. Acknowledge receipt of same on delivery. Stop. Martha.

"Using the New Philadelphia route this time. You will have to take the wagon to Alliance the day after tomorrow. The last boat doesn't leave until Monday next week, so we'll have just enough time to get the package aboard before the boat sails."

The knot in his back muscles tightened. Another arduous trip, and another game of chess with the authorities, he thought. For just this once, couldn't someone else go in his place? But as in every other time, he submitted to the mission. Exhausted, he plodded along the two city blocks to his grandmother's house, knocking and immediately entering, as was his custom.

"Grandma Polly!" he called.

"In here, Marcus."

Polly sat in her favorite chair, the curtains open to let the late afternoon light stream in, an oil lamp burning, adding its golden glow across the room. She held an unfinished project on her lap, her fingers busily working the needles and looping the yarn into its pattern. She didn't look up, intent on the pattern.

"Marcus, please light that other lamp and sit here with me. A busy day today?"

"It was. I am so tired, I just want to collapse."

"Well, dear, before you do that, please get a log or two on the fire for me. Now, what has brought you to this condition? Did you hurt yourself?"

"My back is tired. But that's not all of it. Mr. Hubbard got a telegram from Martha. I have to take the wagon to Alliance and pick up another delivery. She says it's just one this time. I wanted to ask for a day off from work and sleep the day. Now I have this."

"Marcus, every time you come here, you grumble about not being more involved, and now when your sister needs you to help, you want to get out of the work."

"My back is sore."

Polly never looked up, concentrated on her handiwork. "I am sure it is, but what about the back of this poor soul you are to bring here? Do you think it's any less sore than yours? What kind of hardships has that back seen?" She didn't wait for an answer, as was her way. Marcus resigned himself that she was about to impart her wisdom as she always did, once again trying to make him see the correctness of her opinions. "You accepted the responsibility of your duties as a conductor, and this person is dependent on your fulfilling that duty. Your father is proud of the work you've done. He says you always discharge your duties faithfully. You have your grandfather's grit. He always saw a thing through also."

"I didn't figure on having to fulfill the duty right away."

She continued to knit, looping the yarn while her fingers worked quicker. "There is always the unexpected, isn't there?"

"You won't let up until I agree to go, will you?"

"That's for you to say, dear. Remember, it is always your choice." She paused, looked up. "And I know you will make the wise choice. My children always do." Then she looked back to her work, fingers nimbly looping the yarn, working the needles. She had done it again. She had convinced him to do precisely what others expected of him, and made him feel as though he had decided his course of action on his own.

"Grandma Polly, you don't have any soup cooking do you?"

"No. What made you think that?"

"Wishful thinking."

"When do you leave, dear?" she asked.

"The day after tomorrow," he said, and immediately he heard his own words. She nodded her head, lost in her work. She had done it again.

"Come by tomorrow, dear, and I will have cooked up a nice potful," she said at last.

He stood up wearily. His muscles already had begun to tighten on him. At the door he stopped and looked back at his grandmother in resigned admiration. Polly always had complete control.

"Grandma Polly?"

"Hmm?" she said not looking up.

"Is that how you got Grandpa George to do things?"

"Do what things, dear?"

"Oh, nothing." And as he closed the door he thought he detected just the smallest hint of a smile crossing her lips. Or maybe he just imagined it.

+ + + + +

Martha and Jacob Connor had kept Nat for one day longer than they had wanted, and it was time to get him out of Granville and to another station. Merely an overnight at the Kelton house had quickly allayed their fears of discovery. The disguise had worked to get him out of the Kelton's custody and on to Granville. But their ruse of passing Nat off as their hired man hadn't gone as planned. It was suspected by most that they were abolitionists if not blatant Underground

126

Railroad conductors, and on occasion, Jacob had been observed making night time journeys. Since he was recognized as an upstanding, devout Quaker, and not given to nocturnal philandering, the natural inclination was to assume instead that he was up to illegal slave activities on those night excursions. But this time was different. In broad daylight, a black man had arrived in their care and was never introduced but referred to in vague terms of his "employment." Neighbors in Granville wanted to meet the new working member of the Connor household, wanted to converse, see how Nat liked Ohio and his new situation. They were immediately rebuffed. When the marshal stopped by to meet him, Nat was conveniently taken ill and couldn't receive visitors. But he received the promise that once he was well, they would be happy to introduce this free man to the community.

And so it happened that three days had elapsed before the scheme was devised to claim his death, and load him into a coffin to send back to his "relatives" in New Philadelphia, Ohio. Nat insisted in boring the holes in the bed of the coffin himself. If he was going to suffocate, it was going to be by his own hand and not by these abolitionists. In truth, he trusted himself more than those that God had ordained to protect him. He lay comfortable on the warm quilt in the coffin and waited for the lid to be nailed.

Martha Connor looked in on him, resting in the wooden coffin. "Nat, I have sent a telegram to Mr. Hubbard in Ashtabula. That will be your destination. You are first to go to Coshocton, then to New Philadelphia. From there you may ride to Alliance. I don't know that you will make the entire journey in this crude box, but however you travel, the glorious result will be your freedom in Canada. I have a brother in Ashtabula. He is Marcus Armstrong and he will assist with boarding you on Mr. Hubbard's shipment to Canada. I will pray for your safety."

Then the lid closed and the nails hammered loudly around his face and down the sides to his feet. It wasn't as black inside as he thought it would be. The air holes he had drilled let in cool air as the box was lifted onto the wagon. A rough slam of the wood onto the wagon bed, and the sound of a whip cracking preceded the sudden lurch forward and the wagon began its journey to freedom. He squeezed his arm along his side, reached for his pocket, felt the ribbon in his fingers, and pulled it up, close to his chin, rested his arms across his chest. He could do nothing now but remain patient, feel every bump and rock, every dip and hole on the road to freedom. He was conscious of no definite passing of time, for the rocking of the wagon and the imprecise airflows made him drowsy. He slept, then was jostled awake. Drifted off again, only to be awakened by another slamming and shaking of the wagon. This broken pattern continued he knew not how long. Finally, the wagon stopped and the lid was mercifully removed and he looked out to afternoon sun and felt the cold November wind wash into his coffin. Jacob Connor offered a hand.

"Nat, it's safe to get out and stretch now. We are in Coshocton, halfway to our destination."

"Whey is dis Coshocton? Be close to Canada?"

"No. Not close, but closer than you were coming from Kentucky. We followed the Erie Canal Towpath, and it was a mite rough riding. I am sorry about that. We must be on the way soon. I am taking you to the graveyard. A conductor named Mr. Powell will take you from here to New Philadelphia. If it is safe, then you may ride to the next station freely. But there are those who will look for an advantage to sell even a freedman into slavery for the right price. So the coffin is still your best option. I don't want to subject you to that any longer than necessary. So, if you are ready, lie down and I'll close you in."

It wasn't a long break, but the sitting up, even for a moment, did his body good and he rested again, hearing a single nail hammered again into the side boards. The feeling that he could merely slide the top aside if necessary lessened his uneasiness. He was ready for the journey. In a short time, he felt the wagon turn off of the main road and he rolled against the wall of his wooden shelter. Uphill, he thought. He lifted the top enough to see the road stretching behind him, the marble, sandstone, and granite headstones, on either side of the lane. The wagon stopped, the lid lifted, and quickly he climbed out to be greeted by Mr. Powell.

"It's safe here for now," Connor said, "but we must be quick. This is Mr. Powell. He will take you on. Nat, it was a pleasure to meet you, and I do hope to meet you again when you are finally free to visit. Don't forget us, for we won't forget you."

"I won' be fergittin' yo' kindness, suh. Bless yo' and de Misses Connor."

Powell was stern-looking, roughly dressed, said very little, and was all about business. He seemed to Nat a person who was guarded, continually searching for any threats. Nervous eyes, highlighted by bushy auburn eyebrows, darted about, never making eye-contact too long with him. He sized up the surroundings, peered into the nearby woods at length and then searched about other spaces, all while trying to load the coffin onto his own wagon. A simple command, "Get in," and he closed the coffin lid on Nat, securing it with four hammered nails. Once again Nat felt the wagon lurch forward and the bumpy ride began. He felt the wagon leave the cemetery and the relative smoothness of the main road started. He tried to lie comfortably in the coffin, seeking sleep which evaded him. Everyone had been cordial, flooding him with empathy and food. They all saw to his needs, trying to erase the mounds of despicable deeds they believed had been heaped on him for his whole life. Though he had been born a slave, and had known nothing but slavery, he had to admit lying in that coffin that he had not had as bad a life as the many other slaves he had known. In fact, he had been so favored by Marse Ashbie that he felt embarrassed for having allowed these abolitionists to suppose otherwise and shower him with extraordinary care when others were still in worse bondage. He lay inside, fingered the yellow ribbon, angry with himself. He wanted no sympathy from these conductors, both white and black, but he allowed that he would persuade them to teach him all manners, customs, spoken skills, anything which would separate him from those with whom he was identified. He determined that he would use his status to request – no, he would demand help to rise in his station. Then he would resurrect the fortune from its grave, seek out Emma, and settle somewhere that he could hold his head high – show Master John Ashbie and the others that he was just as worthy as they. Maybe even help free those in bondage, if the war didn't free them first. In his own personal ark, riding the Nile to his own destiny, his daydreaming persisted until he fully developed in his own mind the plan for his own advancement, just as he arrived in New Philadelphia.

The wagon stopped, and once again the cover was removed from the coffin. Night had fallen and Nat climbed out of darkness and into darkness. His eyes adjusted readily to the surroundings. He was beside a church building where the November air was chilly, yet a comfortable change from the muggy warmth of the coffin. Powell again worked quickly, looking about, nervousness on his face. He said nothing, but pointed to the side entrance to the church. Nat quickly walked to the door and inside. He listened for any movement, saw a dark figure in a dress come down the aisle from the

130

front pulpit. Powell closed the door behind him and Nat heard the wagon drive away.

"You will be safe in this sanctuary. I have food for you, here." The woman held out a basket with a small loaf of bread, an apple and a small block of cheese. "In an hour you must be on your way. Travel at night is our best hope for you. I have a map here. This will get you to the Ohio and Erie Canal. Follow the path north, and if anyone finds you, throw this map in the canal or destroy it immediately. You will stop at the cemetery in Massillon. Now, eat and refresh yourself, study the drawings and then be off with you. I can say no more. We have been watched." The tension in her voice was punctuated by her quick movement in the darkened sanctuary. She rushed out before he could thank her. Maybe it was just as well, he thought. He hungrily ate everything she had given him, the first food he had taken since early morning. He pored over the drawing as best he could see in the limited starlight, and finally followed the fence line to where a lane led him to the canal. Here he stumbled onto the path and began his trek northeast.

Soon he approached Zoar Village. In the distance across the Tuscarawas River, a few candles still burned in the homes' upstairs windows. Though he wanted to find a place to sleep, he thought it best to avoid the distant village and keep to the canal. The night air had settled cold on the deserted canal and a steam rose from the warm still waters. Unfamiliar lands lend their own trepidations to a night time traveler, and Nat fought the fear overtaking him. He kept moving, silently as possible, but occasionally betraying his presence with incautious steps snapping small branches. An occasional dog barked out his alarm, and Nat ran all the faster, using the darkened woods along the path to plunge in and out; hence, he was on the path no more than necessary. He slipped past the ruins of Fort Laurens and moved on, stopping only briefly to consult the drawings on the map. He didn't know how long he ran, but the fear kept him moving steadily on until he came to the village of Massillon. Off to the right of the river he saw the tombstones faintly against the dawn sky. He was out in the open and would soon be recognized as a runaway. He dashed for the cemetery, rushing through the open iron gate and up on a small rise. He chose the largest tombstone and lay on his back at its base, sucking in the cold air, his lungs prickling with each breath. He felt his leg. The knife sheath he had carried with him since Kentucky had chafed at his calf, and the skin was raw and itching. He reached up and untied the lacing, dropping the knife and sheath on the grass beside him. The leather was damp with sweat and he rubbed his leg through the trousers until the itch subsided, and he drifted off to sleep, clutching the comfortable handle of the knife at his side.

+ + + + +

Ridgeway Haines had received the telegram the day Marcus arrived. His plans were altered immediately and he sent Marcus to Massillon with the wagon. At the cemetery he was to call the name of Nat and wait for the answer. Then he would bring Nat, a passenger from Kentucky, by way of his sister near Columbus, back to the Haines house. It was too dangerous to move on to Hanoverton. Albert Harvey had been contacted by his cronies in Columbus who informed him of the delivery. Jude Simon had left Ashtabula and could be expected in Hanoverton with the local marshal in tow. Marcus had driven from the Haines house and now approached the Massillon Cemetery. He cautiously looked about and then called out. No answer. He drove for the highest elevation, called again.

"Nat! Is that you, Nat?"

The black face appeared from behind the tombstone, said nothing.

"If you are Nat, then I am here to help you. You met my sister in Granville. Her name is Martha Connor, and she sent you to New Philadelphia. I am here to take you to Canada. But we must be quick about it. If you are Nat, then get in."

"I's Nat. Who you?" Nat grabbed the knife, holstered it back in the sheath and strapped it around his waist with the blade extending down his back.

"I am Marcus Armstrong. Get in, Nat. We have no time to lose." The wagon lurched forward and Marcus turned east toward Alliance. "You are my hired hand, employed by my father, Seth Armstrong, and you work wood."

"I's a blacksmit' by trade."

"Not if you want to stay alive. No doubt the slave catchers know you are a smith and where you come from. For now, you are a free man from Wooster who has been hired by my father. That's all anyone needs to know."

Marcus drove the wagon along the road to Alliance and shared with Nat his duties with the Underground Railroad. Nat told of his sale to Kentucky, his escape, and his flight from Ripley to Columbus. He let Marcus know he could also drive a team of horses and understood horses better than any white man he knew. Marcus immediately liked Nat, enjoyed his company.

"Onliest t'ing fo' me is to git along in schoolin'. Dey's a gal I's meanin' to see agin someday and don' wanna be a no'count fo' her."

"Someone you are sweet on, Nat?"

"Da's about right. I's gwanna git me my own house and mebbe marries her if'n she has me. But she say I's talkin' likes de field han's an' she don' like me so much."

"I must say, Nat, you give yourself away. When you get to Canada, they have schools that will teach you properly. You have desire. That's, I suppose, the best requirement."

"But I's not wantin' to git to Canada."

Marcus looked at him in silence. He had never met a runaway who didn't want to get to freedom in Canada.

"Da's right. I's be wantin' to stay right he'e in de nort' fo' apiece. I has me a secret need to gits back to Alabama one day. "

Marcus was attentive. "Can you share the secret, Nat?"

"I don' know you dat well."

"Fair enough."

A horseman appeared on the road ahead, riding at a full gallop.

"Remember, you are hired out. Say nothing and let me do the talking."

Marcus watched the horseman closely, then the dawning – it was Jude Simon. "I know this man," he said quietly. "Say nothing!"

Simon rode up, yanked on the reins, his horse rearing, then laid his hand on the cheek piece of Marcus's horse.

"Who's that with ya' Armstrong.?"

"Actually, he's none of *your business*, so kindly let go of my horse and be about your *own* business."

"I am about my own business! This nigger is a runaway and I have been sent to arrest you and take him in shackles to the marshal in Hanoverton!"

"I know the law, and you have *no* arrest authority."

Simon pulled out a document from his saddle bag and handed it to Marcus. He swung his leg over the saddle and jumped to the ground. "*There's* my authority! This one done run from Kentucky and has been runnin' up here for nigh on a week. We been waitin' for you to make your move on him so we could make our move on you. When he's in chains and I have my bounty, you'll be facin' the court for violatin' federal law. Unless of course you and your daddy and some o' your abolitionist friends want to buy you out. The marshal and me, we ain't above bein' helped out financial, if you get my drift. 'Course you kin jes' hand him over now and get your share in the reward money. That should help you with your college expenses, I think."

Nat heard the deal and slipped down from the wagon seat, crossing slowly in front of the horse.

"You stay there, Nat," Marcus said. Then to Simon, "He is not going to leave with you!"

Jude stepped closer to the wagon, drew his pistol and aimed it at Marcus's chest.

"Yes, he is! And I ain't askin' your permission neither!"

Marcus cautiously laid the reins on the foot rest before him, warily raised his arms in surrender. Nat's left hand lunged for Simon's left hand at the cheek piece, and Simon turned his gun toward Nat. In that same instant, Marcus thrust Simon's right arm high in the air and the gun discharged, startling the horses. Again in that same instant, Nat's right hand drew the knife from the sheath on his back and he shoved it deep into Simon's side, splitting the first rib with a sickening crack, the point appearing at the side of his back, and blood gushing from the two wounds. Simon groaned loudly and tried to pull the trigger again, but Marcus wrenched the gun away. Simon reached for Nat's throat, had time to utter, "You black..." and was silenced by another thrust, lower this time, deep into his thigh. He collapsed onto the road, the red pouring out of the wounds and staining the dust at the horse's hooves."

Nat wiped the long blade clean on Simon's coat. "Ain't nobody takin' me back," he said firmly.

Marcus gaped in shock. He saw Nat drag the body off to the side of the road, staining the dirt a deep crimson, leaving him to bleed out. He watched him tie the horse to the back of the wagon. He sat, stunned by the savagery of the moment and stared at the bloody scene while Nat climbed back in the wagon seat and grabbed the reins.

"Which way?"

Marcus stared at Nat mutely, then back at the body.

"Which way?" Nat repeated louder.

"Uh-h-h, th-that way." Nat shook the reins. The confusion and trauma vanished in the instant that the horses lurched forward. "No, wait. We can't go to Alliance now! Not after this! We have to get away – as far away from here, in as short a time as possible. Anyone who is searching for you along your route will stay east. No, we head due west. Nat!" Then after a beat, "You didn't have to kill him."

"Dat so? What would yo' do, Marcus? He would'a killed yo' if'n he had a chance."

Marcus sat quietly entrenched in thought as Nat gripped the reins, drove the wagon fast and hard, the crime scene disappearing in the dust behind them. He tried to justify it all in his mind. Nat did have to defend him, he thought. But he *couldn't* justify it. This wasn't just helping a runaway – this was murder. Of course, there were no witnesses, but someone knew something. Someone knew where Jude Simon was heading. Someone knew Jude Simon was meeting Marcus Armstrong and a runaway named Nat. And when Simon didn't return, someone would soon seek him out. Justice would eventually overtake him. He had to put distance – miles and miles of distance – between himself and justice. He worked it over and over in his own mind. A matter of self-defense, wasn't it? But he was breaking the law, and now a murder yoked itself to the original offense of aiding a run-away. No. He couldn't justify it. He could only run himself.

Hours passed.

"Nat?"

"Yas'm, Marcus."

"We go to Mansfield. I have a friend there. He will help us."

PART TWO

Chapter Sixteen
Camp Buckingham Mansfield, Ohio   November 1861

The Ohio militia had been ill-prepared for war when the hostilities began, and it needed adequate training. Senator John Sherman had answered Governor William Dennison and President Lincoln's call for volunteer regiments by seeking out land for Union training camps. Near his home in Mansfield, Ohio, Senator Sherman acquired the ground bordering the Baltimore and Ohio Railroad spur. Appointed colonel of the new 64th Ohio Volunteer Infantry, Sherman served with them from September until November, organizing the companies and establishing the army base. Camp Buckingham stretched south across the cleared farm land of E. A. Stocking at the foot of the sloping hills just outside the small city. Access to the railroad provided transportation for the army traveling south to the battlefront. The hastily constructed wood housing and city of Sibley tents quickly developed into an active training facility. Marcus and Nat arrived in Mansfield on that cold midday where the clouds had painted the sky a milky white. Nat drove the wagon through the muddy lanes spotted with deep pools of rainwater that slowed all animal and wagon traffic to a near standstill. On a hill to their left a tall brick house, ornamented with seven white-trimmed gables, faced the sloping ground where the extensive camp spread out in a muddy display of martial activity. The empty home of businessman John Robinson was a commanding presence over the sprawling south end of the camp. Below this hill, a haze of wood smoke, undisturbed by the higher elevation breeze, lay like a grey veil over the field, the peaks of white tents poking through the smoke. The smoky aroma of wood fires serving the camp wafted up on the cold breeze, and the sweet perfume of bacon and distinct fragrance of brewed coffee tantalized the men. Nat pointed to the tall gabled house.

"Dat be de gen'ral's house?"

"Don't know, Nat. But what I do know is I'm getting us some of that bacon I smell."

"Dat's fine by me. I's powerful hongry too."

"I had no idea the army here was so big. Don't know if I can find Adam in all these soldiers, but if he's here, he'll help us get something to eat."

A short, squat, pinch-faced middle-aged soldier wearing sergeant stripes sloshed through the mud to the wagon. He carried a metal cup, a volume of steam rising from it, stopped with the cup half raised toward a drink, grinned, showing dirty brown teeth, looked at Marcus.

"Ye here to enlist, boy?" The *b* punctuated the speckles of food that exploded from his face.

Marcus wiped his cheek with his sleeve. "Not sure. I am actually looking for a friend by name of Adam Watling. I thought he might be in this camp. He is from around these parts."

"Can't help ye there, boy. Ye may have to ask at the colonel's tent. That's where the muster roll is kept."

"And how do I find that?"

"Jest look for the tallest walled tent you can find, down that way along the tracks."

"Much obliged."

"Who's the Negra?"

"He is my personal servant."

"Slave?"

"Not anymore."

"He can't join up."

"Yes, thank you for your help."

The wagon ambled on through the muddy ruts and down the hill to a lane running alongside the railroad tracks. The further Nat drove the wagon, the clearer the view of the large camp spreading out, an immense tent city that fascinated him. This many soldiers preparing to fight the rebel army would certainly strike fear into the hard hearts of the slaveholders. He felt as safe here in the midst of the commotion as he had felt in many years. By the first tall square-sided tent, they tethered the horse and wagon to a telegraph post along a company street. The corporal working for Colonel Sherman found Watling's name assigned to the 6th Ohio artillery battery.

At the extreme northern end of the camp the artillery batteries pointed across an open road toward a looming rocky hill. The cannon stood in a short imposing row of polished brass and gleaming black iron. There sat Adam Watling on a caisson, scooping food into his mouth in a most uncouth manner, and Marcus immediately saw the change. This was not the proper college chum he had known. In a matter of weeks, he had become a rough-looking, bearded soldier in blue, grubbing food like he hadn't eaten in days.

"Adam?" he shouted.

"Marcus!" Adam tossed the empty tin plate aside, wiped his mouth with his sleeve, and jogged through the thick mud, grabbing Marcus in a great bear-hug. "What are you doing here?"

"Adam, we need to talk. Can we go someplace where no one will hear?"

"No. There's no place of real privacy. But just talk anyway. We are all brothers here and they won't listen in on conversations."

Marcus lowered his voice, "I am – that is we – Nat and me, we're in a heap of trouble, and we need help." He told Adam of helping Nat to freedom, of being thwarted by Jude

Simon, now lying dead in a field aside the road to Alliance, of his escape, and of his complete trust in Adam's discretion.

Adam recoiled at word of the killing. He could not condone a murder, though he allowed that in court a self-defense argument might be used. Nat, of course, would get no fair trial. He murdered a white man, who represented the federal slave law, while trying to apprehend a runaway. If it could be proved that Marcus had done the deed himself in self-defense, then he could *possibly* be set free. However, the snag was that Marcus would have been acting in self-defense against a man who was enforcing a federal law – the Fugitive Slave Act. This could allow either one to receive the full punishment of the law.

"It's a conundrum," Adam said.

"If I am caught, then I will assume the responsibility. Nat will get no fair trial and will be hanged immediately. I will at least get a fair trial and maybe even avoid hanging."

Adam's eyes suddenly brightened. "You have another option, Marcus. Join us here! Yes!" He clutched Marcus by the shoulders, animated with a cheerful insistence. "You would be remarkable in the Union blue. We will soon be ready to go off and fight the Rebs, and you'll be out of Ohio for a spell. This war is going to end quickly, so when we come home, slavery will be a distant memory and all may be forgiven."

Marcus looked about at the mud, the filth on the artillery horses' legs, the soldiers' legs spotted with brown and their shoes caked with pounds of grime. He saw the men beginning to stir from their noontime dinner and dressing in their accoutrements, ready to begin the afternoon military activities. Saw the camp conditions, the dingy white tents, the stack of muskets with their gleaming bayonets locked together in a sort of tepee of weaponry. He looked at Nat, dependent on him for his protection. Once hopeful, his eyes now disclosed a helpless window into a dubious future. His repugnance at the conditions paled in comparison to the nausea he felt at seeing Nat hang while he had the ability to stop it, paled in comparison to the fear he felt at facing a trial for murder. He clutched Adam by the shoulders.

"Where can we get some of that bacon?"

Adam yelled a loud "huzzah," and ran toward a cooking fire. "Follow me."

"Nat, what was your trade?" Adam asked as he threaded chunks of bacon onto a ramrod.

"I's a bla'smit'"

"So you know something about horses?"

"I knows 'bout all dere is to know 'bout dem hosses. Mules, cows – it got fo' legs, I's wo'ked wit' 'em."

"Marcus, we have some contraband already showed up in the camp. That's what they're calling the blacks that escaped and showed up here for protection – contraband. Not a lot of them, but there's some. They can't join the Army, but they work here at the camp. Mainly, they're orderlies for the officers, like servants. A couple of them help the cooks. No pay, no uniform, and they are free to leave if they want. So far they all have stayed with us. 'Course I've only been here three weeks."

"Do you think Nat can work here with the horses?" Marcus asked.

"It's worth a try. What do you say to staying here with the Union Army, Nat?"

"Cain't say's dere be anymo' places to go. Dis here be 'bout as good as anywhere's be, leas' fo' 'while."

"There's Captain Bradley. I'll ask him."

Captain Cullen Bradley had risen through the ranks, promoted to the rank of sergeant, had served in the Mexican War with battlefield experience, and had finally received his current rank with command of this battery of six guns. But he had no authority to take in any contraband. Instead, he referred the two men to Colonel James Forsyth of the 64th Ohio or Colonel Charles Harker of the 65th Ohio. As Marcus had just been to the field headquarters upon arriving at Camp Buckingham, he chose that officer's tent for his enterprise. He walked there first, leaving Nat in the care of Adam and the 6th Ohio Battery. Major James Olds listened patiently to Marcus's plea to allow Nat and himself to stay with the Army. He conveniently avoided telling the whole truth of their escape and of the death of their pursuer, but admitted that this Nat was a runaway who had a blacksmithing trade and was skilled at handling wagon teams, and might be of value to the regiment. His ultimate goal was to live freely in Canada, but recent circumstances had forced him to postpone his trip. Marcus's resolute salesmanship was rewarded and he procured a job for Nat to drive supply wagons. When forced to elaborate on his own Quaker upbringing, he expressed his sentiments about slavery, about the necessity of preserving the Union, about his personal aversion to fighting in the war, but also about his desire to serve in some capacity. He left the meeting with orders in hand. He would drive ambulance wagons to wherever Surgeon John Kyle and the 65th would need his service. He found Nat at the campfire, surrounded by soldiers of the 6th Ohio Battery, some taunting this uneducated runaway, others defending him in a sort of moral tug-o'-war. Some of the men of Holmes and Tuscarawas County revealed their bigotry in a kind of flaunting pride that offended Marcus.

"This your Negro, boy?"

"He isn't mine. He isn't owned by anybody. But he has just been appointed as a teamster."

"Appointed? Ha! Get him. Appointed!" the private nearly doubled in laughter, triggering loud guffaws from the men.

"Well, what is the word you use," asked Marcus, "when Major Olds has just ordered this man to drive your supply wagons for you?"

"I'd call it insane," said another.

Adam spoke up sternly. "Perhaps you'd like to tell Major Olds himself that you believe him to be insane. I can go fetch him for you."

The laughter died and the men began to drift away with the excuses muttered that they had to clean the two new artillery pieces before inspection. The brass already shone like a polished golden mirror, and the excuse had a comedic effect.

"Dat cannon am so clean now, I's afraid to look at it in de sunlight and strike me blind," Nat whispered to Marcus.

"I have secured our place with the Army. Nat, you will drive a wagon team, and it looks like you'll drive it when the Army takes the war down to your home."

"Dat ain't my home no mo' Marcus. Look like dis here army be my home now."

"I won't always be with you, Nat. I am to drive one of the surgeon's ambulances with the 65th regiment. I suppose I will always be somewhere near you, but we have different duties."

"I's gwan travel wit' you, dough, Marcus?"

"I don't know for sure. But we are both safe from the slave catchers as long as we stay with the army."

Adam grinned, "Well, Private Armstrong, it looks like you finally joined the cause."

"I have joined the cause, but I am not a private. I mean, I didn't join the Army so I won't be on the muster rolls, for obvious reasons. Anyone looking for me will discover I am indeed difficult to find."

Captain Bradley's eyes narrowed, his forehead wrinkled. "Your name Armstrong?"

"Yes. Why?"

"Are you any kin to Lieutenant Johnston Armstrong? He's with Company B."

"Not aware of any kinship. I am from Ashtabula, Ohio."

"Small world if you were, I s'pose. How 'bout you, boy? You named Armstrong too?"

"No suh."

"Your named Nat what?"

"Jes' Nat."

"But you belong to somebody. You have to have a last name. On your plantation, what were you called?"

"Nat."

"Nat what?"

"I's done wo'ked for Massa John Ashbie. He call me Nat Ashbie. He gots de big plantation call Cypress Grove. It twixt Bridgeport and Huntsville, Alabama. But you ain't gwan send me back to Massa Ashbie," he said, clutching the empty ramrod menacingly in his hand.

The captain recoiled, "I have no such intention."

"I ain't called Nat Ashbie no mo'!"

"I understand about your name, and it's all right, Nat. I'll tell you somethin'. I'm not really Captain Bradley." The three men watched him, curious. "My real name is Cullen Bradberry, but the army got it wrong in their records when I first enlisted, and I have been Cullen Bradley ever since. No sense in changing it back. The name doesn't make you who you are, Nat. You are still yourself, however you're called. You make your own name for yourself, and let the reputation follow that name. I believe it's not so important what name you're born with. It's the name you die with that people will remember."

"I's s'posin' one day som'uns 'members me."

"If they remember you kindly, that's about all you can wish for. I guess most all the men here would say they want

145

the Sherman Brigade to be remembered. So they do their duty to bring honor to the brigade's name. Do *your* duty, men, and leave the rest of it to sort itself out. Now, you two get over to the cooks and tell them I ordered you to eat your dinner. They should have plenty of pork and some of that bread from the Mansfield bakeries. They take good care of us here, so get some dinner. Then you report to the colonel's headquarters for your billeting orders."

At the mess tent, the two men got more than they had eaten in the last two days, and were completely satisfied. Later, Major Olds assigned the two, sending Nat to Springmill Road, where the teamsters had lined the baggage wagons into two orderly rows. Marcus reported to Surgeon Kyle's tent, and there he received his sleeping arrangement in one of the empty ambulance wagons. Not comfortable, Marcus thought, but it will be better than sleeping on the ground or in one of the crowded Sibley tents. He wanted out of the clothing that he had worn for several days and that immediately identified him as a civilian. The quartermaster provided him with a new Union blue uniform, lacking any stripes, any trimmings of any kind. Though he wasn't on the muster sheet, he felt a bit of pride in finally wearing a uniform like Adam Watling or Tump Haines. He hadn't known exactly how he would feel, but the pride in the uniform had an emptiness about it. To him this uniform was merely a disguise, a clever ruse to keep the slave catchers and the lawmen bewildered about his complete evaporation. Even his family didn't know where they might find him. He was a nameless non-entity in this ocean of blue. And his pride humbled in the acute understanding that he was merely portraying a soldier alongside these heroic members of the 65th Ohio Volunteer Infantry.

Chapter Seventeen
Camp Buckingham Mansfield, Ohio   December 1861

Disease had struck the camp, and the boys who had never been off the farm suffered along with the boys from the colleges and the cities. Some medicines were available, and well-prepared food was abundant, yet the regiment began to lose men who had no immunity to the diseases. The cold, wet conditions invited pneumonia and other infections into the camp and began to thin the ranks of the companies. Marcus's head was splitting. He lay in the infirmary, closed eyes watering, nostrils clogged, and wheezing through his dried lips.

"Yo' sho' soun' terr'ble, Marcus."

Marcus blinked his eyes, focused on the smiling black figure seated beside his bed. The hand reached out, laying a cold damp cloth on his forehead, and he flinched.

"Sure could use a drink right about now," he murmured.

"T'ought yo' might be wantin' sumptin' like dat." He held out a tin cup, but the aroma of coffee couldn't pierce through the fog of his stuffed head. "I gots dis from a campsite out yonder and say it be fo' de lieutenant in here. Dey lets me keep it. Yo' migh' as well drinks it, 'cause I ain't gwan' nowheres fo 'while 'til yo' do."

"Wish I could smell it."

"Dat's awright. I smell it fo' de two of us."

He held Marcus up and let him drink deeply. The hot coffee and steam had the desired effect. Marcus coughed heavily, a kind of sneeze-cough combination that cleared what felt like every ounce of fluid between his vocal cords and his brain. He spat thickly on the wooden floor. His voice immediately cleared.

"That's just downright ugly, Nat."

Nat chuckled, "Better out den in, dey say."

He handed the cup back to Nat, and lay back. "How has it been going for you with the wagons, Nat?"

"Dey, fine, Marcus. I tol' you befo', I can handle any beast wit' fo' legs. It's jes' dem two-legged 'uns dat puzzle me."

"Are you treated fairly?"

"I's 'spec' I is treated better 'en somuns is...."

"But...?"

"I s'posed freedom be diff'ren' den dis. I ain't been w'ipped at all, and I gets to eat reg'lar food dat de w'ite so'jers eats. It jes'...." His voice trailed off. He looked about the large tent, every bed taken by a sickly soldier, some snoring, some staring through their delirium at the roof. He lowered his head.

"Nat, what is troubling you?"

"I's been meditatin' on it. All but a few o' dese so'jers, like Adam and yo' and de cap'ain, and sech, axe like I's anymo' den one o' dem field hand niggas back on de plantation. W'en dey gwine treat me like a man? I's treated real good by mos' dem ab'litionists dat he'p me gets to Ohio, but mos' o' dese here'uns axe like I's no better'n dem mules out on de road." He pursed his lips, a furrow forming on his forehead, and a tear showed in the corner of his eye. "Marcus," his voice cracked, "w'en it be *my* time?"

Marcus sneezed, cleared his throat, spat again, propped himself on his elbow, spoke quietly, "I don't know. I wish to heaven I had an answer for you, Nat, but I don't. This war, we hope, will end slavery for all time. My grandfather fought for its end for nearly forty years. Many times he said that abolishing slavery was within reach, but changing people's hearts – that had to come from within. We can't do it for them."

"Wishin' I could."

"Me too, Nat. Me too." He cleared his throat again, coughing heavily. "Let me make this observation. Don't give them anymore reason to treat you like less than a man. Hypocrites with the prejudice of color in their eyes will do so anyway. But you may sway the hearts of those who are merely followers. You still sound like you're a slave of the master on your Alabama plantations, Nat. Be a man – not in *their* eyes – be a man in *your* eyes. I think you see yourself as the runaway slave. I see you as a black man – one of God's creation. *Act* like a free man, and eventually most will *treat* you like a free man. You can't sway all, but you can sway enough. Maybe then your time will come."

"You he'p me?"

"In what way?"

"Emma say once dat I's talkin' like dem field hands and she tries to teach me what words to say. Only she ain't here now, so you teach me?"

"It would give me great pleasure to do so, Nat." He collapsed back onto the bed, staring at the roof of the tent, his head swimming again. "Just as soon as I can get free of this infirmary."

+ + + + +

Colonel John Sherman had stood before the men whom he had overseen in their preparation to become the sixty-fourth and sixty-fifth regiments of Ohio's volunteer soldiers. Satisfied that their training had started them toward becoming capable soldiers, he had answered President Lincoln's request that he return to duties in the U.S. Senate. He formally shifted command of the camp to Major R. S. Granger, now promoted to the colonelcy. Colonel James Forsythe became commander of the 64th OVI. Sherman's impassioned speech called upon the love of their native state, inciting them to deeds of valor. The speech was posted throughout the camp as a public notice so men who could read it would find inspiration. Of his brigade, he said that he could

...take pride in its achievements and feels assured that they will reflect the honor upon the state from which they come, and upon the country they serve.

Marcus read it to Nat as they stood near the mess tent. Along with the stirring words, a notice had been posted by the camp commander. Nat's most recent state of residence had called for help from the Union Army. Enough of the Union sympathizers had convinced the governor that Kentucky's neutrality was in jeopardy and they cried out for the Union Army to address the secessionists.

"It appears as though we won't stay in Ohio much longer, Nat. How do you feel about returning to Kentucky?"

"Wid an army behind me? Shoo-eee! Dat be a sight dey never fo'gets. Y' s'pose we go to Maysville?"

"Hard to say. But we are indeed moving south very soon. I wouldn't fret about Maysville. We won't get close enough to the plantations where anyone will recognize you. Besides, I will stay close as I can."

"Marcus, I's been waitin' fo' yo' to gits healed up, and...."

"What is it, Nat?"

"Now dat you's up and about..." He paused, tried to find the right phrase. "Kin you l'arn me to read too?"

Marcus laid his hand on Nat's shoulder. "We can start today, Nat."

There at the mess tent, Marcus began his instruction, pointing out letters which Nat hungrily read and repeated over and over. He could easily see that this uneducated free black man had intelligence coupled with a desire to improve his station in life, but it was the way he attacked this rudimentary schooling that astonished Marcus. He knew the alphabet, said one of the house slaves had secretly taught him as a child, but he hid that knowledge from all whites. Now he burned to string letters together, to make words, to make real sentences, and the fire was unquenchable. Nat had memorized a dozen words by the time the surgeon sent for Marcus to assist him in preparing the medical supplies to take into the field with their departure. Nat returned to the baggage wagons and approached his mules armed with his own self-confidence.

The army mule lived up to its stubborn reputation, and though the mule drivers most often resorted to the severest corporal punishment they could lay upon their hides, it rarely had the desired effect. They watched and mocked as Nat talked gently in their ears, and then were awestruck when, with a slight prodding, he made four mules pull as one. It was a specter to behold, one muleskinner reported to the captain. What he whispered to them was open to conjecture, and the muleskinners, who were never at a loss for adjectives to describe anything, ran off an entire dictionary of unflattering descriptions about Nat's skill. The captain surmised that Nat had been treated like the mules to get work out of him, and he was paying out in kindness the wages that he had never received. Maybe so, they said, but he had a way with them, there was no doubt of that.

Marcus had helped load the medical provisions into the surgeon's wagon, taking careful note of the inventory. Surgeon Kyle, impressed with his efficiency and initiative, praised him repeatedly to where Marcus felt uncomfortable. Just doing his job, he had said.

"Were you ever a student of medicine, Marcus?"

"No, sir. I had studied at Oberlin College to pursue the study of the law eventually. My grandfather was dying and I went home to Ashtabula to help my father and grandmother with his affairs. I stayed at their request and had hoped to return to college."

"What has prevented it – your returning?"

"I violated the Fugitive Save Law. Not very good for someone studying the law. Eh?"

"Oh, I don't know. It depends on to what extent you were in violation, I suppose."

"No, there is no *extent*. The law is black and white, and a violation of any part of it is a violation of it entirely."

"Well, Marcus, I can only speak from a medical background and tell you there are shades of gray too. Not everything is clear-cut."

He spoke quietly, his voice hesitant. "I helped transport – runaways. It was on what we call the Underground Railroad. They knew – Many of them knew I could handle a wagon, and when they asked, I joined."

"You sound ashamed."

"I am not, but it is the law. I had to find a place to hide to avoid arrest. So, I am here."

"And the Negro you brought with you, is he one of your passengers?"

"Maybe, maybe not."

"Marcus, you have no fear of me. I am not an abolitionist, but I am certainly more in sympathy with the cause than you might suppose. I would turn in no one."

"I am not at liberty – for his sake – to divulge much more. A death occurred – he or I might be blamed for it. The man was white, so Nat would get no fair trial. I might get a fair trial, but helping a runaway would sour a judge and jury. That's why we're here."

Kyle squinted his eyes, an inquisitive gesture, like examining a microscope slide. "Hiding?" he asked.

"One might choose to believe that," Marcus said quietly.

"I choose to believe that. Anyway, there are few better places to hide than in a regiment of soldiers. Your secret is safe with me – my 'hypocritical' oath." He chuckled at his own humor, setting Marcus at ease. "Still, I should think you may want to at least let your family know what has become of you. At the least, they deserve that. So many soldiers have gone off to war only to lose all contact with home until the casualty lists are posted. I know it happened at Bull Run. Marcus, let them know."

"I suppose they won't try to visit me if they know they could be followed."

"Then let them know the regiment will march soon and you won't be here by the time they come."

"Is it thus?"

"It is. The 64th will begin to leave immediately, and we of the 65th will soon follow."

"What about the baggage?"

"If you mean your friend, he will drive with the wagons eventually, but for now he and the other muleskinners will leave with the rest of us. You'll see him again. In order of march, we will follow directly behind the artillery caissons, and the mule trains will follow well behind us. If he is carrying ammunition, he will be close behind, if tents and personal belongings, far behind."

"I have no idea what his assignment is yet, just that he will drive a wagon. I will write to my father immediately."

"That would be wise, Marcus. Do so tonight after supper."

As the campfires blazed in the evening chill, Marcus huddled inside the ambulance he had made into his own personal lodgings. He carefully penciled the words to his father. Apologetic, claiming responsibility for his passenger, he excused his actions as the best course under the circumstances. He veiled direct reference to the murder, but chose instead to explain his joining the 65th Ohio Volunteer Infantry as an ambulance driver as his way of helping the Union cause without picking up the rifle. He hoped his grandfather would have approved of his wanting to help suffering. He trusted that his father and sister would agree. He shaded any references to Nat in words that would confuse the slave catchers, leaving them all to infer that Nat had run off toward Canada after *"...the incident of which you have undoubtedly heard."* He trusted that the man was now safe somewhere, *"...free from his chains and working with the animals, he loves, as is his calling in life."*

The letter sealed and posted with the regimental post office, Marcus wandered back through the camp. The fires dimmed and the subdued melodies from guitars and fiddles accompanied the voices of men singing harmonies of home and loved ones. Then the patriotic and melancholy tunes began, picked up in chorus from squad to squad, by those who sang perfectly in tune, and also by those whose monotone added feeling if not actual function.

Chapter Eighteen
Cincinnati, Ohio   December 1861

The train chugged to a stop amidst the hiss of steam brakes, the clanking metal of couplers, the jolt from the suddenly shifting weight of twenty rail cars slamming into each other. The rail journey from Mansfield through Columbus and arrival at the Ohio River town had been a lark, an excursion for the men who had seldom seen anything beyond their small world at home or at Camp Buckingham. Now they had made the journey to Cincinnati, where they would begin to take the war into Kentucky and beyond. The men were lighthearted and happily waved to the few townsfolk who gathered at the station at midnight to see another regiment of Ohio soldiers arrive in the darkness. It was cold, and the men shed the blankets and quilts with which they had cocooned themselves for the long journey from Columbus. Marcus stuck his head out of the ambulance where he had spent a restful few hours buried under several blankets, happy that his duty had given him a sleeping place off of the boxcar rooftops. For there, cold-interrupted sleep was attended by flying sparks from the engine's conical smokestack. Officers began to gather alongside the train, greeted by a few dignitaries, and meeting in small clusters to receive their orders before organizing the men. Marcus slid out of the ambulance, climbed down from the flatcar which held four more wagons. Men who had burrowed themselves under the wagons in their coverings which they had received from home now correctly concluded they would need to carry these heavy blankets on the march.

"Armstrong," called one corporal from Company B. "Let me load my quilt in your ambulance. I'll get it back when we get to our camp. May I?"

"Put it in here," Marcus said, pointing to the back of the wagon. At once he realized he had opened a floodgate. Several other privates of the company queued up behind the corporal, his singular permission being a blanket statement to all. "Remember," he said, "just until we reach camp." In minutes the ambulance overflowed with quilts and blankets – gifts from wives, sweethearts, and mothers – looking like an overstuffed sutler's wagon.

Assistant Surgeon John Gill saw the piles of cloth hanging from the wagon. "This is a good thing you did, Marcus, but it cannot continue when we are ready to do battle. This wagon will be needed for the wounded, for the dying. Be firm and remind them when they ask again. They will either carry it with them, or they will find some other transportation for their goods."

The other goods were already being unloaded from the boxcars when Marcus found Nat, working with three other contraband volunteers hefting crates onto a waiting wagon.

"Peaceful trip, Nat?"

"Slep' fine wit' de hosses in de car. Some o' de sojers bellyache about bein' put in wit' the animals, but I don' mind so much. Been working hosses all my life. I been tol' we get our new pack mules and wagons when we get to Kentuck'. Takin' dis here truck down to de riverboat now."

"I imagine you are nervous about going back into Kentucky?"

"Not so much. We nowhere's near Mayesville. Anyhow, I 'spect dey done quit lookin' fo' me long time ago 'round dese parts. 'Sides, I is with the Union Army now," he said proudly brushing the straw from the front of his blue uniform.

"I guess the uniform makes all the difference."

"I 'spect it do. Oh, I knows I is not one o' dem reg'lar sojers, but dey give me de blue suit to make me look like one o' dem, and dat is fine wit' me. If'n black men gets to join fo' real, I is gonna gets me a bit o' colored ribbon to wear too. Den I wants to march in to Alabama and shows de massa I is jes' as good as him. Lawdy, dat will be a sight."

"I want to see it with you, Nat."

Marcus joined in with the three black contraband workers, helping load the wagons with boxes of rations, ammunition, officers' tents, everything to keep the army supplied for its invasion cross river. Dozens more white soldiers were soon recruited to help unload the rail cars and stack the local wagons with the supplies. By three in the morning, the wagons were stacked high and bound with ropes to keep the top-heavy bundles from shifting as they descended toward the river's edge. The 65th Regiment of Ohio Volunteer Infantry marched through the town, the regimental band playing "John Brown's Body" to the cheers of citizenry. Awakened by the blare of horns, they rushed to their windows and doors, then ran to the streets to stand under the dim street lights and wave white handkerchiefs and American flags. The soldiers returned the greetings with their own boisterous cocky cheering. Nat proudly drove his wagon slowly behind the treading soldiers, and seeing the waving kerchiefs, felt into his blue trouser pocket, pulled his own white handkerchief stained with black ink drawings and wrapped in Emma's yellow ribbon. His future fortune rested there in his palm and he couldn't hold back the wide, tearful smile of satisfaction and pride. He would soon enter the Confederacy as a conqueror. Oh, if Emma only could see him now. He carefully returned the ribbon and cloth deep into his pocket. At the riverboat landing the soldiers again unloaded the supplies, working through the night and stacking them on the deck of the steamer *Telegraph*. By early daylight, the soldiers had boarded the paddle-wheel, the lines cast off, and the 65th Ohio turned into the current and steamed downriver toward Louisville, where the 64th Ohio had landed a day earlier. There they would wait to be joined on the morrow by the 6th Ohio Battery.

"Beautiful country on that side of the river," Marcus said.

Nat leaned against the side rail and somberly stared across the river to the south. "Dey is parts dat is real pretty, but I don' recollect all dat many."

The Ohio side of the river was dotted by a few on-lookers who came down to see the grand Union army off "to whip the Rebs." Many young girls stood along the riverbank, wearing their finest, most colorful cotton dresses and wrapped with colorful, heavy shawls against the cold early morning air. They waved and called to the soldiers and Marcus called back, waving broadly.

Nat elbowed Marcus in the side. "W'ich one o' dem is yo'rn, Marcus?"

"I'll take the one in the bright lavender dress with the red and black shawl over yonder," he said, pointing to a girl who waved broadly toward him.

Nat looked at him bewildered. "How yo' knows her?"

"I don't yet."

"Yo' have a girl back home?"

"No. Oh, I have some I like back in Oberlin at the college, but none I would say I courted. No time, what with all the studies. I expect to settle down sometime, but when grandfather died, it just got set aside for awhile. What about you?"

"I never seen much future in it. I wanted one gal, Maggie, but she done got sol' off to some place in Georgia, so I don' get too close to any'uns. But den I met Emma. She a house slave to de Richardsons, and she done got sol' off to a speculator who sol' her into Kentucky. I gots sol' off to de same speculator and he brings me to Kentucky and done sol' me to de Marshalls. Dat's where I seen Emma again. And dat's when I gets to thinkin' I's done bein' sol' off. So, Emma and me, we clears out o' dere at first chance and heads fo' Ohio. De Revrun Rankin, he sends Emma north to Canada, and he sends me to Columbus and den to you."

"I am sorry I didn't get you all the way to Canada yet."

"Is awright, Marcus. I ain't goin' t' Canada no ways. I gots me a treasure to get first."

"I don't understand."

"Looka' dere, Marcus." Nat pointed off to the Kentucky shoreline where small clusters of men stood waving Confederate flags and banners, jeering at the soldiers.

"Colonel," one private called out, "Can I try out this musket just once?"

Colonel Harker looked at the shoreline, saw a large heavily bearded man astride a small horse, menacingly brandishing a sabre, looked at the private busily preparing his musket. "That isn't a wise choice, private. They are non-combatants. Besides, I have seen you shoot. You might miss and hit his horse." The men laughed loudly.

"But it's a Confederate horse, sir."

"He didn't choose to be. The answer is still, no." The murmurs of protest soon subsided.

Nat continued to point. "Dat de reason I is not goin' to Canada. Dem people who kep' me a slave takes all de money I saves fo' myself to buy my freedom. Massa Ashbie has me bury it fo' him so's he can git it a'ter the war. So, fust chance I git, I takes it back, and I buries it in a different grave." He turned to Marcus, pulled out the handkerchief, held it guardedly against his coat. "Dis where it be. And first chance I gets to go back to Alabama, I digs it up and buys me some land o' my own. Den I asks Emma to set up housekeepin' with me when we all is free."

Marcus looked at the map. "That's quite a plan, Nat."

"I gots it all worked out. We ain' goin' be slaves forever. De day will come when dey is all set free. And I is jes' proud to be a part of it. Massa Ashbie goin' t' remember Nat."

"They will all remember Nat Ashbie," Marcus laughed.

"Only I ain' goin' be Nat Ashbie no mo'. Dat a slave name. I goin' be som'uns else."

"And who will that be?"

"I'll think o' sump'in. It like dat Cap'n Bradley say, it don't matter what name you born with. It what name you make fo' yo'self make de difference."

The *Telegraph* rumbled on downriver, the men in their own way facing the reality of leaving the relative comforts of Mansfield, Ohio. Some men continued their boisterous incendiary taunts at the Confederate sympathizers on the Kentucky shore, most by now too distant to hear them. Others quietly meditated along the side railings, gazing off at the disappearing Ohio shore. Still others had found places of refuge to throw their blankets and curl up to catch up on the sleep they had missed on the Columbus to Cincinnati train ride. Each man prepared himself to finally enter the life of a real soldier, to face the elephant and stare it down. But Nat stared somberly at the Kentucky soil, and Marcus discerned a sense of vengeful anticipation in his manner. It showed a singularity of purpose fixed in his own mind. It might be prudent, he thought, to keep Nat in sight when they first camp on enemy soil. He did not want the embarrassment of having this contraband take a walk, leaving him to make excuses. He had risked much, had put his own life on the line for Nat, and he wanted to see this through to a conclusion, whatever that conclusion might be.

The afternoon passed with men eating rations, drinking from their canteens, many of which, Marcus observed, were decidedly *not* water-filled. But the resulting raucous laughter was a welcome contrast to the quiet, uneasy introspection. As time inevitably wore off the canteen effects, the men settled into various states of rest and continued this way until sunset. At just after sunset, the men began to stir and Nat shook Marcus awake. Glowing torches and street lamps on the shoreline welcomed the *Telegraph* as it chugged up to the dock. Lines secured and the ramp extended, the general officers left the steamer while the men continued to roll up blankets and quilts, pack away personal belongings, and wipe down muskets in anticipation of immediate battle. They wanted to form into ranks right here on the boat and march off to find a Reb and shoot him. All the training, the constant marching, drilling, firing was about to pay off for them. Marcus sat back on a small mound of packed Sibley tents and watched. He had no rifle, but he would soon receive his new ambulance that would transport the rifles' victims. The soldiers stirred as the lower ranking officers came back aboard and barked out commands. The regiment now fell into place in the ranks, shouldering their muskets in anticipation of their orders. Then the order came. The men would not disembark this night. It was too late to march inland and set up camp. Instead, they would remain aboard the steamer, sleeping wherever they could find a space until morning. Roll call at 5:00 a.m. and then they would march out. The usual grumbling started, but it subsided as the more reflective soldiers convinced the rest that sleeping aboard was a hands-down better alternative to pitching tents in the dark. Marcus pulled blankets up over him and nestled down on the pile of tents. He spied Nat gazing into the darkness from the railing.

"Nat, you going somewhere?"

"I's jes' thinking. Wonder when I gets m' wagon, and when I gets to drive it wit' de sojers."

"That's important, is it?"

"Tis to me. You al'ays drives as a free man. I al'ays drives as a slave. Now I drives as a free man too." He turned from the rail, walked to Marcus' side and stretched out on his back beside him, resting his head on his cupped hands and staring at the night stars, the "Drinking Gourd" low in the sky.

"A few months back I followed dem stars to freedom, Marcus. Now I leaves dem fo' somuns else to follow. I's back here to show m'self as a free man. Yeh, Marcus. It dat impo'tant."

Chapter Nineteen
Louisville, Kentucky   December 1861

Just outside of Louisville, Kentucky, the Union camp, christened Camp Buell after General Don Carlos Buell, commander of the Army of the Ohio, was busy with welcoming activities. The 64th Ohio greeted the arriving troops of the 65th Ohio with a feast they had prepared for their welcome, and the men dined with their corresponding host companies. The two training regiments, the Siamese Twins they called themselves, now came together once again. Only this time they had planted themselves in the enemy country, and the men boasted how they were there to end the war. Their new camp resembled the plan of Camp Buckingham and the men of the 64th already had become accustomed to its layout, easily navigating its few company streets. Marcus arrived an hour behind the infantry of the 65th after helping transfer the medical supplies from the boat to the waiting ambulances by the docks. The mule drivers would have to wait even longer for the requisitioned supply wagons and mule teams to arrive, so Nat helped Marcus, then climbed into the wagon seat beside him for the ride into camp. But eating arrangements were a separate issue. Nat left Marcus at the hospital tent of the 64th and walked off to find the camp's contraband section. Here he could eat with those of like color without the intimidation that attended the mixing of the Union soldiers. A sergeant offered Marcus a place at his table with the other regimental hospital orderlies. Marcus declined.

"Where'll ya' eat? We have good grub ya' don't wanna' waste."

"I won't lack for food. I am going to join my friend with the Negroes' camp."

"That's contraband only!" the sergeant insisted.

"Well, I'll take my chances. If they ask me to leave, I'll be back."

"What kinda fool are ya' anyway?"

"I'm an a-bo-lition-ist." He pronounced it slowly and with as much sarcasm as he could paint on the word, then left it to drip dry. There. He had said it and need not hide his activities any longer. Marcus had grown weary of masking his beliefs. He was an abolitionist, a proud purveyor of persons of color from slavery to freedom, and he haughtily strode from them toward where he had seen Nat go. At the extreme edge of the camp where the officers' horses were penned up in hastily built split rail corrals, he found Nat among the chattel that had wandered into the camp as their first line of refuge. Several of them had procured pots and pans and had a good fire going, cooking a strong meaty smelling bean soup.

"Marcus," Nat called his greeting. "Yo' jes' in time. Dese here contraband sho' know what cookin' pots is fo'."

"I should hope so! I could eat half a hog myself. Can I join you?"

"Sho' can. Dey gots a loaf o' sof' bread for all o' us'ns. Here." And he tossed Marcus a whole loaf of bread, which Marcus shamelessly assaulted.

"Dis here boy done come from the Marshall's farm," Nat said, pointing to a young boy of a caramel hue and light sandy brown hair. "He say dey done quit lookin' fo' me awhile back, and dey believes Emma and me is in Canada," he said with a great, satisfied grin.

Marcus saw the danger in Nat being recognized, even by another runaway. "Do they know where this boy is now?" Marcus asked Nat.

"Dey don' know wher' I be," the boy said between mouthfuls of beans. "Dey look to de river, but I goes to where I hears de sojers be, and here I is. Dey los' all sign o' me. I been wit' de sojers here 'bout fo' days now, and I ain't seen none o' dem pattyrollers. And den you'uns come and, Lawdy, it look like de who' Union army be here now." He ripped off a hunk of soft bread from his own loaf and greedily stuffed it in his mouth.

"If'n dey don' know where dis boy is, den dey sholy don' know where I is, neither."

"What's your job with the army here?"

"I's been settin' up de tents dat come in fo' two days no' and den I's been he'pin' de cooks feed de firs' white sojers what come here. I's gwan he'p de gen'ral if'n he let me."

Nat's eyes widened. "Gen'ral?"

"Gen'ral Byool, dey calls him. He not here yet, but I keeps waitin' to meet him, and den I's gwan offer m'self to him. I kin fetch and do all sorts o' truck."

"And if the general can't use your service, then what?"

"I 'spect I's gwan get some sorta work from de sojers, so I jes' keeps rat here and does w'ats needed doin'."

Marcus and Nat separated themselves from the contraband for private conversation. Marcus had written his father in Ashtabula, advising him of their situation, and had apologized to him for bringing shame on the Armstrong name in the county. He acknowledged his father's teachings that violence against another was violence against God and asked forgiveness from his family. But Nat's first thought was that he had now given a clue as to their whereabouts.

"Confessin' to him might be good fo' you, Marcus, but it not gonna do me any good when he let people know where you is."

"My father would never tell where I am, Nat."

"He don' gotta tell, Marcus. Dey find what's written in dat dere letter of your'n and dey will follow us here."

"Confederate sympathizers would get nowhere near a Union army camp, Nat. Anyway, I just couldn't let father think

165

I was dead some place. The worst thing for him would be for me to die somewhere and him to not know about it."

"Still, we needs be watchin' fo' two enemies now – dem Rebs, and dem slave catchers."

Over the next days, Camp Buell grew by thousands as more soldiers arrived from Kentucky, Indiana, and Illinois. Louisville, which was heavily pro-Union, welcomed the soldiers, though intrigue still lurked in the citizenry. Barely settled in, the soldiers began to drill daily, and the curious on-lookers trickled by the camp to watch the spectacle, many of them intending to report the numbers and the disposition of the troops to the Confederacy. Then the rains came. During the next weeks the soldiers contended with less and less food, more and more training. And mud. The sickness followed the cold and damp, and before long Marcus had settled in as a hospital orderly, helping care for the sick as the surgeons required. In his off hours he had begun in earnest to teach Nat a new vocabulary. Now that someone knew exactly where to find them, the disguise had to be greater. They drilled as much with speaking as the soldiers drilled with line of battle. Nat began to show marked progress, changing his speaking, changing his whole bearing.

The requisitioned mules finally arrived, a surly lot that tested the muleskinners' fortitude. John Bumbaugh of Company E. of the 65th, a burly German of broad shoulders, hardened hands and even more hardened speech, took it upon himself to teach Nat how to break in the "mools" and force them to do his bidding. Nat passed on the offer, content to follow his own devices when his wagon and mules would also arrive. Nat finally received his wagon, and along with it a team of six cantankerous mules. Training six to pull as one team tested the patience of all the mule-skinners, and even Nat found his team was a bigger chore than he had ever handled. He drew the scrutiny of the muleskinners and some of the non-commissioned officers who had waited for a chink in his armor to show. One particular mule refused to be broken, and as the sodden days slopped by, Nat's attempt to handle her garnered even more attention. Every time he thought he had her harnessed to a practical position for her temperament, she bucked and kicked, once nearly taking both his kneecaps off.

On one particularly rain-soaked morning just before Christmas, Nat had become the entertainment spectacle for the soldiers, huddling under their rubber raincoats and pup tents to watch stubbornness go head to head with determination. The word had spread and soldiers began laying bets on who would be broken first, Nat or "Dolly" the mule. Imprecations were of no use. Cajoling had lost its luster. Three days of struggling, and Nat was flustered to the point of violence. He knew all eyes were on him, knew of the bets being made, knew that he would face the taunts of the soldiers if he did not show his mastery of the team. He suspected that he might even be removed from the contraband volunteer teamsters if he failed. Believed his days with the Union army might be numbered already. Through the driving rain and the thick sticky goo of mud in the camp, he worked, repeatedly untangling the harness and the long lead line of reins.

"Thought you were so good with the animals," one soldier barked out.

"Yeh, boy. Finally met your match?" another mocked.

"Mebbe you need the ones from back in Ohio, ain't that right?" Laughter.

Nat dropped the reins and the long whip, stared through the drizzle. "Might be right, sojer," he said. "Atter all, these here are Seccesh mules. This one don't want no part of a

Union team. But I ain't licked yet. Tomorrow I have them work as a team, or kill 'em all tryin'."

"Well, if they all be Seccesh mules, might just as well kill 'em anyway." More laughter.

Nat climbed down and led the mules by their reins through the muck and slop, nearly losing his shoes as the mud sucked them down with every step. Eventually, through much braying and kicking, he moved them to the opposite side of the camp and into a corralled area, removing the harnesses from the more temperate beasts first. Dolly, the most volatile of the team, he left to wander around the corral with the leather collar resting heavily on her neck. He trudged back to the contraband camp and climbed up into his wagon, shivering with the cold and wet, angrily determined to pay Dolly a visit in the evening after supper.

It was well after the rains had stopped and the cooking fires had dwindled to dim glowing embers amidst the surrounding mud that Nat slipped from the contraband camp, excusing himself past the guard on picket duty to find Dolly in fatigue from the heavy collar still on her neck. "Dolly'" he said quietly, "You be still now. Nat knows what's best fo' you."

The morning air was cold, damp, entirely disagreeable, as the men stirred from their sleep to muster for morning roll-call. Near the scene of the previous day's escapades the soldiers watched dumbfounded as Nat drove his wagon of six mules through the muck, all the animals pulling together mightily – pulling as a team. Some cheered, others cursed at losing their bets and accruing debts until the paymaster would arrive. Nat drove his team on, as though leading a whole parade of supply wagons, a self-satisfied smirk mortared to his face. The cat-calls and taunts began immediately from the debtors who mused how-in-the-hell Nat had finally broken Dolly's spirit and got her to pull with the rest of the team in only one night. Nat never answered. He merely drove on, passing admirers and detractors alike, content that no one had examined close enough to discover that it was no longer Dolly pulling. For Dolly had been covertly swapped in the middle of the night for a former member of the 51st Indiana.

Chapter Twenty

The 65th Ohio now finished the last day of its orders, building and repairing roads one hundred and twenty miles south of Maysville. The ten days here had been frustrating for the soldiers who thought they were to join the fight against General Braxton Bragg's Confederate Army. Marcus alleviated his own boredom by spending time tutoring Nat in reading and writing. It was his own personal crusade against bigotry, believing that in educating Nat, he would remove the blight of hurtful words from time to time heaped on Nat's ears. But he went beyond mere literacy. For it was Nat's request – more than that, it was his persistent pleading to Marcus that he teach him to speak as genteel as he remembered Emma's voice. This was more of a challenge to Marcus, and he insisted that Nat listen much and say little. In listening, he could learn to mimic the voices of the Ohioans. He confessed to Nat that he didn't think it could be done, but Nat was determined. Marcus accepted it as his own personal test. He had for a long time wanted to do greater things for the runaway slaves that he transported, never relinquishing them until he was sure they had reached safety. And even after that, he still had wondered if he couldn't do more. But this time was different. He felt a responsibility for introducing Nat into Northern customs of living. After the war, the authorities might still search for the runaway who had murdered the white slave catcher, and a whole new language would practically insure his disguise. He would not relinquish Nat until he determined that he had safely changed Nat's speech and, consequently, his identity.

"Repeat after me. I am going to find it." Marcus said slowly.

"I am going to find it," Nat repeated.

"Good. It is no longer 'I's gwanna find,' but 'I am going to find' something."

"I am going to find something." Nat watched Marcus for approval.

"Good. What are you going to find?" asked Marcus.

"I's gwanna find my treasure."

Marcus sighed.

Nat flashed a large grin. "Just sportin' with you, Marcus. I am going to find my treasure. When we gits to Alabama..."

"When we *get* to Alabama..." he corrected.

Nat continued, "I needs – uh – *need* for you to help me dig up the treasure I buried."

"The one you say you stole from your master?"

"That be – *is* – the one."

"Nat, I've thought on it, and I don't know that I can abet a theft. Helping you to fetch it is akin to condoning larceny."

"Condoning Lar -- ?"

"Larceny. Tolerating Stealing. I can't in good conscience approve of theft on any scale."

"You gots – *have* – you *have* too much of a conscience, Marcus. It'll get you in trouble someday," Nat advised.

"That may be, Nat, but I'll take that as it comes. If you think the treasure is owed you, then maybe you best get it on your own. I'm just uncomfortable with helping you."

"You can have some of it..." Nat led.

Marcus merely stared at him incredulously.

"You sho'ly can, Marcus. There's enough to go 'round, and you can consider it payment for you teachin' me."

"I can't believe you just said that," Marcus said and walked away shaking his head.

"Just consider it, Marcus," Nat called after him.

Marcus threw up his hand, deflecting the words as he continued on his way. At the medical tent, Surgeon's Assistant Gill greeted him. "I have had two patients today. I swear some of these men don't know anything about using a spade. One nearly sliced his large toe off. Can't walk much on it now. I may have to send him home on medical furlough."

"Maybe that was his intention," Marcus said sarcastically.

Gill considered this. "Maybe. Oh, you have a letter over here. Delivered just after you left this noon. Looks like it's from Ohio."

Marcus opened the letter, the bold red and blue banner on the stationery reading *The Union Forever.* He recognized his father's hand in the penciled salutation and immediately sat to read. His father had received his letter and had taken care to not respond too quickly. He thanked Marcus for his openness about the assault on Jude Simon, but he and Nat were *not guilty* of murder. Simon had survived. And ever since his wounds healed, *"...he has been now actively seeking you and Nat for full prosecution. The house has been watched, and even your sister is under suspicion in Columbus. It is supposed by many that Nat has been spirited away to Canada and that you have in fact joined the Union Army."* His father now believed it wouldn't be long until they tracked him to his current regiment. The federal marshal was no longer alone in the pursuit, for this had now become a personal vendetta involving Albert Harvey, Jude Simon, and a young man from near Salem by the name of Stevens. Father didn't know him but wrote that he always wore *"...a slouch hat with an unusual thin rabbit fur hat band on the crown."* Seth cautioned him to be aware of anyone who might inquire of the two of them.

His stomach convulsed in a shudder, and he felt the sweat beading up on his brow. His gut ached and he nearly doubled over.

"Bad news, Marcus?" Gill asked.

"Yes. Request permission to find Nat, the mule driver?"

"Go on. I have no need of you at the moment. We will be readying to march soon, so be back when the regiment begins to strike camp."

Marcus found Nat harnessing his mules to begin the trek with the Army toward Nashville.

"Nat, I just received a letter from my father. The good news is that Jude Simon lived."

"Is that what you call good news?"

"Don't you see? We're not guilty of murder."

Nat stood up at once from the harnesses, stared quizzically.

"The bad news is that now Simon is searching for us both and knows we – or at least I might be with the Union Army. Father advises caution."

"I done tol' ya' not to let 'em know where you is – uh – are."

"Had nothing to do with that! If I hadn't let father know, I would've never found out from him that we're marked men. Now that we know, we must be vigilant."

Nat slapped the knife sheath hanging on his belt, clenched the handle. "I ain't goin' back."

"I ain't lettin' you go back either," Marcus said. In that moment he felt an intense protectiveness. More so than he had ever felt for any of the charges he had spirited away from slavery. Inexplicably, Nat was stronger bonded to him than even his own family. He had vested too much of himself now. Nat *was* family to him.

"I'll *fight* to keep you safe, Nat. You will *not* be returned to slavery, on my word of honor."

"You always carin' for me."

"I can't do any less."

"And I'll always care for you, Marcus."

The order shouted, the drum tattoo snapped loudly across the camp, and the 65th Ohio assembled to strike their tents, pack equipment, rations, and ammunition. The infantry formed and began the march toward Munfordville, Kentucky. Marcus fell into the back of the line with his ambulance, happily empty of excessive baggage for the journey. Nat drove his team of six mules near the rear of the extensive column, along with the dozens of other muleskinners who urged their teams on, slogging through the thick mud, the unwelcome consequence of the winter rains. Like a slow serpent the column stretched itself out for miles, slinking its way toward the rebel army.

The route was a test of fortitude. The column continually slowed to a halt. And each time, cursing, complaining soldiers fell out of line at the order to unload the supplies and help muscle the wheels of the baggage wagons past a stretch of impassable mud-slimed road, only to carry the supplies forward and heft them back on to the wagons. Over and over, mile after tedious mile, the column snaked along, repeatedly unloading and loading. The mules rebelled and even Nat had unusual difficulty making his team obey. Yet the journey at last had finished, and the rain-soaked, mud-weary army dragged into the camp. Here they would spend weeks cutting down trees and constructing corduroy roads for the army and stay in readiness to support General George Thomas's corps engaged in battle at Mill Spring, Kentucky. The fight was small in scope compared to reports of other battles in the East. Casualties from Mill Spring nevertheless began to flood into the camp. It was here that Marcus encountered his first bloody carnage of war. Rather than nauseate him, the wounded and dying curiously roused in him the same passion he held for the runaway slaves, a passion to do more – more than just observe. He had grown weary of merely caring for the dozens upon dozens of sick soldiers, many of whom died from the diseases that accompanied the labor on roads through swampy grounds. He soon volunteered his ambulance to journey to the battlefield, retrieve soldiers in need of medical care, and then transfer them from the makeshift field hospital to a more permanent surgery. When the duties were at last fulfilled, he and two other ambulance drivers rejoined the 65th. Though the guilt pricked his conscience, he privately hoped for another battle, one in which the 65th OVI would gain glory for themselves, and in which he could earn his own personal glory, performing miraculous deeds while saving the wounded. Yet with each passing rain-drenched day, the boredom of building roads and tutoring Nat took a depressing toll on him. Nat was making steady progress, but Marcus grew weary of it all. At times he longed to leave the 65th and venture on to wherever the enemy was in a desperate struggle with his Union Army. *His army*. With them he could use *his* medical wagon to make a name for himself. His hometown of Ashtabula, his college in Oberlin, the Underground Railroad conductors, all would hear of the deeds of Marcus Armstrong on the battlefields, saving the Union one soldier at a time. He drifted off to sleep each boring night with visions of receptions where he would be the guest of honor, lauded for his heroism. He would brave the shot and shell, the Minie' ball, the canister, the bayonet, the slashing sword, the horse pistol, all for his chance at immortality. The visions were reinforced when the body of Confederate General Felix Zollicoffer, killed at Mill Creek, came under flag of truce through the camp on the journey to his final rest in Bowling Green. Another rebel officer had died, and Marcus felt the flush of satisfaction in the loss of yet another defender of slavery. The encounter drove him deeper into reflection that evening. As he lay in the back of his dried-blood stained wagon, his imaginings occupied him until he drifted off. The dream of glory recurred to him again and again, every night until the regiment loaded onto the trains to journey to Munfordville, Kentucky. On February 13 they arrived, and there the regiment rested at Camp Wood until the army recaptured Nashville from the Confederate Army.

Wherever the Army of the Ohio went to set up camp, the sutlers' tents were not far behind. Merchants who gained favor with politicians or with the general staff received carte blanche in hawking their wares. Sutlers' tokens replaced money in many camps and soldiers procured as many of these as necessary for trade. Here at the suttlery, soldiers used their tokens to purchase items not provided by the Army. Most of the soldiers purchased tobacco, coffee, and sugar when the sutlers had a large enough supply. Because Marcus was not on the roster, he could not be paid. He was simply a volunteer whom the Army fed and clothed in exchange for his skills. At Camp Morton, he persuaded Adam to give him tokens enough to get tobacco and coffee for him in exchange for half of the coffee bag. Though he did not partake of tobacco for himself, a stockpile of tobacco would eventually come in handy for bartering for other necessities. These he promised to share with Adam.

The sutlers' tent was bustling with soldiers looking over the goods, haggling prices. Marcus and Nat stood just outside the throng of men waiting their turn. At the large chuckwagon before the tent, one of the clerks was boisterous and rude toward the soldiers, who in turn mocked him and his obvious speech impediment.

"They're sure giving him a good riding," Marcus said loudly to Nat.

Nat didn't see the humor in the situation. "They don't like him only 'cause he don't talk like them soldiers?"

"They're just sportin' with him. It's the way of it, Nat."

"Why does it have to be that way?"

"I guess it doesn't have to be. It just is."

The taunts rose above the loud bartering between soldiers and the other clerks.

"W'at that on your hat? Ith that a bunny rabbit?" a soldier mocked.

Another piped in, "Naw, I think it ith a thquirrel tail!"

"Naw," said another, "Ith a pieth of a ol' hare for a hatband!"

Loud guffaws.

"Fooled me," said the first voice. "I thought the hare wath on hith lip!"

An officer moved through the ranks to maintain order before the ribbing got out of hand. Marcus strained to see who they were taunting. A slender figure wearing *a slouch hat sporting a piece of thin rabbit fur on the hat crown* stood red-faced against the men while trying to make his sales. Marcus immediately remembered his father's letter.

"Stevens!" He blurted out. "Nat! Get out of here."

"What?"

"Get out of here!"

"I want me some sugar."

"Nat! Don't argue. Please! Get back to the supply wagons. You can't be seen with me. I'll explain later. I'm going to slip away and get back to Adam. Please, Nat. Just do it."

Nat reluctantly left, and Marcus pulled his Kepi hat down over his eyebrows, lowered his head and hunching his shoulders, losing himself in the mass of blue uniforms. When he made his way back to the camp of the 6th Ohio Artillery battery, Adam confronted him.

"Where's my tobacco and coffee, Marcus?"

His voice was urgent. "Adam, I need your help! I saw one of the sutlers, and he matches the description father sent me of a man named Stevens, one of the Ohio slave catchers!"

"Where is he?"

"I just told you! He is with the sutlers!"

"Calm down. Did he recognize you?"

"I don't even know if he knows what I look like. But he's here, regardless."

"If it's him…"

"Adam, it can be nobody but."

"You think he's here looking for you? Maybe he's just a merchant and happened to be here."

"I didn't stay to find out."

Adam thought on it. "Hmm… Give me my tokens back. I'll go get the provisions and see what I can learn of him and what his motive is. At least you'll know."

"If you talk to him, don't mention Nat."

"Marcus, I think you know me better than that."

As Adam headed for the sutlers' wagons, Marcus, took a meandering route to the baggage wagons in search of Nat. He found him uneasily sitting on the wagon tongue, scraping his long knife on a stone.

"I'm sorry that I had to be so short with you, Nat. I recognized the sutler as that Stevens fella that father described in his letter – the one who is looking for you and me. He may in fact be a sutler by trade, or he may be hiding his intentions by traveling with them. I don't know that he knows what either of us looks like, but he is here."

Nat looked up from his blade, gaped at Marcus for a moment. "Ya' sure? It's really him?"

"I wasn't waiting to find out. But if it is him, and he is here, we're both in danger. Don't know what he can do to us inside a Union camp, but I know he can report it to whoever he's working with outside of the camp."

"What you want me to do? I ain't goin' back!" he said, clutching the long blade.

"I won't let anyone take you back. And I'm sure the colonel won't let anyone take you back." He looked long and hard at Nat, "But then, he doesn't have to take us back, does he?"

Nat spoke low, menacingly. "You want me to take keer of him?"

"No, I'm not suggesting any such thing!" he said in a strident whisper. "I'm suggesting he may take care of us."

"What do we do?"

"We wait. Adam is trying to determine his motives and will let me know. Presently, we just wait. And we also stay clear of the sutlers' tents. Get someone else to buy for you and me, and keep a low profile."

Marcus walked back to the surgeon's tent and nervously occupied himself with medical utensils, pretending to be busy and occasionally looking out the tent flap, searching for – he knew not what: Adam, the sutler Stevens, the colonel, a local marshal, a squad of armed soldiers, Nat? His imagination flitted about. His conscience displayed the image like a tin type: Jude Simon lying bloody in the road. And now this Stevens was in his camp, looking for him. Inside he felt his stomach turning, he grew pale and he began to shake. His brain reeled, his legs felt weak, and suddenly he collapsed onto a cot.

"Marcus?" a hospital orderly said. "Are you well?"

His brain was fuzzy. He tried to focus on the soldier. "No," he said simply.

+ + + + +

Marcus opened his eyes in the dim yellow glow of the oil lamp affixed to the central tent post. Around him lay several soldiers, all of them covered in wool blankets, shivering with assorted maladies. Outside, the rain spattered against the sides of the Sibley and the loose flap tossed open on occasional wind gusts. He pulled the wool blanket up to his neck, licked his dried lips, tried to speak.

Adam Watling stood over him, a metal cup poised at his face. "Drink this," he said.

The aroma awoke his senses. Marcus sipped the coffee slowly and with effort propped himself up on his elbow, "How long have I been here?"

"I 'spect about three, maybe four hours. Not sure what you have, but you sure were exhausted."

"What did you learn of the sutler?"

"You have a right to be concerned. His name is Stevens, and he's from Ohio too. He was asking about you."

"What did he learn?"

"Evidently, not very much. A few said they had heard of you, being from Ohio, but no one knew where you were now."

"Did he talk to you?"

"No," said Adam. "He left with another sutler by horseback on toward Nashville. They said he was seeing about securing positions with the army setting up camp in Nashville."

"What of Nat?"

"I suppose he didn't ask about him at all. No one mentioned it."

"Where's Nat? I need to tell him."

"No one has seen him. I tried to find him near where the other teamsters are, but they said he had lit out on horseback."

His eyes widened. "Stole a horse?"

"Don't think so. They say he looked like he was off on an errand for the captain."

"Adam, did he ride off toward Nashville?"

Adam paused. "Oh, no, he wouldn't…."

"He is determined to not be taken back. No, he couldn't go after them alone."

"He'd be a dead man, Marcus."

"No. I don't think it's in him."

"What about the fella out on the road in Ohio?"

"That's different. He thought he was defending me."

"And what's he doing now, if not defending you?"

With some effort Marcus was soon layered in heavy clothing, a rubber raincoat draped over his shoulders, and a wool floppy hat tugged down over his head, his collar pulled high. Using one of the borrowed cavalry horses, he rode at a gallop toward Nashville two miles distant.

Chapter Twenty-One
Near Nashville, Tennessee   March 1862

Marcus reined in his horse and pulled off the turnpike toward the figure crouching in the woods. "Nat! What do you think you're doing!"

"Nature called, Marcus."

"I don't mean that! I mean, what do you think you're doing leaving the camp the way you did! You want to be shot for desertion?"

"I am not a soldier Marcus, I can't be held as a deserter."

"Nat, you stole a horse!"

"Borrowed. And it ain't much of a horse. I've rode better ones back in Alabama on the Richardson place."

"So what do you think you're doing, *borrowing* a horse, *not* deserting, and heading toward *Nashville* where I know a certain *sutler* rode?"

"Just paying my compliments."

"Not with a knife!"

"No. With this here pistol." He pulled a Colt revolver from his belt and held it out.

"You stole a pistol too?"

"Borrowed," he said, returning the pistol to his belt. "I got it from that German fella, that muleskinner. I told him I'd bring it back when I's done with it."

Still lightheaded, he tried to make sense of it, stared incredulously at Nat. There was no logic to it.

"Marcus, that man is after you. Probably me too. He not gonna quit until he got you locked up and me dead."

"This isn't the way, Nat."

"And what is, Marcus? Hm? What is?"

"Well, not this. We have courts...."

"Courts! Oh, Marcus, when you goin' to see the world? You done showed me how backward I am in talk and writing and cyphering and such. But you're backward too. You don't know much about the world. All you know is *your law*. *Your courts*. Well, that's fine for you white men, but what about us? Hm? What about us? We got no courts! And we're goin' to see the same thing for ages to come. That's *my* world. That man isn't here for the law, Marcus. He's here for vengeance!"

"Vengeance is *mine*, says the Lord. *I* will repay."

"Yeh, you read that Good Book of yours to that sutler fella when he's standing in front of you with a rifled musket. See if you can convince him when his finger is tightening on the trigger."

"Killing a man makes you just as bad as him, Nat."

"It make me still *alive*!"

"Not this way, Nat!"

"What you want me to do, Marcus? Huh? What you want me to do?"

"Not this. We can avoid him. He most likely thinks you're safe in Canada by now, so he's not really looking for you. As for me, if I'm caught, I can face the courts. I committed no crime except violating the Fugitive Slave. Many of us on the railroad did that, and not all have faced jail. We have lawyers who are in sympathy with us. But you go out there and try to stop him on your own, they will soon know *who* you are and *where* you are. Just stay low and keep working your wagons. We will be safe."

He instinctively recoiled when Nat pulled his pistol and took aim at a horse and rider coming toward them at a full gallop. It was Adam.

"Thank God I found you two."

"What's wrong?"

"Nothin's wrong, Marcus, except the regiment is moving out. General Garfield ordered us to march immediately for Savannah!"

"What's in Savannah?"

"Boats. General Grant is moving on Corinth and needs us in support. So we catch the ferries there in Savannah."

"Is it safe for the two of us to be back in camp?" asked Marcus, indicating Nat.

"You're part of the Army. The command won't give you up to any vigilantes while there are battles to be won. You're expected back there. Now, let's move!"

The Army was in a state of hurried packing when the three returned, and within an hour, the 65th had stepped out on its way to Savannah. The sutlers had packed their wares, destined for Nashville where the rest of the Army camped in and around the city. Beyond the city, the rebels had put up a "minor resistance," as the men called it, but had removed themselves when the overwhelming numbers began to arrive, abandoning Nashville without a shot fired inside the city. Reports from scouts and civilians friendly to the Union indicated General Albert Sidney Johnston's army had fled southeast and the rest of the Confederates under General P.T.E Beauregard had moved southwest toward General Ulysses S. Grant's forces near Corinth, Mississippi.

Marcus still carried the anxiety of discovery with him, but the draw of a coming battle and anticipating his own heroic deeds now smothered his deepest fears. He soon dismissed most thoughts of the sutler. His need for glory once again recklessly drove him to forget that notoriety was not a desirable ambition. Visions of heroic rescues of the wounded propelled him into action. He eagerly packed his ambulance with the readied supplies, hitched his team of mules, and fell impatiently into line behind the infantry already slogging along the quagmire that feigned to be the Nashville Pike.

Wherever the Army was headed didn't matter. It meant finally he would face a battle. Now he could do his part and show the conductors at home that he was every bit as heroic as his grandfather had been. His heart raced, for he would soon save many lives for the glorious cause.

Nat still carried with him – along with the handmade gladius accessibly strapped to his waist – the compulsive craving to end these slave catchers' mission for all time. Privately, he hoped for a final confrontation. He envisioned that violent bloody moment when he would exact revenge, and it attended him on the muddy route. At times he jerked out of his reverie when the mules balked at a difficult stretch in the road, where the beasts wandered off the path and rebelled against their burden, kicking and braying. He calmly coaxed them back toward their path, tracking in line with the extended baggage wagon train, repeatedly earning the awe of the other 'skinners. Mile after tedious mile, they slogged on. Time and again he wandered back into that dream, saw himself struggle against his foes and vanquish them. Then Emma would be proud of him, would cheer him as her hero. And he would take her to the gravesite where he had buried his fortune, there under that tree in a hayfield in Alabama. Together they would resurrect the coffin. Then he would allow her to open it. He would see her eyes sparkle as she beheld his treasure – her treasure. The silver tea service, the gold coins, the silver table settings: These would set her heart racing. He would at last be worthy of her. Then he would ask her hand in marriage. Then they would buy a house – a house bigger than Master Ashbie or Master Richardson even. Then they would be free to hold their heads up high. Then he would set up his own farrier shop. Then the white folk would come to *him* and pay *him* money for *his* skills. The plan unfolded in his mind, and he fairly laughed aloud as he saw it before him like a massive painted mural. But then on the canvas Jonah Kenton's face appeared. The evil image of that whip-wielding son of Satan obliterated the vibrant colors. Well, then. He simply would kill him.

+ + + + +

The regimental march had consumed nearly a week by the time the soldiers finally arrived in Savannah, Tennessee. During the journey, Marcus had transported nearly two dozen troops who had fallen out one by one, suffering from sore feet, legs, and backs, sore throats, heads and sinuses. He was not alone. All of the hospital wagons and many of the baggage wagons had eventually carried their quota of soldiers who through age or infirmity had succumbed to the weather and deplorable roads of Tennessee. Many died along the way, while others were given their discharge and sent back to Ohio. Even officers who had started with good intentions and full of bravado had succumbed to disease, boredom and battlefield anxiety. They chose to resign their commissions and return to civilian life before any major confrontation could challenge their fortitude. Marcus watched new officers continually added or promoted in a seemingly endless cache from the rank and file in hopes they would successfully lead where others had faltered. In his opinion, the rebels were winning.

The 65th Ohio gathered at Savannah, Tennessee and set up camp, awaiting the ferries that would transport them downriver to link with General Grant's army. The April rains had left much of the main road a soft rutted mess. The rebel cavalry under Nathan Bedford Forest had taken advantage of the weather's effect on the slow-moving army and destroyed what bridges they could in their attempt to impede these invaders. Those independent small cavalry units harassed the wagons, forcing more soldiers to be reassigned as guards for the supplies. Most times the defense was successful. But many wagons still fell into Confederate hands when Union soldiers simply abandoned them, running to save their own lives. The harassment slowed but never completely stopped the flow of supplies. Nat had returned the pistol he borrowed, and more than once wished he had not done so. A few Confederate riders came within pistol shot range, and he merely ducked for the cover of the baggage while Union soldiers fired their rifles to drive them off. When the remaining baggage wagons finally caught up with the regiment, they had little time to sit idle and recover from the raids. Colonel Harker announced the Army of the Ohio's orders to support General Grant, now fully engaged in a major battle at Pittsburg Landing on the Tennessee. It was the evening of April 6, 1862.

"Those bullet holes?" Marcus asked.

Nat sat on the upturned wooden bucket, poking at the fire with a long iron rod, stirring the embers. He glanced over to the wagon where the glowing campfire revealed several jagged holes in the side wall.

"They are," he said.

"I'm glad there are none in you," he said as he drew up a wooden keg to sit.

"Not any more glad than I is," Nat said.

"*Am*."

"...than I *am*."

"Was it much of a fight?"

"It warn't much, but it was a scrapper. Times I wish I had me a gun."

"I bet." He sat, uncomfortable, quiet, reflecting. Finally smiled weakly, "Well, I'm glad I didn't have to come get you and carry you in my hospital wagon."

"Me too."

"Don't want any black blood staining the inside of my wagon," he said slyly. "Especially yours."

Nat thought on this. "I'll tries hard to not disappoint you," he said softly.

They sat quietly, contemplating the flowing river, their highway to the impending firestorm at Pittsburg Landing. "Looks like we'll be returning to your neck of the woods soon enough, Nat."

"That so?"

"I hear it that we're marching on Alabama once we whip the Rebs down this way."

"Well, I tol' you before that I was from around Huntsville, but I don't think they'll be wantin' to go that way."

"Adam tells me that his captain told him they want to move on Chattanooga and trap the Rebs there, but that General Johnston isn't cooperating. He won't sit still long enough for us to beat him."

"Mebbe this here battle we will."

"Either way, we'll have our work cut out for us."

"How's that?"

"You taking a wagon full of tents and food for the men, me taking the hospital wagon to set up the hospital, the regiment taking the fight to the Johnnies. We all have our work cut out for us."

"If'n we get towards Huntsville, I have some work cut out for you and me. That is, if'n we can slip away for a bit."

Marcus sat quietly, stared at the fire. Waited. Nat had spent more than enough thought on his plan to find Emma and dig his treasure. He inevitably had fallen into despair when he reasoned that he might never find her in time. The impulse to claim what he believed to be rightfully his – payment for forced servitude – finally outweighed all measured caution. He resolved that he must ultimately trust in Marcus.

The voices of the men singing quietly around the various fires blended together to permeate the stillness of the camp. Nat looked about cautiously, lowered his voice.

"Any chance you 'n me can get away for a bit? I don't mean to run away or desert – jes' get clear of the camp for awhile when we get to Huntsville."

Marcus peered around warily. "Go on..." he said.

"You've been teaching me real good and I'm grateful, but I need your help even more down there, Marcus."

"You're scheming about something, aren't you?"

"Member when I tol' you 'bout that treasure I hid? I been thinkin' that might be a good time to fetch it. I know that country like the back o' my hand, and we can find my field and get that coffin. But I need your help again, Marcus. First we get it, and then we hide it in the back of my wagon. I'm still the onliest one what unloads the wagon, and I can keep it hidden with my own goods."

"Someone will notice, Nat."

"Don't think so. I can keep it buried under so much truck that no one will be the wiser." He waited.

Marcus looked off at the fires around him, watched the men going on with their muted laughter at soldiers' jests and stories. He saw them prepare themselves mentally for the inevitable battle, saw them so full of faith that they would at last generate peace, and then go home to make their own separate peace back on the farms or in the cities. But where would this man he bore from slavery to freedom go after the war? What separate peace would he find? He had nothing to restart his life. Nothing. Nothing except the treasure he believed was rightfully owed him. He could teach Nat how to speak, how to read and write. But then what? How could Nat begin afresh? He wasn't white. He certainly had no advantage to speak of. Nothing except that buried coffin he had fixed in his mind as his start as a free man.

"When the time comes that you want to try for it, let me know. Don't go off on your own."

"I will need your help, so I am asking you now. Help me."

It had gone against his own beliefs to agree, yet he heard himself speak as though detached from the words. "I will assist you in any manner I can, Nat."

Chapter Twenty-Two
Pittsburg Landing, TN.   Just before 12 pm, April 7 1862

General Wood's division had begun loading onto the arriving ferries early in the morning. Infantry arrived first, but the few supply wagons that could fit onto the ferries rolled onto the boats before them, allowing the soldiers to pack themselves in wherever they could find a place to sit, stand, or lie down. Most stood in anticipation. Col. Harker and the men of the 65th regiment shuffled into their places on the boats, and then they waited. By the time Marcus had his hospital wagon aboard with several of the supply wagons, the waiting had taken its toll.

"Why can't we just leave?" he asked Surgeon John Kyle.

"Patience, Armstrong. You'll see your battle soon enough. The entire division must move as one. When the entire brigade is ready, we will coordinate with the 64th."

"But surely they are in need of the hospital supplies."

"Listen. Do you hear the thunder down river?"

Marcus strained to hear above the commotion of the army positioning themselves on the transports.

"Barely."

"That artillery is the sound of carnage. You don't want to be in that yet, do you?"

"Yes," he blurted out. "I do. I am of no use sitting on a boat tied to the shore."

Kyle stuffed his surgical case into the rear of his wagon. "You will be of no use if you get there ahead of the men and get yourself wounded or killed, either. We will go when we are ordered."

"But we might miss the fight!"

Surgeon Kyle looked up abruptly. "God willing," he said.

"But the wounded –"

191

"There will be enough to go around, Marcus. You'll get your share of blood and shattered men."

"I didn't mean —"

"Yes, you did, Marcus. Since we first arrived in Kentucky you have wanted to jump into the fray. I've seen you. You are good with your team, you drive the wagon well, and you have no revulsion at getting your hands bloodied carrying soldiers from the field. But adding your impatience to that duty is a dangerous combination. We will get to the battlefield soon enough, and when we do, you must restrict yourself to following orders. It is for your own good as well as the brigade's."

Marcus said nothing. Of course he disagreed with Kyle, but the surgeon was his immediate superior, and if he was to continue with the brigade, he must of necessity follow orders. Nat leaned in beside him at the stern rail, the large paddle wheel towering over them. He elbowed him and grinned. Marcus was not in the mood.

"What?" he said tensely.

Nat continued to grin. Marcus studied him curiously. Still the grin. "What?" he repeated.

He spoke softly. "White officers ordering you around too."

Marcus dropped his eyes, hung his head, shrugged, "Got to follow orders, I suppose."

"We all do, Marcus. Lemme ask you somethin'. Why you want to jump onto that battlefield? You got a death wish?"

"No."

"Then why?"

"Why do you want to retrieve that treasure that isn't yours?"

"That's no answer, Marcus."

The smoke began to belch heavier from the tall stacks rising over the deck. The wheel slowly turned and the

192

paddlewheel pulled out from the dock, cheered by the soldiers on deck, heroic slogans shouted above the engine's chugging, and the loud whooshing from the water churning beneath the wheel.

"See, all my life I've heard how heroic my grandfather was. His name was George, and he fought with Oliver Perry, the naval hero of the last war against England. He didn't talk much about it, but my grandmother told me all of the stories. Father too, and others I didn't even know. But they knew him. He had done something important – helped build ships, rescued his cousin, helped fight a ship on Lake Erie, saved his home in Erie. That's in Pennsylvania, Nat."

"Like the lake?"

He nodded. "That same lake I was to take you to for your freedom. And I saw something very profound, Nat."

Nat's eyes narrowed.

"It means very thoughtful, Nat. At his wake, I saw two women whom I didn't even know place two ribbons on his chest as he lay in the parlor. It made no sense to me at first. They honored him for what he had done, not just in the war, but I think for his work in rescuing slaves like you. And there was something else. I saw freedmen come in and stand around his body and sing hymns to honor him. You see?"

"And you want them to put a bit of colored ribbon on your body and sing hymns around you too?"

"I hope not. No, I just want to be remembered in some way. Everything we do for the slaves is in secret. Even traveling with the army I must also do in secret."

"Because o' me."

"No. Well, not entirely. I just want to feel I am remembered like grandpa George is."

"An' you think savin' soldiers on the battlefield will help, do you? Is that why you are here? I thought we were here to hide out from them slave catchers."

Marcus couldn't answer. Stared at the wake the paddlewheel churned behind the boat. Nat had hit it. And once he heard it voiced, Marcus couldn't admit to the truth of the words.

"And the work helpin' us slaves? Was that so yo' chillun' and grandchillun' could tell stories about you and how you rescued po' nigga' slaves a-lookin' fo' freedom?"

The words slapped him in the face, and he was struck speechless. Nat's reversion to his past field hand dialect was done for effect. He understood that. Nat's condescension hurt. For one of the few times in his life, he felt humiliation. But for the words to come from the man whom he had rescued, the man for whom he had risked his life, this pierced him deeply. Nat's homemade knife couldn't have done the deed any cleaner.

"I may jes' be a uneducated nigga' from de Sout', but I kin feel what way de win' blows." And then the effected dialect stopped. "Marcus, I thought that you *cared*!"

Marcus glared long into the rush of the churning water, heard Nat's shoes fade away, stared deeply into the big wheel's wake. At length he discreetly wiped his sleeve across his eyes. What indeed *was* he doing here?

+ + + + +

Shiloh

The boats steamed downriver, the musketry and sporadic cannon firing growing louder, and the men tensely gathered at the side rails, listening. They clenched their muskets in anticipation, peering toward the distant cluster of gunboats anchored in the river, roaring to life with black smoke and orange-white muzzle blasts. The steamers drifted past the landing, began wide turns in the river to turn back against the current to dock. But by the time the steamers made the circle past the gunboats to unload the brigade at Pittsburg Landing, the distant musketry had faded, some in volleys, some in intermittent cracks now far from the landing. The gunboat cannons had silenced. Even the usual blue-gray pallor of black powder smoke had dispelled in the light breeze. The ramps swung out from the boat and the men ran down them to the cluttered, muddy shoreline, forming into companies under tersely shouted orders. They would march at the double-quick to support Grant's army which had checked the advancing rebels and now were driving them back. The 65th would not join the battle which was all but over, but would reinforce the army now claiming its victory. Marcus swallowed his disappointment as he readied his medical wagon, drove down the ramp and up the bank. Union soldiers soon appeared in a thin line, marching with bayonets at the ready, escorting dozens of rebel soldiers, most lacking any real semblance of uniforms. Marcus looked long at the weary faces, black powder streaks smudging the side creases of their mouths from biting off cartridge ends. They held their tired heads high with a defiance that impressed him. He wanted to talk to them, get questions answered, to try to know this enemy who were also his countrymen. But they trudged on past, down the bank to the landing, there to be transported to northern prison camps. For them, the war was over.

For still others, the war was over too. Marcus continued up the steep bank on the muddy road, following the 65th, and he passed row after row of bodies torn asunder, bearing the marks of exploding artillery shells and musket fire. These were already retrieved from the battlefield, unrecognizable, but he knew still other soldiers lay ahead, crying out for his help. Following the rushing line of blue uniforms, he drove on, looking for the makeshift hospital tents that would have posted themselves to the rear of the fighting. More captured Confederate soldiers arrived at gunpoint, moving to the prisoner holding area, passing his wagon, some despondent, others defiant. One of the soldiers caught his eye. He was a tall, lanky young man with bushy side whiskers. Much like other rebel soldiers, he was unremarkable except he bore an old, deep scar running from his lower lip down to below his chin where no whiskers grew. Marcus focused on the chin as he passed by, staring, trying to recall where he had seen that face. An open wooden coffin lay by the road, void of inhabitants. The coffin triggered it. The man at the tavern. Where was it? Uniontown? Name? "Isaiah?" he said half aloud.

"Yeh? Who are you?" the young man sneered.

"Uh—oh, I was thinking aloud. Sorry." He couldn't hold back. "Have you ever been in Ohio?"

"That's where I lived for a spell. Why?"

"What are you doing here with the Rebs?"

"My mama and daddy is from Tennessee. I came home to he'p 'em after the Yankees invaded. What's it to you?"

"Nothing, except I saw you once, Unionville it was. You were rummaging through my wagon where I had carried a coffin for burial. You didn't seem too intent on helping me."

"I don't remember you."

"Well enough, I'll just leave it at that. I suppose they'll parole you so you can get back home – Ohio or Tennessee."

"I think it'll be back to Ahiya. I've had my fill o' fightin'. Why'nt ya jes' go on back home too and leave well enough alone?"

"Can't. I tend to the wounded, and can't leave while other battles are about."

"Then maybe the Yanks can jes' go on home and you can follow 'em."

"Can't do that until we put down this rebellion."

"All *that* for a bunch o' slaves –"

"Yep. All *that*."

196

The soldiers escorted the prisoners into a haphazard stockade of split-rail fencing, hastily thrown together. And as he drove his team on toward the battlefield around Shiloh Church, Marcus felt a distinct queasiness churning. This Isaiah fellow would be paroled would return to *Ahiya* as he called it and tell the story of Shiloh and how he met a fellow Ohioan. A federal soldier from around his county. A federal soldier who had once carried a coffin in Unionville. Someone would trace him to this Army of the Ohio. He now regretted even speaking to the soldier. Once again his mouth had cast a beacon on his whereabouts. His low profile kept standing up, and he agonized that it may have stood up too tall this time.

Chapter Twenty-Three
Near Corinth, Mississippi   May 1862

Nat had skillfully served as a wagon driver, had distinguished himself above the other muleskinners and contraband with his handling of the teams, and he had grown proud of his reputation, enjoyed the notoriety and the small rewards, extra food, better shoes, the freedom from extra duties. The captain of the supply wagons had at length learned of his prior work as a farrier. Every company kept two smiths, and Nat was selected to replace a burly German smithy who had succumbed to the pneumonia which had repeatedly swept through the camps. Nat set his farrier's wagon with its bellows and iron works in an open area near the horse and mule corral, and there he plied his trade. He had at long last arrived at his comfortable place. Doing what made him happiest, and alone with the animals and his thoughts, he carefully plotted out varying scenarios for recovering his treasure.

This army had the rebels on the run. They would chase them out of Corinth, were in fact doing that very deed with increasing casualties. Yet a swelling sense of ultimate victory had roosted over much of the camp with the resulting cockiness being the rule and not the exception. Soldiers who at one time had seen the contraband only as teamsters, orderlies, and cooks essential to the cause now began to openly question why they weren't currrently serving on the battle lines as infantry alongside the white soldiers. Those who had believed the contraband not equal to the white soldiers eventually doubted the entire truth of that premise. Though deep-seated prejudice still gripped their perception, many were willing to allow the "darkeys," as they called them, a chance to bleed too. Some even requested it. The brigade had received word that President Lincoln was considering enlisting these men of color as soldiers to fight for their own freedom. Nat pondered the question.

"Would you do it?" Adam repeated.

"I might," he said.

"You'd give up the job as farrier for a chance to get killed?"

"I see it as more of a chance to kill those soldiers that defend slavery."

"Nat, don't you have a wish to live, to make your freedom amount to something?"

"Oh, I s'pose it will amount to something when it's all over and done with, but I got some scores to settle first."

"Revenge first, eh?"

"Don't like the word *revenge*. Call it *retribution*."

"Big word, Nat. You know what it means?"

"Adam, I'm not as dull as some think I am. I know exactly what it means."

"It means revenge."

"No. It means justice. And I aim to get my piece of justice portioned out on them that never gave me justice."

"Picking up the rifle and charging an enemy isn't going to dole out your justice on the men who hurt you. They ain't on the *battlefield*. They're over in Alabama on their plantations and on their farms."

"Mebbe we'll get over to Alabama."

"But charging a regiment of rebs ain't gonna make any difference. It's just gonna get you killed."

Nat laughed quietly, cocked his head, looked calmly at him. "Adam, you trying to protect me?"

"I guess I am. But I think I'm protecting Marcus even more."

Nat puzzled over this. Marcus needing protection?

"Looka here, Nat. You didn't know Marcus before he found you in that graveyard in Massillon. You don't know what he's done to make sure all of you runaways got safely to your freedom. He would do anything, *anything* to see you all reached Canada, even if he had to row you across Lake Erie himself. I've known him – better'n you even. He's a devoted abolitionist. More than that, he's relentless. He's sacrificed himself more than most anyone I know. He can't stop 'til he sees a thing through, like when he's teaching you to fit into free society. It would kill him to see you die on a battlefield instead of getting to use your freedom. He'd take it personal. Like *he* had failed. You do this thing, and you'll let him down. And he ain't *never* let *you* down!"

Nat sat, straddling the tongue of the blacksmith's wagon, the smoke from the cooling forge embers rising in a wisp of gray above his brown slouch hat, the ash settling on his coat. His thoughts drifted. He saw Marcus, diligent with the lessons, teaching him to read, to write, to cypher, to speak. He saw Emma, firmly teaching him *patrollers*, not *pattyrollers*. He saw Big Jim, patiently teaching him his smithing trade. He saw the many others who had taught him about the animals, how to drive a team, all those who had a hand in his present position with the 65th Regiment of the Ohio Volunteers. But through all the visions he also saw the whip-wielding Jonah Kenton, who taught him about cruelty to humans. Saw John Ashbie, who taught him not to trust a master, no matter how close and friendly they seemed to be. Saw the slave catchers and home guard, who taught him they would kill or maim to reap their reward money. They all had taught him their life lessons, and he had learned them well. But who was the better teacher?

"Adam," he said at length, "Whatever I do, I'm not going to let Marcus down either."

"I hoped you would say that. He doesn't need to be worrying about you."

"No need."

The inner drive to repay the violence had abated, and Nat fixed his gaze on his original plan to exact justice on the institution that had started his life's journey. The buried coffin waited still. Receiving his own rifle, becoming an actual soldier in full uniform would give him just the authorization he needed to recover his treasure, backed of course by the invading Army of the Ohio. He could surely see his way clear at some opportune moment to pay a visit to a farm in Alabama as the rebels ran before them. Collecting his treasure was only a matter of time.

Marcus could afford no more time for Nat's lessons. The wounded from Shiloh and the disease-ridden divisions from the Army of the Ohio and the Army of the Tennessee had turned Corinth into a combination hospital and morgue. Marcus's wishes of serving the Union troops in some grand fashion were now granted to him by the wagonful. He slept only when he could slip in a few minutes between the multitude of journeys from the battlefield or the camp sites in Corinth to the various makeshift hospitals set up for the overwhelming casualties. He was diligent, but he found himself wearing down much easier than when he first stepped off the boat in Kentucky. The rebel army finally abandoned Corinth, allowing the division a chance to regroup and prepare to pursue General Earl Van Dorn's forces. Hundreds of slaves had escaped their masters and flocked into the city under the protection of the Union Army, and Marcus felt lured to abandon his ambulance duties to help in the relocation of the former slaves. Yet the work of caring for the wounded consumed his waking hours.

The summer was hot, humid and sticky; the work, relentless. The brigade labored to repair the Memphis and Charleston Railroad, torn up by fleeing Confederates while the rest of the Army of the Ohio chased the rebels toward Tupelo, halting at Booneville. Cavalry scouts reported that the army had begun to work its way north toward Kentucky, and the 65th regiment once again was left behind to guard and repair railroad track and bridges. Except for what the men felt were only a few minor skirmishes, the soldiers fell into the apathy that inevitably accompanies boredom and the perceived lack of leadership. Marcus sought out Nat to work with him on his reading. Nat placed his finger under the text, followed the words as he read aloud to Marcus.

"Come, how will you trade about the gal?—what shall I say for her? – what'll you take?" Nat stopped, thought on the words.

"Go on, Nat. You're reading real well. Keep on," Marcus reassured him.

"Mr. Haley, she is not to be sold," said Shelby. *"My wife would not part with her for her w—w—"*

"Weight," Marcus prompted.

"...weight in gold."

"Ay, ay! Women always say such things, cause they ha'nt no sort of cal—cal—calculation."

"Calculation," he repeated. *"Just show 'em how many watches, feathers and trinkets, one's weight in gold will buy, and that alters the case, I reckon."*

Nat re-read the words, looked up at Marcus.

"That's true enough, Marcus."

"True?" he repeated.

"I seed – saw it happen."

"For years I have heard the stories from my grandfather of the buying and selling."

"You'll know nothing like it until you live through it yourself."

"I suppose Mrs. Stowe saw it enough to put it in the book."

"I reckon so, but I mean I saw what happened when the lust for money took hold of Mrs. Annabelle back on the

Richardson place. She sold Emma away for the money she'd bring. Money for *her* trinkets and feathers!"

"Emma liked the Richardson's?"

"Yes, very much. They taught her to read and write, to talk like a gentlewoman. Emma said they al'ays treated her humanely."

Marcus took the book from Nat, flipped a page, read aloud, *"...and there is no end to the odd things humane people will say and do..."* pointed to the book. "Mrs. Stowe saw through them all, Nat," he said.

"No one listened to her."

"Many of us did. That's why I joined in with my family and the Railroad."

Nat took the book from Marcus, read silently over the passages, looked up, "Do you understand now why I must do what I have to? That treasure is earned wages, Marcus. It belongs to me – and it belongs to Emma. We're going back to Alabama, I heard the captain say, and I need time away from the regiment to gather my wages."

"It's dangerous business, Nat."

Nat looked at Marcus pointedly, "Not with two of us."

"I assume you have a plan already worked out?"

"Look, Marcus, the captain always lets some of us go out foraging for food, right? So we get on with the soldiers who are foraging and then we slip away real casual like and head over by the Richardson farm. I know the way, been there dozens o' times. We take along a shovel, gather up the crops we can, and dig up that little coffin alongside." I can wrap my treasure up in my pup tent or blanket. We got no cause for needin' blankets right now, so it'll be freed up."

"Nat, those people are not goin' to just let you forage for food around their farm without trying to stop you!"

"I'm a soldier in the Federal Army. I can do what I damn well choose to do!"

"They probably got home guard 'round those places that will put up a fight. We need more than just the two of us."

"Can we ask Adam? I trust him."

"We can ask. Then we'll get a couple more – whoever Adam wants to bring. He won't ask anyone who will use us to an advantage."

"The captain will send a squad of men, so there will be plenty of soldiers. We just need to slip away from them without them gettin' suspicious. I don't have any desire to split up my treasure with anybody – 'ceptin' maybe you."

"Nat, it is yours. I have no need – no desire for it." He breathed deeply, held it, exhaled in a burst of air, a reluctant gesture, Nat thought.

"I'll help you, but we do it quietly, we do it safely, we harm no one. That's my terms."

"Now where's the fun in that?" Nat grinned.

+ + + + +

Adam sat on an empty crate between the two 4-pounder Parrotts, trimming a new cloth on the sponge ramrod and listening calmly to Marcus and Nat's plan.

"Why me?" he asked.

"Because I know I can trust you with this profound secret."

"You know you can always trust me, but stealing gold and silver goods...."

"You won't be stealing," Nat interrupted.

"They're already stolen," Marcus added.

"So, we're returning them to their rightful owner?"

Marcus looked furtively at Nat, then to Adam. "In – in a manner of speaking, y—yes," Marcus said.

Adam laid the ramrod against the barrel of the gun, bent forward. "You're hedging," he said.

"I'm asking you to trust me, Adam," he said quietly.

Adam leaned back against the cannon's wheel, clasped his hands behind his head, patiently waited. "Not 'til you tell me who the owner is."

Nat cut in, "It's me."

Adam looked at Nat, silent, looked at Marcus who nodded in agreement with a subtle wink, looked back to Nat. Then the realization. With a loud laugh, he wiped his hands on his coat, extended his hand to Nat.

"Well, count me in."

Chapter Twenty-Four
Memphis & Charleston RR near Bridgeport, Alabama
August 1862

In June the 6th Ohio Battery moved on to Stevenson, Alabama, as the Army of the Ohio pursued General Bragg's Army of Mississippi. The 65th Ohio was ordered to do what it had done best – guard railroads and generally drift into boredom. So they marched on, passing near Huntsville and camping near Bridgeport, Alabama and the Memphis & Charleston Railroad. Though fairly well supplied, the army frequently foraged wherever ready vegetables existed, taking whatever grew. With that knowledge, Nat and Marcus joined the early morning foraging details that left camp. Three wagons with accompanying soldiers were prepared for the foraging troops. Sgt. George Howard granted Adam and two of his "pards" from the battery permission to ride along in Nat's wagon. Adam chose Charles Wicks and Henry Collier, two of whom he could trust, but only telling them that they were to forage for as much food as they could bring back for the soldiers.

"Ho' kin you be sher thet there's food where you be takin' us, Nat?" asked Charles.

"Because I know these here parts. I drove these roads for the Ashbie's farm many a-time. I know this road all the way to Stevenson and to Huntsville. If they have any crops out, I'll find 'em."

"They be sesesh out there on those roads too," he countered.

"Why, Charles, when did secessionists ever bother you before?" said Adam.

"Bothered me some at Shiloh."

"Did you shoot back?"

"I did."

"Do you have your musket with you now?"

Charles held it out high, gripping it firmly with a defiant shake.

"Well, then, you have permission to use it again if the need arises," Adam said.

The travel on the road from Bridgeport was quiet as the men kept a vigilant eye and ear to the surrounding fields and woods. Though they had confidence they could meet any individual secessionist opposition, they remained wary of the prowling Confederate cavalry. These mounted units still probed about for weaknesses in the federals' defenses, and they attacked their stretched out train of supply wagons with relative impunity. A cavalry scout might stumble on them, and they would soon surely be outnumbered.

After two hours, the sun had risen high enough to steam the countryside in its heat. The wagons plodded on, stirring up eddies of dust as they passed corn fields already mashed into stubble by scavengers pounding the countryside in the name of the Confederacy.

"You sure you know this country?" a soldier in the trailing wagon called out to Nat.

"Like the back of my hand."

"Well, looks like it's as bare as the back o' yer hand, Somuns outcheer done rode off with our food. That's what I'm a-thinkin'."

"Looks like they just hit this main road. There'll be plenty of foragin' for us on one of these side roads not far from here."

"How far, Nat?" Adam asked quietly.

"Awhile. Then awhile further."

Marcus saw Nat's appearance begin to change subtly as they drove on, closing in on the farms where he had once been enslaved. His jaw set, his brow furrowed as he glared ahead. His hands gripped the reins tighter, a nervous tension in his wrists, not shaking, but strained, as though he wanted to clench his fist and hit something. Or someone. Marcus recalled the many wretched runaways he had helped, the stories they had shared with him. But he didn't really know Nat, for he had never let him enter his world, the sordid details of what he had witnessed. Nat had bottled that up inside, had borne that flask of bitterness these many months since they had first met in the Ohio graveyard, and had never once poured out its contents. Occasionally he had sipped on that cynicism which kept him suspicious of anyone's intentions. Yet he had remained fixed on the singular purpose of recovering his treasure. He had recited the goal so often that Marcus understood it as an obsession.

The familiar hills drew him on, past the lane to the Richardson farm – Belle Vista, past *his* lane where the stone arched bridge spanned the small stream. He recognized the hill, the grove of cypress trees, the broken tree limb laying on the ground, free of its hinged bark, the branches in the air beckoning like a bony hand. He elbowed Marcus, nodded toward the lane.

"I think we'll try up this lane," he called.

"Nat, you want us to follow?"

"We can cover more ground if we split up, but stay in gunshot distance," Nat said.

Marcus shouted back to the other wagons. "Any shots fired, the rest of us ride to the sound of the guns."

"Where you think we should go?" Corporal Benning yelled from the second wagon.

"There's a crossing road up ahead apiece. See that, and you'll take the right fork. There's a big field there hidden behind a hill. Bottom land it is, and can't be seen from the crossroads. Likely no one has picked it clean. We'll catch you up if our pickin's are slim."

The trailing wagons passed by and Nat turned his wagon team up the lane toward the stone bridge. The sweat stung at his eyes, his heart raced, clammy hands gripped the leather reins. He peered over his shoulder, blinked away the tears, surveyed the distant tree lines, scoured the fields on all sides, vigilant for any observers. The two escorting wagons faded in the distance and turned at the crossroads nearly a quarter of a mile ahead. Suddenly he shook the reins, quickened the horses' pace, rapidly closing the distance to his prize. At the knoll, he leaped from the wagon, ran ahead as the others climbed from the wagon, muskets readied and alert for rebel soldiers or home guard. Nat reached the hilltop and stopped quickly. He dropped to his knees, half out of sight.

"Nat!" Marcus yelled.

"C'mon, Marcus! Help me!"

It wasn't a shout, but a wail that resounded from the grove. Marcus ran up the ridge to the grove of cypress trees. On his knees, Nat clawed at the ground, grasping fistfuls of clay, and throwing them back down in front of him, moaning. Dirt had been piled in small mounds and rounded smooth from months of weather changes. The deep impression in the ground attested to an empty grave. Marcus stood speechless, the crushing realization stimulating tears for his friend.

Adam, Charles, and Benjamin dropped from the wagon and joined the spectacle at the grove of trees. Adam quickly comprehended.

"Nat, where do you think it could've been taken?"

Nat knelt in silence, tears dropping from his cheeks.

"Nat, are you sure this is the place?"

Marcus turned on him. "Of course he's sure! He has his map with him! And anyway, the ground has been dug up!"

"Maybe it just settled from rain over time," Benjamin offered.

"Mebbe yer map is faded out over time...." A scowl from Marcus. "Uh—le's jes' digger rightcheer," Charles said and sank his shovel into the soil.

"Marcus, it's possible the Rebs found it when they were foraging for their own supply. This land has been pretty nigh picked clean. See these old wagon tracks across the field? These are weeks old – maybe even a month," Adam said.

Marcus knelt beside Nat, his arm around his shoulder. He spoke quietly, nearly a whisper. "Nat? What do you want to do? We're here to help. What can we do about this?"

Nat looked sullenly into Marcus's eyes, then through clenched teeth, "We go to Marse John Ashbie's farm and we ask him."

He strode down the hill, climbed into the wagon seat, tugged the reins and wheeled the horses smartly about, starting the drive back down across the bridge toward the road junction. The soldiers ran behind and vaulted onto the tailgate, pulling themselves onto the bed as the wagon sped forward.

Within twenty minutes the wagon had passed onto the long lane to Cypress Grove. The familiar trees were still cluttered with clumps of Spanish moss and the strands hung weeping from the bent branches. Dark greens and deep grays, exactly as he recalled they drooped nearly thirteen months ago, that day Ashbie sold him to the speculators who chained him in the back of the wagon. The lane was deserted now, and from his perch on the wagon seat, he saw no workers in the fields. The wagon pulled up in front of the big house, and John Ashbie stepped out onto the massive porch, stood between the massive columns, a rifle held firmly across his body. The men in the wagon readied their rifles and casually aimed them in his direction. Adam held the reins and Marcus gripped a pistol lying on his lap. Nat jumped from the wagon seat, removed his hat, slapped it against his Union blue coat, scattering small puffs of dust, and in long strides proudly walked to the porch.

Ashbie relaxed his finger from the trigger, his eyes widened. "Nat?"

He replaced his hat, stood imposingly before him, legs spread apart, arms folded across his blue uniform.

"Thank God it's you Nat!"

"How are the boys?" Nat asked.

"My boys? They've gone and joined up with Bragg's army. They ain't here, Nat. What are you doing with these Union soldiers?"

"I'm asking the questions this time, Mister Ashbie! Are any of the boys here?"

Ashbie tightened his grip on the rifle and tensed his shoulders.

Nat looked at the figure. "No call for that, Mister Ashbie. I just want to know if the boys are about."

"I just told you. They are not here, Nat."

"Good. Don't want any of them to get hurt for doing something stupid. Where's Marcella?"

"Run off, along with most of the field hands when the Yankees came through."

"Whatever happened to that coffin I buried for you, Mister Ashbie?"

A look of fear coupled with a pale sort of sickness showed on Ashbie's face, like he would soon double up and vomit. He dropped the muzzle of the rifle and let his left hand hold the stock, dangling the weapon to the porch floor. His voice shook.

"What are you g – going to do, Nat?"

"I said I'm asking the questions now." He waited for a response. Finally repeated, "The coffin?"

"It's where you buried it, Nat."

"I don't want to ask again, Mister Ashbie," Nat said.

"It is where you buried it," he said, an uncharacteristic high pitched nervous strain leaking from his voice. "If you forgot, I – I st – still have the map if you will let me g – go inside and retrieve it," he said turning toward the door.

Nat was calm, not a trace of malice in the voice. "I know where it *was*, Mister Ashbie. I want to know where it is *now*."

Ashbie stopped, his eyes widening. "What do you mean *was*?"

"I'm asking the questions," Nat repeated. "I went to the gravesite. It was dug up. I want to know where you took it."

Ashbie's face showed panic. "I don't know where it is, Nat. I swear before God!"

"I'm not accustomed to asking more than once, and you've already used up my patience," Nat said evenly. A sound of clicking musket hammers snapped behind Nat, and Ashbie looked past him to the soldiers by the wagon.

"I s – swear to you, Nat. It sh – should be there. I'll get the map." He started again for the door.

"I don't need your map! That map is no good anyway. You think I would tell *you* where I had buried all that treasure? *I moved it, Marse Ashbie!*" he shouted, the words dripping with sarcasm. "I buried it in another grave because it was MY compensation – *mine* – for all the trouble you gave me! For all the trouble you gave *all* of us! For selling me off to make you richer! And I came back to fetch it, but now it's gone, and neither you nor I have the goods I buried – unless you're holding out!"

Ashbie's gun fell from his grip, clattered to the porch floor. His voice was incredulous. "You stole from me?"

"How's that sit with you, *Massa!*"

Nat stormed off the porch and strode heavily to the stables, the men watching, while Adam trained a rifle on the stunned John Ashbie. Fearful for Nat, Marcus jumped down from the wagon, tucked the pistol into his belt, following after. Before he could catch up to him, Nat appeared at the door with two horses in tow, willingly following Nat's familiar coaxing voice. Marcus noted one was a beautiful black Tennessee Walker. He quickly helped Nat tie their ropes to the tailgate of the wagon.

"Nat!" Ashbie yelled. "Nat! Where you going with my horses?"

Nat and Marcus climbed into the wagon seat. "Requisitioned for the Army of the United States, *John*!" Nat called. "Git up!"

"Nat!" Ashbie's pleading voice ceased at the sight of three muskets trained on his dusty green waistcoat, his tarnished gold watch chain quivering under his heavy sighs, and as he leaned tearfully upon one giant Doric column, a whimpering sob resounded on the big house's front walls, amplified by the high white ceiling and the low dark porch.

And the wagon lurched forward, passing down the dismally ornamented lane, the charcoal gray Spanish moss weeping from the Sweetgum and Live Oak limbs, mourning the righteous judgment decreed upon the expiring dynasty that was once Cypress Grove.

Chapter Twenty-Five
October 1862

With the scavenging of hundreds of Federal soldiers, the supplement to the regular fare increased and those who could supply their own companies with fresh produce rose in esteem. The pickings were indeed slim, but Nat's sojourn into the countryside was one of the rare successes. Though Nat had returned without reclaiming his treasures, the treasure of corn the men had claimed in the name of the Union carried far greater importance to the soldiers of the 65th. All of the wagons had returned with ears of corn overflowing their sides, a bounty of belly filling food.

September saw the soldiers more relaxed than they had been in weeks and beginning to endure camp life as much as possible for being far from home. For the short term, well fed and well rested, they settled down to an otherwise mundane existence of guarding the railroad and rebuilding the partially burned great bridge over the Tennessee. But in time the food supplies once again began to dwindle, and as most of the countryside had been picked clean, no food remained for the army and the horses and mules. Soldiers complained that they were as hungry as the Israelites coming out of Egypt. There were even fewer pleasures to encourage the men. Occasional letters in out of camp renewed their spirits, and the men anticipated every infrequent delivery.

News rapidly spread through the camps, usually about some major battle that transpired sometime with somebody fighting somewhere, and the men took full delight in spreading the gospel. Great excitement greeted them one warm afternoon. Colonel Harker had led the men of the 64th Ohio and the 51st Indiana in a great triumphant battle near Stevenson, Alabama! The word spread like an infestation of lice. Many casualties had been inflicted on both sides! The reported numbers of dead and wounded swiftly grew. The medical tents must soon prepare to fill the beds with the poor wretched casualties! But when the rumors of the great battle were skinned away to the bare bones, the truth was much simpler. A picket had shot a wild pig.

While camped between Bridgeport and Stevenson, the soldiers also took advantage of the Tennessee River and finally bathed regularly. Those who didn't care to bathe were generally encouraged to participate, usually at the point of a bayonet. Lice and vermin demonstrated no partiality in the conflict, and had plagued both of the armies in equal measure. Men on both sides of the river, shedding both the blue and the gray uniform, took to the waters of the Tennessee in a spirit of peace and cleanliness. Though they were still mortal enemies, their challenging banter back and forth across the river never escalated to enough excess where one was compelled to grab his musket and answer an insult with lead. With all the reverence of a revival-tents-baptism-turned-party, they immersed themselves in the river and scrubbed away the depredations of camp life. The men of the 65th put their trust in the waters and the lye soap to rid them of the sins of the six legged "gray-backs" that kept them scratching their heads, chins, armpits and orifices.

Across the river, one Rebel soldier yelled amidst his comrades, "Hey, Billy!"

"Yeh, Johnny?" Marcus called back.

"You fellers comin' over this away fer to git your asses whupped?"

"Maybe," Adam called.

"You fellows keep running all the time, and you don't give us any show for a fight," Marcus yelled.

"Well, when you gonna do it?" yelled a Rebel youth.

"Do what?"

"Come over here."

"When are you going to give us Chattanooga?"

"We ain't!" another gray bearded soldier yelled.

"Reckon we'll just have to come over and take it," Adam called.

"When?"

"Some fine mornin' before breakfast!"

"I allow y'all 'll git mighty hungry if'n you's to wait fer yer breakfast til ya'll git Chattanooga!" said another.

"Just be patient, Johnny. We'll get there soon enough."

"Hey, Billy!"

"Yeh?"

"Is that there a nigger washin' in the river with ya?"

Nat scowled, tensed his jaw, took a stride toward the rebel. Marcus touched his elbow, calmed him with a look.

"Yeh, he is," Marcus yelled.

"Don't that bother the fish?" the gray bearded Rebel sneered to the delight of his companions.

Marcus searched slowly, studiously around at the water as if meticulously inspecting it, then affected a thick deliberate drawl. "Wal, so far they ain't been killt off by you 'uns warshin' in the river, so I reckon they ain't gonna pay *him* no never mind."

A roar of laughter from the Federals, followed by splashing and slapping the water as the men returned to more horseplay, ignoring the rebel soldiers engaged in their own silliness.

From his vantage point, Colonel Harker did not see this banter, but did note where Almond Allerton, a private from Company B was splashing in a nearby stream with his comrades. Though a white soldier, Allerton had darker skin than the other soldiers, and from a distance Harker took him to be mulatto. He was indignant that a naked black man was frolicking about so near his headquarters. He sent a guard to arrest the offender. When the guard returned with the explanation that the private was indeed a white soldier, Harker became the butt of good humored teasing that took weeks for him to live down. Lt. Wilbur Hinman said that Colonel Harker for a time often had even told the joke on himself, much to the amusement of his staff. Marcus and Nat could not see the humor in it.

On August 29 the regiment had finally received orders that would relieve them of the monotony of merely guarding railroads. General Garfield ordered the brigade to march back toward Louisville, Kentucky. Scouts had discovered that General Bragg had left Tennessee to invade Kentucky in an attempt to threaten Cincinnati and recruit more Confederate sympathizers along the way. The 65th abandoned the Tennessee River guard post to join the chase after the rebel army. Marcus had finished securing his medical wagon when he saw Nat's blacksmith wagon approach. He pulled alongside and the two covered the width of the road with their teams.

"How those rebel horses working out for you, Nat?"

"Just fine," he smiled. "We go a long ways back and they like to hear my voice. Makes 'em easier to work when they trust me."

"Looks like we're finally going to face those Rebs, Nat," he said.

"For the first time, I wish I wasn't leaving Alabama."

"Mind set on searching out your treasure?"

Nat nodded. "How can I ever set up a home for Emma if she knows I have no money now?"

"You think that will matter to her?" Marcus asked.

"Matters to me."

"Maybe you should ask *her*."

"Don't know where she is anyway."

"I do."

"Whoa," Nat called, and stopped his wagon. Marcus reined in his horses.

"How?"

Marcus reached into his coat, pulled out a grimy envelope which had clearly seen a few miles of handling. It was addressed to Nat, in care of Marcus Armstrong, 65th Ohio Volunteers. "Got this today, and I received one too. They're from my sister Martha in Granville. Remember? It was where you stayed. When several of the boys were on leave back to Ohio, one of them brought the letters with him. She wrote that she met Emma and encouraged her to write to you."

Nat pulled his horses off the road and tore open the letter. Marcus drove his wagon ahead to an open area beside the road, walked back to Nat's wagon.

Dearest Nat. Please have Marcus or someone you trust read this to you. He smiled, "She doesn't know I can read by myself, Marcus." *I traveled as far as Station 99 and Mrs. B. When I told her I did not want to go any further, she grew angry. But my mind was fixed and I told her to send me anywhere else. By some friends, I went to 97 and was finally taken to Mrs. C. I have lived with her family and have been this past year working for her. She told me of Marcus and your journeys with him. He seems to be a good person. Mrs. C. surely is. I hope this letter finds you safe and willing to settle with me if you are still agreeable to that arrangement. May God protect you until we meet again. Emma.*

"She wants to be with you, Nat. Clear as a gold piece in the well water. What are you going to do?"

"Looks like I need to get me some money to set up housekeeping. I think maybe after this war I'm just gonna keep these two horses John Ashbie gave me."

"An appropriate wedding present if there ever was one."

"Hey! Move along you two! The rebs ain't waitin' for you to read your mail!" a passing mule driver yelled.

Nat pulled out the rolled up yellow ribbon. Looked it over, winding it around two fingers, unwound it, stuffed it back in his pocket. It had been his good luck ribbon, her last gift to him to keep him safe. Now it was his compass, a bit of colored ribbon to keep him resolute until he reached Emma at last. He shook the reins, and Ashbie's horses responded willingly to Nat's voice, a more encouraging voice than Marcus had heard in several days.

+ + + + +

The march north to Louisville stretched out for over three weeks as the army once again struggled on roads, off roads, by-passing destroyed bridges, avoiding prying cavalry scouts, working its way toward the army of Braxton Bragg. The drought of the area left the army with practically no sources for water. Men and animals alike died along the way. Marcus now used his ambulance as a hearse to transport the bodies of soldiers who had died of heat and dehydration.

Then near Perryville, Kentucky, the army finally came face to face with the rebels who had maneuvered themselves for a major battle. By the end of September the brigade had positioned itself to engage and finally trap the Army of the Tennessee. However, for the 65th it was, as usual, another reserve duty, held out, to be commended to the flames of battle only if the need arose. The need never arose. And Marcus again was relegated to sitting by his medical wagon, tending to minor scrapes, foot sores and the extreme exhaustion from the lengthy march. In his self-absorbed focus on glory, he never recognized his importance to the men who suffered from thirst. Instead he wondered aloud if he would ever see the grand duties on the battlefield which he justly deserved.

The enormous array of baggage wagons had camped near the pike, guarded by the 64th and 65th Ohio, and the 51st Indiana. They listened to the distant report of the muskets and artillery. Several miles to the north, the army had fully engaged in a clash with Bragg. Under General Buell's orders, General Garfield held the brigade in reserve, and once more Bragg slipped through their fingers. The retreating Confederate army had won the field in the battle but saw its position compromised and drew back into Tennessee, leaving Kentucky finally and solidly in the hands of the Union army. Buell tried to sell the news of the battle as a major Union victory. President Lincoln disagreed.

While the lengthy train of baggage wagons moved on to Nashville, the rest of the army settled in to await orders. Due in part to General Buell's indecisive results, the Army of the Ohio was once more reorganized. On October 24, 1862, General Buell was relieved of command and the Army of the Cumberland was placed under the command of General William Rosecrans. The men took the reorganization indifferently, for he was perceived as just one more officer who would bumble his way into heavy casualties with minimal success. Only the comradery of the companies kept the soldiers glued together.

More and more runaway slaves had streamed into camp, some expecting food and clothing, but most only wanting protection from slave catchers. Defying General Buell's wishes, some of the Union officers accommodated whomever they could, as they were always in need of mule drivers, cooks, and assorted helping hands. Though the old deep-seated prejudices remained, Nat had felt more welcome by many of the soldiers within the battalion. He continued to spend his early morning hours free of the infantry's incessant drilling, taking full advantage of his free time to work diligently with Marcus on reading skills, more intently on writing skills, and above all, language skills. In the end, it was always about Emma.

Private George Rankin of Company B had befriended Nat and Marcus, had respected the ongoing education and marveled at Nat's change from the time at Camp Buckingham. One afternoon he ran into the medical tent where Nat and Marcus were engaged in a reading lesson.

"Marcus, Nat. I just heard!" he panted, trying to catch his breath.

"Must be important," Marcus said indifferently.

"Oh, it is!" He gasped for air.

"You going to die on us before you tell all?"

Nat and Marcus waited, annoyed with the interruption.

"Yes?" Nat asked casually.

"You will not believe it!" he said.

"Will you let us be the judge of that?"

"A courier just brought in the telegraph news. Those rumors *were* true! President Lincoln is freeing the slaves!"

"Wha-?" Marcus stood.

"I saw the message myself. Captain Austin had it and was reading it aloud. It will be in all the newspapers soon."

"Glory, hallelujah," Marcus said quietly.

Nat sat dumfounded. If George was right – He couldn't believe it was finally true. Private Michael McBride burst in.

"Armstrong, did you hear? Oh. I see you did."

"This is real? No soldiers' rumors?

"It's true," said McBride. "Of course, no one knows what will come of it."

"What do you mean by that?" Nat asked, rising with his book in hand.

"Here in Tennessee the President's proclamation means nothing. Captain says that Tennessee is an occupied state by articles of war and is exempt."

"Exempt?" Nat asked.

Marcus shook his head in disgust. "It means they don't have to obey the President here."

"No, but it means that what we're fighting for is now all changed," said Rankin. "It was to preserve the Union. Now if the rebs don't quit fighting by the first of the year, all their slaves are freed!"

Nat thought on it. "And what if they do quit fighting?" he said quietly.

"What? " McBride said.

"What if they quit fighting?" he repeated.

"Then the war is over," said Rankin.

"No! I mean if they quit fighting, then what happens to me? And to all the others?"

"I would expect that they stay slaves," McBride reasoned.

Marcus saw Nat's look change, his eyes angry, grip tightened on the book.

"And all of this," he said waving the book high, "is for nothing!" And he slammed the book down on a wooden box, causing several bed-ridden soldiers to flinch.

"I didn't mean that, Nat," McBride said. "It's just that – "

"He means for us the war is over, and we can go back to Ohio," said Rankin.

"And where do I go?"

Marcus studied Nat, glanced at the others. "You go home with me, Nat. Emma is sure to be waiting."

"So are the slave catchers, Marcus," he said.

"But you're not a slave, Nat."

"You explain that to 'em when they come to chain me an' carry me away!"

Rankin interrupted. "They'll never agree to it, Nat. So this is all just speculation."

"Speculation?"

"Guessing," said McBride.

They were indeed guessing, but no one had guessed how the rest of the soldiers of the brigade would react. It took a short time for the news to spread through the camp like a measles outbreak. Soon everyone had an opinion. Nat saw the change in the soldiers. Some were delighted at this, the fruit of what they were fighting for; others were appalled, wanting to quit and go home in protest. To emphasize their hatred of the President's "abuse of power," two hundred men of the 2nd Kentucky deserted all at once and joined the Rebels. Others threatened to do the same. To try to restore order to the camp, the officers assured them that it was just governmental talk and nothing would come of it anyway.

For the present, Nat tried to remain patient. If the day of deliverance did come, he must personally prepare for it. He knew he could not impress Emma with his vanished wealth, so he revisited his former notion of preparing for the only goal over which he did have control. Now that he had given up driving the supply wagons and was comfortably settled into his blacksmithing duties, he worked to better train himself for his future job once he could return to Ohio.

Armed with the knowledge of President Lincoln's overstepping his office duties, officers ordered escaped slaves, as contraband of war, out of many of the camps. Rumors had said that Nat was an escaped slave, others that he was a freedman from northern Ohio. The brigade needed Nat's blacksmithing skills, and the other smiths had welcomed him to lighten their load, and so for the time being he was passed by. After his studies in the morning, the hours stretched long into the evening. Where some of the smiths avoided working late hours, Nat used the night to his advantage. He depended on the darkness to guide his eyesight in heating the iron to its ideal orange glow for forging the horseshoes, or forming the metal bands used to repair wagon, cannon, and limber wheels. Occasionally the melancholy would visit him. He witnessed escaped slaves turned away to fend for themselves or turned over to local authorities to appease the white population. In his depression, some days he skipped his studies with Marcus and slept in late. Then he attacked the forge's bellows with a heated vengeance, striking in anger at the hot metal, working out his despondency and pent up rage with hammer and anvil. It would eventually subside. But Marcus reminded him that he was now in school, that every experience he learned would pay off in the future. Though it wasn't a formal education, which was his desire, the experience was educating him and changing him for the better. As the cavalry officers' reports of his farrier's skill spread, he grew especially proud of his work. He hoped that Emma would be proud of him too.

Chapter Twenty-Six
Nashville, Tennessee
November 1862

Before being relieved of command, General Buell's action and inactions had divided his army. Don Carlos Buell hated abolitionists, was in fact a supporter of slavery. He had grown intensely critical of Lincoln's proclamation that would take effect in January. He saw it his duty while he was still in command to return any escaped slaves to their masters, if they could be found, or merely turned over to vigilante authorities on the pretext of keeping peace with fellow citizens. The Army of the Ohio soon took sides. Many abolitionist sympathizers began to stand up to be counted among Marcus's friends. They became more outspoken.

Eventually Nat's presence came to the commander's attention. Newly recruited non-commissioned officers were detailed with investigating Nat. Was he a field hand? Was he a runaway? Those soldiers who knew him from Mansfield said he had arrived with Armstrong and had been told he was a freedman who showed great skill with the horses and mules. The report created an image of the perfect blacksmith. He had a way with horses and had kept two for himself from a farm they had raided. They would answer only to him, and if anyone tried to ride them, the horses instantly and painfully discouraged from attempting it again. Nevertheless, Nat was a curiosity that bore closer observation and the supporters of slavery watched for any signs of the subservient personality. If he was a runaway he must be cast out with the others. Marcus feared for him, but feared more that Nat's discovery would mean his discovery too. Unconsciously he began to distance himself from Nat.

+ + + + +

The news spread about the camp faster than a telegraph message. General Grant was advancing to take Vicksburg. But once again the men would not see the elephant. For General Buell's final orders had sent them back to Nashville to guard the railroads and keep General Braxton Bragg's army at bay. But because General Bragg had once again slipped through the porous net Buell had set and had moved south, Washington had finally replaced his ineptitude. This guarding of railroads and rebuilding bridges as fast as the Confederate cavalry could destroy them had a singular monotony all its own. The routine criticism of the dim-witted officers who prepared these senseless orders continued unabated. They had marched south to chase and capture Bragg's army. He had slipped away. They heard reports of his invasion of Kentucky, and so they turned around and marched north in pursuit. At Perryville, the Federals had routed the rebels but failed to pursue, once again allowing them to escape. And so they marched north yet again. Finally reaching Louisville, they faced the crushing temptation to just slip over the Ohio River, have done with it, and go home. Yet, to a man, the soldiers stayed. Officers however, owned the luxury of quitting the Army by merely resigning their commission and going home. Many took advantage of it and left for Ohio and the life of privilege they believed they had earned. Surgeon John Kyle left the regiment and was replaced by Surgeon John Todd. Marcus liked him immediately. Eleven years older than Kyle, he had a gentle manner with the soldiers in his care that Marcus emulated. The desire for glory began to fade as he accepted more responsibility with the disabled. It came at a cost. He began to see Nat's education as a burden to his medical work. But Nat persisted.

"Marcus, will you have time to help me with my language lessons today?"

Marcus slowly wrapped a corporal's ankle tightly, ignoring Nat. Then he re-wrapped it, admiring his own handiwork. He sighed, "Nat, can you see that I have this man to care for?"

"I didn't mean at this moment, Marcus. I only axed if you have time…"

"*Asked*. You *asked* if I had time," he corrected.

"That's right," Nat snapped. "I *asked* if you have time – "

"I wish you would get it right,' he interrupted. "Just once."

"I did get it right *just once*. That's why I keep asking for help."

Marcus covered a blanket over the soldier. "Come outside, Nat," he said. He walked to the empty ambulance away from the field hospital and stopped at the tailgate. Nat followed like an obedient pup. Marcus scowled at him. "I go over it and over it, and I am getting pretty tired of going over it. I have given you all the tools to build a man who will fit into Northern society."

"Seems that's what we all did back at Camp Buckingham. We went over it and over it at the camp until the soldiers learned to march and shoot like soldiers. And those officers didn't seem to mind drilling these men to make them proper soldiers. It was their duty."

"Yes, well, you are *not my* duty!" Marcus snapped.

"You said you would teach me."

"I said I would get you to Canada! You see how far from Canada we are? That wasn't my doing!"

"You took me to Mansfield."

"You left me with no choice!"

Nat's fear began to swell inside. He saw a dark curtain drawing over all of his dreams, and there pulling the cord stood Marcus. They silently studied each other. Marcus, defiant, and Nat reading the emotion that Marcus tried to mask.

"What is this really about, Marcus," he said gently. "It sho'ly ain't about you taking time from the hospital. What's it *really* about?"

Marcus looked down, hesitated.

"What?" Nat repeated.

"I've heard from home," he said at last.

"And?"

"Father is sick. Father is sick," he burst out, "and I can't go back to Ohio to see him!"

"Why can't you?"

Marcus looked at him dumbfounded. "Nat!"

"I'm not as stupid as you think I am. I know they will be looking out for you. But why can't you go back? You're a soldier and can get a furlough. Look-a-here, you said you were always good at hiding us runaways. Can't you hide yourself just as good?"

"It's not that easy. Everyone knew me and I could go about anywhere. But I have no one, Nat, no one that everyone else knows who can secret me into Ashtabula and then back to Columbus."

"Write your sister."

"No. It was her letter told me of my father. She warned me to stay away, that Albert Harvey would be looking out for me to come home."

"She don't want you home?"

"She wants me alive, Nat."

"So you gonna' stay here?"

"That's my choice, Nat. I don't like it, but that's my choice. It's a conundrum."

Nat looked at him, a sly smile beginning. "Well, now. Since you're staying, you can help me."

"In time, Nat. I have plenty of time."

"Well, I don't. So I won't be waiting for you," he said and returned to his forge, leaving Marcus, leaning on the back of the ambulance.

Marcus sighed. "At last," he thought.

A week passed and true to his word, Nat didn't wait for Marcus. He continued to read on his own, to practice his writing and took every opportunity to talk to cavalrymen, teamsters, officers. Anyone who could carry on a conversation with him, while he carefully chose his speech to emulate those he identified as educated. He felt comfortable in his new identity. He was forming himself into who he wanted to be, not who Marcus wanted him to be. In short, he was becoming an individual.

Then more news arrived. They now had a new designation – the Army of the Cumberland. Some of the men had high hopes for this General Rosecrans. Most couldn't care any less than they already did. If he brought them victory, he would earn their respect, and in no other way. Victories, after all, are everything.

For his part, Nat enjoyed having a place to settle in and ply his blacksmithing trade. He never had a lack of work, as the army by its very nature used the smiths to keep them in repair. However as Nat kept himself busy, Marcus had kept himself scarce from the medical tents. Surgeon Todd's initial influence wore off in a short time, and Marcus detested the habitual treatment of blisters, cuts and bruises, and illness which had carried his boredom to extremes. He daily excused himself on errands for different companies of the 65th.

"Nat, Captain Bradley sent me to see if you had started on that limber wheel yet."

Nat pulled once more on the bellows, sending a rush of air into the fire. "Finished it already," he said, pointing to the metal hoop on the ground.

"Looks good. I'll tell him."

"You can take it to him if you like."

"Nat, I'm sorry I haven't had the time to work on lessons with you."

Nat returned to the bellows, pulled hard on the chain, another rush of air roared the fire to life, began choosing his words.

"You heard me? I'm sorry about my time."

Nat poked a long rod into the fire, stirred the coals, sparks erupting and rising into the air. "I heard you."

"I just don't feel like I've been able to change you much recently."

"Change me?"

"You know, to sound like the others."

Nat shoved the iron into the coals, turned on him. "Listen to yourself, Marcus!"

"What did I say?"

"What have you been doing in these lessons all these months? What have you really been trying to do?"

"I don't understand – "

"Emma wanted me to be educated, to not sound like one of them field hands. She corrected me on my talk because she was proud of me and wanted me to not sound like a slave anymore. I asked you to help so she would accept me."

"I've done that – "

"No, Marcus. You haven't. You wanted me to blend in so I wouldn't be caught and give you away."

"That's not true," Marcus said.

"It is true."

"See here! I could've had you safe in Canada, Nat, but you had to lose your temper and stab that Jonah Simon."

"How were you going to get me into Canada? Huh? How were you going to do it? That man was going to kill you and take me! It's no worse than what these boys are doing out here with these Rebs."

"But you didn't want to go to Canada."

"I did at first."

"Emma changed that."

"Yes she did. And you, Marcus, you showed me what I could be. But you lost your vision. I am not some experiment that you can do in your college!"

"That's unfair!"

"Is it? You are so full of wanting glory for yourself, that you will do anything to make yourself a name. I know you, Marcus. You want someone to pin a ribbon or medal on you to be honored like your granddaddy was."

Marcus was seething, the truth now flushed his cheeks red and he trembled in anger at the reproach.

"Marcus, you have been a blessing to me, and you never see it. You get angry when I don't learn everything just the way you want it. Oh, Marcus! You can't fix everything the way you want it. You must open your eyes and see that you can't control every outcome. No, let me finish! You say you want me to fit into this new world of mine. Well, I have been discovering that on my own – without you. Never think me ungrateful. I would've never known where to start without you. Yes, you have changed me, and at the same time I have been becoming my own man."

The pent-up frustration had finally tumbled out. Inwardly, Nat feared for their friendship, and at the same time felt that their friendship must now be on an equal plane. In his life as a slave to John Ashbie, he could have never talked like this to any person, black or white. He owed this newfound strength of character to Marcus. He respected him, and he desired Marcus to respect him in return. With this outburst, he feared the damage was done, but he trusted time to repair it.

Chapter Twenty-Seven
Battle of Stones River
Murfreesboro, TN
January 1-3, 1863

Winter in Nashville was wet, guarding railroads, boring. But the men of the 65th did their duty. Marcus cared for the soldiers who took to beds, the hospitals completely taxed by the camp illnesses. Pneumonia, often fatal had spread through the town, and the Southern winter had gripped them. Still, rather than stay in winter quarters as the Army of the Potomac was prone to doing, General Rosecrans was ordered to seek out Braxton Bragg and destroy him. General Halleck, overall commander ordered that if Rosecrans didn't do so, he would find someone who would. The day after Christmas, under chilling gusts of wind, the men stepped off in the frigid march toward Chattanooga. Nat remained in Nashville while the Army moved on. His duties would remain with the blacksmiths until more teamsters were needed. Comfortable with the stables and the warmth of his forge, he continued his studies on his own, borrowing books from anyone willing to loan them. Marcus led his horse from the corral, saw Nat.

"I have something for you," he said, reaching into his haversack.

First time in weeks that he has spoken, Nat thought. Marcus thrust out his hand, a book of poetry.

"Thank you, kindly. I'll cherish this."

"Just read it. I'll be happy with that. We can discuss it when I return from this march."

Nat thought, It's still the dead of winter, but there's a thaw in the air. "I'll read it while you're gone. Gives me something to do while the cavalry is out chasing Rebs."

The ambulances once again slogged behind the divisions toward Murfreesboro where General Bragg's army had concentrated, placing itself between the Union army and Chattanooga. Light skirmishing between mounted cavalry and forward pickets slowed the Union army, but they never halted. After five days of navigating the quagmire of Tennessee roads, and the harassing rebel ambushes, the three columns gathered near Stones River, only two miles from Murfreesboro. The 65th quickly engaged the rebels near a rise called Wayne's Hill. Being thrown back, Harker's brigade settled into a defense against further attack. Marcus finally had seen his combat, had rushed near the hill to retrieve wounded, saving some, reluctantly leaving others to enemy capture as the rebels drove the regiment from the field. It was disheartening to watch from afar and see the wounded gathered up by Confederate soldiers. He was powerless to go, and through the following day he chafed at the fetters of the army's orders that bound him to the regiment. He took his ambulance toward the center of the Union camp, seeking a way to circumvent orders and drive to where the wounded might lie on the battlefield. But he found himself near a brick kiln, an easily identifiable landmark close to General Sheridan's headquarters. From here he could not rush out unobserved, and so he waited for the opportunity. They would eventually need his service.

It was December 30, and the men concluded that at least through New Year's Eve they would probably stay in camp long enough to allow the general officers of each army to plan attacks which would obliterate the enemy. Then the New Year would present them with more blood-letting. Marcus collected his courage, mentally preparing to once again rescue the perishing. To pass time and clear his head of the visions of wounded that plagued him at night, he lay back in his ambulance and re-read the letter from his sister.

All is well here. As you are aware, Mr. Lincoln's proclamation has been met with great rejoicing. With Christmas coming this week, and as we prepare for the nativity, we know now the New Year will finally see the end of slavery, and we are anticipating much celebration. Father has read that Mr. Lincoln needs another victory to satisfy the Congress enough to support the Emancipation. We watch the newspapers daily in anticipation of such news. I trust you are remaining safe and well to help in your capacity.

Jacob and I have enjoyed Emma's company immensely. She has been a fine worker for us, and we have decided to sponsor her. She desires to attend Wilberforce College and study to teach children. We wish to make that possible. Father is in agreement. She will begin next term and we hope that will be agreeable to Nat.

Nat had said nothing to him about this. Did he even know? It had been weeks since they had talked, so it was probable. But this was important news. Nat would surely share it with him, wouldn't he? Undoubtedly Nat still held a grudge against him.

He sought out Adam's counsel, and Adam had used the word *arrogant*. Had he really been that arrogant toward Nat? He had dismissed his manner as merely Nat's anger over missing Emma. He wasn't arrogant. Or was he? What was that Arabian proverb: If someone calleth thee an ass, pay him no mind. If two calleth thee an ass, get thee a saddle. Still he couldn't accept he was arrogant. Yet Nat had thought so, and it was important to Nat. He set aside the letter, thought on Nat's words: "You can't fix everything the way you want it." I suppose I have tried, he thought. His soul searching ran into the night. His recurring headache had started again, his temples thumping hard with every heartbeat, decided he would think about it tomorrow.

The military bands had begun their customary nocturnal serenade, the melodies intended to grow courage in the faint of heart. But tonight was different. The Confederate military band was out there in the night, not too far away, encouraging their hearts with tunes of hearth and home. Close by, the Union bands had begun. They traded music in the dark, two pugilistic serenades, each attempting to best the other in song. Almost an hour passed and neither side's bands would surrender their control of the night, answering each song with song. The men had taken notice, had ceased their talk to listen to the tunes of celebration, the tunes of melancholy. And with his temples throbbing, Marcus moved outside of his ambulance, sat on the back, his legs dangling and listened, as if trying to listen through canvas had somehow impeded the sound.

Voices spoke up from inside a nearby pup tent. "I suppose our boys can larn them a thing or two about tootin' them horns," one soldier said to his pard.

"I don' know 'bout that, Tom. Them Rebs is purty good theirselves."

"But they don't come up to home in my ears."

"Mebbe they ain't tryin' to come up to home in your ears. Mebbe they just tryin' to please theirselves."

"Still, our boys kin teach 'em."

"Now, Tom, why on earth would they wanna sound just like our boys? They're playin' purty good just as they are. And I allow our boys are just as good. I think it's just the difference is what makes 'em both good."

Marcus had never heard the enemy bands play, and frankly he could not judge between the two sides. He listened to them trading familiar songs until a band in the distance began "Home Sweet Home." He couldn't identify the band, Confederate or Federal. But he allowed they were very good at their music. The familiar tune seemed to envelop the winter air between the two enemies. Then Marcus heard something profound: Another band started in the same key, followed by another, and another, until it seemed the heavens had come together with angelic instruments to gladden the hearts and quiet the spirits of these who would too soon meet in the killing fields.

December 31 greeted the Union camp with a heavy blanket of frost. The crisp air magnified the breath streaming from each soldier who stirred about trying to make his morning coffee on hastily built campfires. Men warmed their hands as they stood sucking in the aroma, as though the scent itself would awaken them. Another morning waited for the men to rise and begin incessant drill, marching, maneuvering, more picket duty, and cleaning weapons – activities to parry away the thrusts of anxiety. Marcus awoke, the remnants of the headache leaving him foggy-headed. He pulled off the woolen blanket, an involuntary shudder shaking him to the knees. He wrapped himself in his greatcoat and strode toward the closest fire, following the distinctive aroma of bacon. A half-dozen federal soldiers sat on wood crates supporting split rails as modified benches. The talk was subdued, not the usual joking of an army in camp. Suddenly, far off to the right, a swarm of dark bodies rushed from the woods and across the fields.

"Run, rabbit, run!" called a soldier as he grabbed his musket from the ground.

"Heh, if I'se a rabbit, I'd be runnin' too!" laughed another soldier.

"See if you can pick one o' them off," a corporal said. "Fresh meat for breakfast."

Then the sound of a volley of musket fire came from the direction of the woods. Next a yell arose, repeated by another host of voices, and the Union soldiers at the extreme right of the camp began to turn and run from the sound. Marcus could see the men, some not yet dressed, running with arms flailing in their white nightshirts. Out of the woods rushed a host of Confederate soldiers, bayonets at the ready, charging into the Union camp, stopping only long enough to reload and fire into the backs of the retreating army. The men near Marcus sprang for their weapons, scattering flaming logs, knocking over iron grids holding iron pans filled with sizzling bacon. No breakfast today. Marcus vaulted up to the wagon seat, looked down to realize his horse wasn't yet harnessed, was tethered to a nearby rope line between two trees. No time. He leapt onto its back, at the same time tugging the reins at its bit. He kicked hard and the horse bolted. He passed scores of men, panic stricken, running without weapons, some carrying their boots in hand, other having on boots and little else. A line of partially-clad soldiers turned near a small stone wall, began to form a line of battle to stanch the flow of rebel infantry. Braxton Bragg had completely routed the right flank of the federal army and the Battle of Stones River had begun.

Marcus galloped on, leaving his ambulance and all its supplies to the attacking rebel army. His letters from his sister, from his father flashed in his head, and he wheeled the horse in a quick thought to rush back and rescue them. Far behind him, the sounds of muskets now combined with cannon fire. Rescuing the letters would be suicide. He'd let them be for now. He sprinted on, crossing the Nashville Railroad tracks and turned north on the Nashville Turnpike. Headquarters sat in a clearing along the pike with a second house nearby, already receiving the wounded from the decimated right flank.

"Where e'r you about?" shouted a bearded sergeant.

"Just came from the fightin' over on the right!" Marcus shouted, slipping from the horse's back.

"Where's yer saddle?"

"She doesn't have one," he said. "She is for my ambulance. We got overrun!"

Surgeon Todd appeared at the farmhouse door. "Armstrong! What are you doing here?"

Marcus couldn't hide the shame. "Sir, I'm sorry. The entire right has been overrun. I left the ambulance. I'm sorry, sir. They just came so quickly. We all scrambled before they hit us too."

"Us too? Where were you?"

"In the center with General Sheridan."

"What in blazes were you doing there? The 65th is on the extreme left! You left your post?"

"I thought I could be of service in the center. There were wounded – "

"This is why we have orders!"

"Get another ambulance and take it to the left! Report to Colonel Harker at once!"

Marcus found four ambulance wagons harnessed and tied off behind the farmhouse and immediately drove his team east toward the railroad where the sounds of battle now increased. The rebuke stirred something inside. A voice whispered above the battle. You ran. No matter what you told them, you ran.

But I can't save anyone if I'm captured. I had to run. There's no shame in it. The rabbits did it.

But you lied. You weren't in the center to save the wounded. You were in the center to save yourself.

I am here to save men. It's my calling.

You aren't man enough.

I'll prove I'm man enough.

And on he drove, stretching the horses to the limit of their endurance, cracking the whip on their hindquarters as if racing against some unseen challenger. Soldiers were dying up ahead and he would never let them down again.

Reining in his team, he vaulted down from the wagon seat and joined other orderlies who had begun running bloody litters back behind the front lines with the maimed. In minutes, his wagon had filled, and he drove it back to the farmhouse where surgeons and orderlies had busied themselves with the wounded. Once again he set out for the frontlines, found the brigade in a double time run toward the center of the Union lines. The center and right were in danger of being overrun, and the 65th now moved its reinforcements in. Marcus took no note of who was winning, who was losing. For him, all was loss. His duty now replaced any emotional attachment. It became mechanical, repetitive, shuttling soldiers from the battle to the makeshift hospitals now overwhelmed by the casualties. It occurred to him that this fight was grander than Shiloh. But then he had arrived at Shiloh after the battle.

Over the next day, the two armies maneuvered for position, killing and maiming, each vowing to hold the ground against the other. Marcus got little rest. When the fighting died down, he tried to sleep, but sporadic firing through the night intruded, leaving him bleary eyed and weak. Picket lines established crude makeshift defenses. Artillery batteries positioned on high ground began destructive fire, the very earth trembling beneath the roar. Soon the rebels broke off all attacks and faded back into the cover of forests. General Rosecrans claimed victory, and the regiments cheered the news that they had kept the field. Marcus surveyed the fields, the spattered rocks "At what cost?" he muttered to no one.

Many of the men he had seen in camp were now dead on the grounds, were lying wounded among the dead, waiting for him, or were carried away as prisoners. The Federals had captured their quota of prisoners too, and many of these

239

would need medical care. Marcus felt overwhelmed that he couldn't attend them all. He couldn't save all, and it brought him to tears. The emotions long held in check now unleashed in a flood of tears, and he sobbed uncontrollably as he searched among the bodies on his field for signs of life. He found few.

Chapter Twenty-Eight
Chattanooga, Tennessee

General Rosecrans renewed the pursuit of General Bragg's army with the overall goal of defeating him. But all the soldiers knew the real object was to capture Chattanooga, however it could be accomplished. So, on Wednesday, June 24, began what became known as the Tullahoma Campaign. The rain came, and with it came the mud. Half of the wagons were left near Murfreesboro, while the other supply wagons followed along with what rations could be added to the principal load of ammunition. Nat brought along his forge. When the army finally entered Chattanooga unopposed, he finally had a semi-permanent camp to set his forge with the other blacksmiths of the brigade.

Four months was a long time to make horseshoes. But June became July and then August. Nat had plied the trade, working the iron, reshaping thrown shoes, making them workable again. He and the other smiths had plenty to do that summer, repairing wagon and caisson wheels and keeping Colonel Robert Minty's nine hundred cavalry mounts ready for action. But on his own free time, his heart soared with every letter he received from Emma. She still had no knowledge of his literacy and he preferred to keep it a profound secret until the day he could reveal all in person. As a result, her letters to him were guarded, understanding that someone would read her words to him. She told him of her desire to complete an education at the African Methodist Episcopal college in Wilberforce, Ohio. She wanted to teach young children in the schools now begun for former slaves. She would be a good teacher, he thought. At least until they married. It crossed his mind that he too could teach one day. But the lure of his own blacksmith shop always drew him back to reality.

But for a few days of rain early in the month, August was hot and dry, and a summer drought had affected the city. The invading army taxed the water sources, and the citizens daily took their complaints to General Rosecrans' headquarters. The Tennessee River still flowed and the army drank from that, bringing on the misery that bacteria-infested water does of consequence. The city could not support an entire army and the commanders knew they would have to go find General Bragg if he didn't come to them. Bragg still wanted to take back Chattanooga, but Rosecrans wasn't about to present it to him. And so the army of occupation had settled in and begun building its own forts to guard the city's southern perimeter, straining the relationship further.

A local blacksmith named Moore had watched Nat at work, saw some skills in him and finally approached him.

"Hey, boy," he said over the clanging. "Hey, boy!" he repeated louder.

Nat stopped, irritated, stared at the hot metal on the anvil.

"You do some fine work there."

"Thank you," he said and resumed striking the shoe.

"No, I mean it. Have you thought of working on your own? I mean, not for the Federals?"

Nat looked up at the man. "I done thought 'bout it."

"I don't know what they pay you, but it can't be all that much."

Actually, he thought, I am still paid nothing since I have yet to enlist. But that was information he never shared.

"I do all right," he said quietly.

"I hear since y'all were freed by Lincoln, y 'all could join the army, 's what I hear. But they still don't pay you what you're worth."

Nat wanted to clear this annoyance away from his work. "And you can?" he asked.

"I see y 'all have skills and my business is fallen off since y'all came here. Now if I could pay you to help me, I might get some business back, and you'd be richer."

"*You'd* pay *me*?" he asked sarcastically.

"Every bit o' what you're worth."

"Well, now," Nat said as he dropped his hammer and cast aside the horseshoe. "A few years ago I was worth a couple thousand dollars. That's Union dollars. You got that kind o' money?"

"I have it in Confederate script," Moore said.

"And what good is that when we here occupy Chattanooga?

"I'm willing to pay y'all in Federal dollars too, at the rate of twenty-five cents a day. Y'all're worth every nickel of it. I seen y'all."

Twenty-five cents? Slave wages, he thought. Nat wanted to laugh aloud, caught himself, looked down and shook his head, looked up. "Mister, uh..."

"Moore," the blacksmith added.

"Moore. Mister Moore, I am deeply honored by such a generous offer, but I will have to say no at this time. See, as soon as the general has your army out in the open, we will defeat it and all of Tennessee will be occupied. Then we march on Atlanta, and I would have to bid you good-bye."

Moore did not appreciate the condescending air from this black Yankee.

"Y'all don't need to go gettin' uppity with me!" he barked.

"I have no idea what you mean," Nat teased.

"Y'all puttin' on airs like y'all're better 'n me."

"But I am," Nat said. "Can't help it." And he picked up the hammer, the tongs, grabbed onto a strap of metal and blocked out the intruder by banging away at it, leaving the angry Moore to sulk away cursing Nat, Rosecrans, Lincoln, and the Union in general.

Nat was daily kept busy, yet he still found time to annoy Marcus to work with him on his books and his writing. Marcus was singularly focused. He still longed for another battle, looked for redemption from his failure at Murfreesboro, was ready to restore more lives from the terrors of battlefield brutality. Often Nat had found him reading his mail, secreted away in the back of his ambulance. To Nat he seemed perturbed whenever Nat came around, book in hand. Nat saw he had changed, and not too subtly.

"Oh, it's you!" he said quickly folding a letter and stuffing the envelope.

"Hopes not to disturb you, Marcus. Gots a question on the poem here."

Marcus heaved a sigh. *"I hope I did not disturb you. I have a question on this poem,"* he corrected.

Nat snickered.

Irritated, Marcus grabbed at the book of poetry, accidentally knocking it to the ground in a puff of dust. Nat retrieved it, slapped it against his pants, clearing most of the dust.

Marcus reached out a hand irritably, "Let me see it."

"No. I think I won't just now."

"You interrupted me, so let's have at it!"

"No."

Marcus sat upright, leaned against the wall of the sideboard of the ambulance. "What is it with you, Nat?"

"I might just ask the same question, *Marcus*."

He held the envelope up, "They know I'm here."

The realization hit him. "But the Slave Law isn't enforceable anymore. The President freed us. And they can't arrest you for a law that's been abolished. You're free too."

"Not from prosecution on attempted murder," Marcus said. "And the army will not protect me from that."

"But you didn't try to kill that slave catcher. I did!"

"You're in Canada. I'm not. It's revenge, Nat."

"Armstrong!" an orderly called from the warehouse.

"Here!"

"Get your ambulance ready. We're moving out."

Marcus slid down from the wagon, stuffed the letter into his haversack. "Where this time?"

"General Wood has ordered us toward Chickamauga Creek and Lafayette to join the division there. Rebs are down that way, and we're going to get 'em. The army will have need of all of us."

Marcus eagerly slammed the gate up on the wagon. Nat instinctively shuddered, held the book of poetry tightly to his chest. "I'll keep this for later," he said.

Near Chickamauga Creek, Georgia
Sunday, September 20. September 1863

Shortly after the church bells had tolled for the morning worship service, the disquieting rumble like distant thunder had turned the citizen's ears from the Gospel to the guns. The Sabbath's early morning meditative air had been fractured by Yankee artillery. The rumbling had been sporadic at first, much like Saturday's tumults. Then it became more sustained. All of Chattanooga had turned with anticipation toward Lookout Valley as a steady line of ambulances and wagons began to arrive, bearing wounded Federal soldiers and captured Confederate prisoners.

Nat had rested the early morning and had taken his breakfast with many of the black contraband workers who had gathered near the main warehouse beside the Western and Atlantic Railroad spur, listening to the sound of distant guns. They were content to stay safely here in the city and wait for the Union soldiers to drive General Bragg even farther from Chattanooga. Nat had used his free time to

245

practice reading to the former slaves who reveled in his ability to make the words come alive. He fascinated them with his command of the language, and more than once they had asked him to teach them as well. Marcus had instilled in him a yearning to educate himself far beyond the basics and now he craved the time to pass his knowledge on to the newly freed slaves crowding into Chattanooga.

"You are free." He had repeated it often. "You have a future those before you never had." He pointed to the distant valley. "You hear that? They're out there wrestlin' for your freedom. What will you do with it?"

Always it was the same message from his heart. How could he challenge them to want more? "I was content being John Ashbie's boy. I learned myself to be the *best* farrier, the *best* blacksmith, the *best* horse trainer, the *best* at everything because it pleased the master and it got me out of the fields. But it counted for *nothing* when it all came out in the wash. Bein' the best for the master isn't the same as bein' the best for yourselves."

The black faces looked up to him as he rose like a preacher and stood in their midst. His congregation. His pupils. *His*. And he felt empowered.

One skinny young boy with auburn hair had sat eagerly soaking up every word. "Since y'all be de bes' den y'all be stayin' wit' de Yankee army, Nat?"

"No. As it goes now, I'll return to Ohio and have my own business."

"Hell," another older man interjected, "you know you cain't hab no business 't all. Color man cain't do dat no how."

"I've seen it. In Ohio I know of a man name o' Parker. He's a freed man and owns his own company near where the Reverend Rankin hid me. If he can do it, any o' y'all can do it."

"Why Ohio, Nat?" the boy asked.

"I got my reasons...."

"Am she purty, Nat?" another asked.

"Very," he smiled.

A captain walked into the meeting. "You boys need to break up the church meetin' and git to work. We got a lot o' supplies to load on the wagons to take out there," he said nodding toward the Rossville road and the battle sounds. "After that you' got to get back to diggin' those rifle pits out yonder. Johnny Reb comes this way, we need to have a defense."

"He be truly comin' dis way?" the auburn haired boy asked.

"Don't know, boy, but it's good to have a plan just in case."

The noise of the battle echoed along Lookout Valley, the report of the guns growing louder as if the cannon would at once burst into full view. From the forge Nat had listened to it for nearly two hours now. The seriously wounded soldiers, beginning as a trickle, now flooded back into the city, the wagons shuttling along the Rossville Road with the bloody results, then returning at a gallop toward the battlefield somewhere beyond Missionary Ridge.

Moore locked his thumbs onto his suspenders, jutted his chest out. "Sounds like your boys in blue ain't farin' so good out there."

"You think so?"

"I got eyes, boy. Them soldiers are comin' like a flood, and y'all 'll jes' have to leave us and skedaddle for home. Leave us to our homes." Moore squinted his eyes toward the morning sun over Missionary Ridge, closed one eye, inspecting Nat like a tiny insect.

"I expect by sundown y'all 'll see Bragg's army swarmin' over Mission Ridge out yonder. Yessir, comin' like a flood they will."

247

Nat looked long and hard toward the steady stream of ambulances rushing along the Rossville Road. Couldn't see Marcus, hoped he had escaped the carnage, had not tried anything heroic. Suddenly he saw a familiar form driving a wagon, a frenzied dash toward the city, said calmly, "Shut up, Reb."

Nat sprinted to the defensive breastworks straddling the road where Marcus raced his ambulance. Jumping from the wagon seat, his uniform soaked in blood, he yelled, "Help me, Nat," and rushed to the rear gate, dropped it open and pulled on a litter's handles. Major Samuel Brown of the 65th Ohio lay wincing with the pain of a head wound, the white bandage, seeping red and worn like a beret, held on by several wraps under the chin. He gritted his teeth as Nat and Marcus struggled to rush him into the makeshift hospital, a railroad warehouse, serving as one of dozens in the city. Marcus felt the major's fingers tug at his knee as he turned to go.

"Thank you, Armstrong," he said. "Performing your duty." He gritted his teeth, formed the word with his lips, whispered, "Admirable," and tightly, painfully closed his eyes.

Three more returns had the wagon emptied and Marcus slamming the gate, latching it and jumping back into the driver's seat.

Nat looked up at Marcus, his brows furrowed. "Marcus, you need time to rest. "

"Those men don't get a rest. I'm not taking time from them."

"Marcus, you take care, and I'll see you on your return."

Marcus shook the reins violently, sped out of the city, passing arriving wagons crowded with wounded. Lieutenant Charles Wilson of the quartermasters called to Nat. "You're a wagon driver, ain't you, Nat."

"Blacksmith, but I can drive wagons too."

"We have need of you. Report to the quartermaster house next to the church over yonder. We need all the teamsters we can assemble to go to Stevenson!"

"Stevenson?"

"The Rebs are driving us back. If we have to defend this place, we'll need much more ammunition than we have. General Rosecrans has ordered us to get to the supply depot there with all due haste. The men will leave within the hour. We have some wagons ready to go. Others will be at Stevenson."

"I have two of my own horses. I'll ride one of them."

"Take both. You may have need. Now go to the quartermaster's! Move!"

Marcus' team galloped down the Rossville Road kicking up clouds of drought-induced dust, choking the late morning air and blending with the blue-gray smoke drifting from the battle. The deafening roar of artillery now mixed with the thunderous cracks of rifles. His heart raced as he sped along the base of the hill separating the returning ambulances from the battle front. He turned onto the lane, nearly tipping his wagon, drove demonically up the small gap in the hill toward the Dyer House. The field hospital's yard now cluttered with the multitude of the Union's wounded and dying. Three hundred yards away, the federal soldiers maintained an intense fire toward the Fayetteville Road and the tree line beyond. For an instant Marcus recognized Adam far out on the right flank with his long red hair and fiery beard, toiling with his artillery battery, loading and firing into the trees.

"Help me here!" an orderly snapped and Marcus turned back to the carnage at his feet. The two carried a wounded corporal, a tourniquet firmly twisted at the knee, the lower leg displaying a gaping hole stuffed at the edges with pieces of shredded trousers. Then another soldier writhing in pain from a stomach wound was loaded, followed by another, and another. Marcus ceased noting the many ways that soft lead could open a wound. It became rhythmic. Bend, carry, load, bend, carry, load. He stood erect, grabbed his back at the waist and stretched. Noticed the blue uniforms pulling out of line, shouldered muskets moving to the left in a run. Odd, he thought. He climbed into the ambulance seat to drive his load of wounded back to Chattanooga. Concluded he'd have to make many more trips.

Then from the woods across Lafayette Road came the howling shout of hosts of charging Confederate soldiers. The brush below the wood line was obliterated by the sudden rush of screaming men dashing toward the positions the Federal soldiers had just abandoned. They came on at a dead run, and in an instant the massive rush split, some charging the battery where Adam Watling toiled, the remainder of the multitude rushing toward the Dyer Field and the field hospital. A wounded private pulled himself up with his one good arm, plopped onto the wagon seat beside Marcus, slapped him hard in the chest and knocked the wind from him, and in terror-filled eyes, screamed, "Move!"

Instinctively, Marcus violently shook the reins, screamed, "Hyaaah!" He drove the ambulance hard up the small rise that led to the gap in the hill. Beyond the Dyers' orchard and to his left on the distant ridge, saw General Rosecrans and several staff officers untying their horses from the rail fence at the Widow Glenn's cabin. Behind him the artillery had ceased and at the top of the hill he looked back, caught a glimpse of Adam's battery scrambling across the field, horses straining to pull the limber and cannon, yelling rebel soldiers chasing at their heels. The Union's right flank was crumbling and the remaining men at the field hospital would within minutes be captured. A helpless sadness and anger swallowed him, and he drove the horses on. One mile outside of Chattanooga, a flurry of riders caught up to him and passed him by. General Rosecrans was in full gallop, followed by his staff with General Crittenden and General Garfield bringing up the rear of the cluster of men.

"Must be pretty bad now if Old Rosie is lightin' outta there!" the corporal jeered.

"Wish I had seen that coming. I would've tried to get more men in here."

"If you'd 'a tried it, you'd be a prisoner yourself. Best leave that thinkin' behind you."

Marcus looked at the man curiously, "There's always more that can be done, isn't there?"

"Don't know 'bout that. But I do know a man has to know his limits. And I sure ain't nobody's hero."

"I saw how you climbed in here quick enough. You left those men back there."

"Yeh, I did! Who are you to judge me? I'm alive, and I ain't been captured, and I can live to fight again. Stay, and my fightin's done – one way or t' other." They charged on silently. Then the corporal turned angrily, "You're not a soldier. You're an orderly! Get captured and who's gonna carry the wounded? You yourself got outta there quick enough too!"

Marcus' face reddened, his eyes tear-filled, a rage inside pushed him the remaining mile to the city, past the picket lines now scrambling to dig rifle pits at the entrance to the city, preparing a defense. Inside he carried his casualties to the warehouse now overwhelmed with wounded. A major with the division stood bent over a table, tying off a suture.

"Armstrong! Where are you going?"

"Back to the field, sir," he said.

The surgeon scraped a scalpel off of the table, tossed it aside into a bowl, wiped his bloody hands, splashing the pink water onto the wood floor. "I need you here, Armstrong. These men need you!"

"Men out there need me too. Listen, sir. Hear it? That battle is far from over, and there will be need of ambulances."

"I cannot spare you. There are plenty of ambulances to carry whom we can."

"But with me, we can rescue six or eight more, sir."

"I need you here! You are staying! That's an order."

Marcus thought, I'm not a real soldier, never yet signed on to duty. I'm a volunteer, can leave when I want. I have more important things to do, men to return so you can hack off their limbs. He stood his ground.

"Lieutenant!" the surgeon called. "Have this man placed in irons if he attempts to leave the city again."

Marcus walked out of the warehouse, the streets now beginning to fill with the wounded, the despondent, some dazed and inconsolable. It was now afternoon and still the distant artillery's echoes bounced off the wooden city buildings continuing to tell the story that had begun on Saturday. He felt the officer's presence, decided against an attempt.

He hunched his shoulders, clenched his fists defiantly. "I'm not helping him!" he shouted. He stood for a moment, listened to the distant guns, relaxed his fists, shoulders drooping in resignation. "But I'm not leaving, Lieutenant," he said at last.

"I know you won't, Armstrong," he said unemotionally. "I'll have you shot if you do."

He resolved to find Nat. His conscience curiously didn't prick at him for not returning to the battlefield, but his falling out with Nat did. He would find him and make his apologies. Nat was not at his forge, and he had never started his fire. At the livery stable he found Mr. Moore, smugly smiling at this well-dusted, disheveled Union soldier.

"Had the Devil's due today, ain't ya?" he said.

Marcus wasn't in the mood. "Where's Nat?"

"He done run off," he said smiling.

"Nat would *not* run off! Where *is* he?"

"That boy's not in Chattanooga. You won't find him here. Hasn't been at his forge all day. Run off, I tell ya'."

Marcus whirled around, ran down the side streets to the edge of the city near where the river formed Moccasin Bend. Most of the baggage wagons were gone. Nat too was gone.

"Lookin' for somebody?" a private called from his picket post.

"Lookin' for a teamster, the blacksmith, name of Nat."

"Oh. They all drove out o' here about noon. Took the whole kit 'n caboodle to Stevenson, they tell me. Ammunition and supplies there, I hear. Should be back in a few days, or so I'm told."

"I knew he couldn't run off," he muttered.

"How's that?" said the private.

"I said, that's what I thought. I expect you're right. A few days and they'll all be back."

But the few days was an illusion. For the men had driven their mules and horses in a struggle past Confederate cavalry, along the valley floor, passing the looming mountains, all on a futile journey to retrieve supplies for an army that would not see them again for weeks.

Chapter Twenty-Nine
Chattanooga, Tennessee
October 1863

The army had been routed. Holed up in Chattanooga, their backs pressed to the Tennessee River, facing a Confederate Army in a large half circle before them. They waited. And they grew hungry. With a good defensive perimeter, General Rosecrans expected to defend a direct assault from General Bragg in an attempt to recapture Chattanooga and its strategic railroad hub. But it was not to be. General Bragg had settled on starving the Union out of Chattanooga.

After his inglorious retreat from the fields of Chickamauga, Rosecrans's army was once again reorganized. On orders from Washington, General Ulysses S. Grant was named commander of the new Military Division of the Mississippi, and he immediately assigned General George Thomas, whom the men and the public at large had nicknamed the "Rock of Chickamauga," to replace Rosecrans. It didn't take long for Grant's wording of the telegram to travel through the camp: "Hold Chattanooga at all hazards. I will be there as soon as possible." It was comforting news to the encircled soldiers. But it was Thomas's response that upset the men: "We will hold the town till we starve." Though he helped save hundreds of soldiers from capture at Horseshoe Ridge, the men didn't really care that he now commanded. They only cared for food, the food that grew scarcer by the day, threatening to make good on Thomas's words. There on the high ground sat the Confederate Army, hurling sporadic artillery fire into the perimeter of the city. The men treated them as a harmless annoyance; nevertheless, they were an annoyance. But on the the strip of land at Moccasin Bend, trading artillery rounds was more than an annoyance. And so they faced the imposing rocky wall of Lookout Mountain and its flashing guns, hunkered down for the siege and listened to their stomachs growl.

Ordered to Stevenson, Nat had ridden with some of the black mule drivers and other teamsters toward the safety of the supply depot. There they met up with the remnant army and the many hundred supply wagons waiting to reorganize and relieve the beleaguered men of Chattanooga. For nine long days Nat had anticipated the return, had wanted to leave on his own with the many wagons already loaded. Felt he'd burst if he couldn't leave soon. They had worked painfully slowly, first loading ammunition from the train depot to the store rooms, from the store rooms to the wagons. Desperately needed food was loaded last. And now Nat itched to get on the long road, to see how Marcus had managed in the city. He tied Queenie and Daniel's leads to the back of his wagon, leaving only Queenie saddled. He breathed deeply in anticipation, and surveyed the preparations. The mammoth supply of food and ammunition waited in ten long rows of covered wagons stretched out in a vast field bordering the pike. Drivers busily adjusted harnesses, the wagons poised for the planned move on Chattanooga to break the Confederate siege. It was the evening of October 1, 1863.

Clem, a slight, muscular mule skinner known to the men as a busy-body, an intriguer, cinched up his harnesses, drew deeply on his corncob pipe and studied Nat's wagon.

"Did the captain say you could take them hosses with you, Nat?"

"Didn't have time to ask. 'Sides, they're my horses and I need them just in case these mules falter."

"We got close to a thousand mules. Can't you get two more to replace your'n?" Clem asked.

"Spect so. But then, I'd still be leaving them back here with the other supply wagons, wouldn't I? I went through too much to get them to be leavin' 'em behind. They'll be all right tied here to my wagon. Anyway, I'm keepin' one o' them as a gift for Marcus. He doesn't know it yet."

"I expect he's still holed up in Chattanooga with the rest of the army?"

"Oh, I know he is! That's why they're goin' with me. I 'spect to make a present o' one o' them to him when we get into the city."

"Word is, they be waiting for food and they may just eat those hosses of your'n."

"Over my dead body!"

"It may come to that too, Nat." He laughed at his own joke, a cruel laugh ending with a deep rattling cough. Nat decided not to place his wagon anywhere near Clem's. Several dozen wagons between him and the man would suit him just fine.

Well over 800 wagons extended over two miles, moving north on the mud caked road from Bridgeport, Alabama toward Walden's Ridge, Tennessee to then turn east. It was the only safe route they could take away from the rebel army and still relieve Chattanooga. The sutlers had sandwiched themselves within the amassed wagon train, looking to ply their wares to the men who would be desperate for any utensils and foodstuffs the army couldn't supply. Here they could collect a small fortune for themselves.

Nat saw a familiar face among the drivers. The slender young man who wore the rabbit fur on his hat crown and had been brokering his merchandise at Nashville now had joined the supply train. Marcus had warned him to steer clear of him. What was his name? *Stevens* – the man who had hunted for Marcus. But now the man had pulled his wagon into line directly behind Nat and his two tethered horses.

"Mighty fine animals you got there, muleskinner!" the man called out.

"Thank you," Nat called over his shoulder.

"Yeh. Mighty fine! They ain't army issue is they?"

"No." He kept his eyes fixed on the wagon ahead, trying to ignore him.

"Where'd you get 'm, if I might ask?"

"Around," came the answer.

"Around where, boy?" The question now became more direct, hostile.

"Around a farm," Nat called back.

"The Army know you stole 'em?"

"Didn't steal 'em!"

The voice now changed pitch, a volatile shrill intended to evoke a confrontation. "Ain't yours, are they?"

"They are now," Nat said cheerfully.

"You stole 'em and you need to be reported to proper authorities!" Stevens had worked himself into a near fury.

"Now, I don' know what you're all worked up about. They're my horses, and the Army and my captain says I can keep 'em. They were a present."

Stevens had pulled his wagon so close that his mules were nearly nipping the tails of Nat's trailing horses. "Who'd give you a present of two hosses?" he called.

Nat looked straight ahead. "A friend I met down here."

"You don't have no friends down here! You jes' a darkie muleskinner, and you ain't deservin' of any two hosses!"

Now Nat felt his anger rising, parried away the insult, would not turn around to face Stevens. "You're right there!" he called. "I only deserve one of 'em. The other one is for my friend and I'm takin' it to him in Chattanooga."

"This friend, he got a name?"

"Name o' Marcus!" Nat blurted it out in the heat of exchange and immediately knew he had said too much.

The sutler's behavior changed immediately. A long pause, and then a condescending voice sounded. "He must be quite a friend for you to give him such a fine animal."

"That he is."

"Which one is his, if I might ask?"

Nat had never really given it much thought, said, "He can take his pick o' the two."

"Hope he don't want to eat it."

"We get these vittles through to them and he won't have to."

The sutler grew silent and Nat could feel the eyes in the darkness, questioning, searching, knifing into his back as he hunched over and drove his mules on. How much had Stevens guessed? He had come looking for a Marcus Armstrong, and this clue to his whereabouts Nat had just given away. He decided immediately that he would have to warn Marcus as soon as they broke into Chattanooga. He had less than two days to plan.

They drove on through the night, taking short breaks, resting the animals and the men. In the early morning hours, it occurred to Nat that there was no cavalry escort with the wagon train. They could be a mile up ahead, or maybe they were trailing the wagons as a rear guard. He felt uneasy that they were so exposed with few soldiers to guard them. This would be a great opportunity for the Rebs if they stumbled across them. Another unsettling hour passed. Up ahead, the sound of muskets rattled. Then a general sound of battle began to drift back along the line of wagons. Pistol shots echoed from the front, and the wagons came to a sudden halt. Men began to jump from the wagons, grabbing weapons, the black drivers, hiding under their wagons or running into any tall grasses where they could hide. The shouts and war hoops grew louder, the mules brayed and kicked, and in the distance, riders appeared. Dozens, riding along the train, shooting indiscriminately, swung sabers and hacked at the mules that brayed in pain. They were slaughtering the mules! A mass of Confederate cavalry now was distinctly in view and Nat had a moment to react. He leapt from the wagon, pulled his knife from the sheath on his leg, and sliced at the ropes of his two horses. A rider approached at a full gallop, saber high over his head, chopped at the mules, splitting the nose from one which brayed in terror. He saw Nat, raised his sword again and swung at him. The blade missed Nat's arm and the force buried it deep into the wood of the wagon. The cavalryman pulled hard to dislodge the sword, while reaching for his pistol with the other hand. Nat pulled at the horse's reigns and toppled horse and rider into a heap. He swung quickly with his blade, lopped the screaming rider's hand off at the wrist. The soldier screamed in agony, clutched at the wrist with his remaining hand and Nat buried the knife deep in the man's thigh. His body contorted, his remaining hand slapping wildly at Nat's shoulder and then reaching to squeeze at his throat. In one sudden thrust, Nat found his heart, and he went silent. Other riders approached, shooting soldiers and mules alike, and Nat pulled the cavalry saber from the wagon's wall, slicing the remaining rope. A cavalry officer rode directly at him, fired his pistol. But it wasn't aimed at Nat. It struck the sutler's wagon and sent Stevens scurrying for cover. Another shot fired at the wagon, one mule reeling in the air then collapsing. Nat snatched at the pistol lying beside the dead rider. He fired wildly, and the officer rode at him with his raised saber. He again fired, this time directly into the officer's chest and he spun from the saddle. Nat clutched the reigns, pulled the horse up, leading him to the sutler's wagon. He held out the reigns to Stevens who climbed onto the rebel officer's horse.

He stopped for an instant, looked down at Nat. "Ain't nobody gonna find you by me, boy. I owe you that much," he said, and wheeled the horse around and rode at a gallop toward the rear of the wagon train as drivers and soldiers scattered into the surrounding woods and fields. Nat leapt on Queenie, holding tight to Daniel's rope and turned to the rear of the train. A bullet whizzed past him, hitting the sutler's vacated wagon. Nat rode for the rear and then cut quickly toward an open field at a full gallop. Daniel's eyes were wide in terror, and he galloped alongside Nat and Queenie as lead whined through the air around them. Nat rode on, hunched down, making a smaller target. Finally he could look back but saw no one pursuing. They didn't need him for they were now raiding the wagons.

General Wheeler's cavalry had made the successful assault at Andersons Crossroads and captured the entire train of over 800 wagons, reportedly slaughtering 1,000 mules and then setting fire to the wagons – after they had cleared the supply wagons of ammunition, food and clothing destined for Chattanooga. Then they found the sutlers' wagons. The spoils of war were shared out among the troops in the form of hundreds of bottles of whiskey. While the cavalrymen congratulated themselves with a drunken party, many of the Federal soldiers and muleskinners who had luckily evaded capture distanced themselves quickly and quietly cross country fleeing to Bridgeport. But Nat had one too many close calls and chose to run to a safe place he recalled other slaves had talked of. He wasn't deserting, he told himself, since he wasn't technically a Union soldier yet anyway. Fine line perhaps, but a line that he decided he was willing to straddle. He had two horses with him that no white man on the planet would believe were his. But Marcus did. And so he wavered between the two routes he knew were right, at least for him. A large cave near Bridgeport would offer him shelter, if he could recollect which path the slaves had talked about. By late afternoon he saw the familiar landscape, the stream that led to an opening in the side of the hill. He tied the horses in the protected cover of the tree line and quietly made his way along the stream toward the opening. Hearing voices from inside, Nat pulled the blade from the sheath and silently tiptoed to the entrance.

"Yo' bes' be droppin' dat blade afo' yo' gets opened wide up!"

The voice from behind wasn't angry, but menacing all the same. He bent over cautiously, stretching to lay the blade, and at the same time pivoted slowly to face his enemy. A burly black man with a thick black curly beard and balding forehead stood poised with one arm stretched out, all fingers pointing stiffly toward him, and the other lofting a pike pole near his ear, the sharpened point also aimed directly at Nat's forehead.

"Uh, uh, uh!" The man warned. With his free hand he indicated the ground, to which Nat obediently released his weapon. It clattered on the rock echoing into the cave, silencing the voices inside.

"I mean you no harm. I hope you'll afford me the same courtesy," Nat said.

"Talkin' like de white man. Yo' ain' from 'round dese parts, er yeh?"

"Yes, I am. Or was. Name's Nat. I worked for years on the Ashbie place over toward Huntsville."

"Yo' dat blacksmiff what was up an' sol'?"

"I'm the one," he said and extended his hand.

The man lowered his spear and called toward the cave, "Hey, Maggie!"

Maggie stepped out of the shadows, walked through the stream that flowed from the cave, and gazed into the fading light. Her eyes brightened and she flashed a bright welcoming smile. Then the tears flowed.

"Maggie! I can't believe it! You! Here! When did y'all git to this place? Where have ya' been?" Nat gushed.

"Nat Ashbie!" she cried. "As I live and breathe! W'achoo doin' here? And in a so'jer's suit too? Will ya' jes' look at him, Everett?" She said, wiping her eyes with her apron. "Dis boy was jes' a young'un when I's sol' off. He was sweet on me! Now, don' ya' go fibbin' dere Nat. I knowed ya' was."

"Wasn't that long ago, Maggie. I wasn't such a young 'un."

Nat told his story as they sat with half a dozen others at the cave entrance sharing their meager food. Maggie marveled on his adventures, marveled at Marcus, his white Abolitionist guardian teaching him to read, how he had almost made it to Canada and how he and Marcus came back to Alabama. Was any treasure worth the risk? Nat assured her it was. He worked as a blacksmith, drove a supply wagon for the Union army but got separated during the cavalry raid and came here so he wouldn't be killed, since many black prisoners could meet that fate. Then he told of Emma, his plan to get to Ohio where she stayed now with Marcus's sister, and then he'd marry her. Maggie watched his face light up as he spoke her name. When she had worked as a laundress, she had gotten to know Emma only for a brief week or two before Ashbie sold her to the speculators, was surprised that Emma too had been sold off. She allowed that Emma was a fine young woman and prayed the best for Nat and her.

For her part, Maggie had finally settled near LaFayette, Georgia, on a small farm having only three house slaves. There she met Everett and the two of them were married by a local preacher who passed through every other week. They had never once considered running off. When the

Emancipation Proclamation was read to the local slaves, the master had freed them both.

"'Y' all jes' as free as me,' he say. We 'uns had no quarrel wif de massa and missus. So we stayed on de farm to work for massa, and he gave us our cabins, vittles and some moneys. But when Masssa James Benton be forced to join de Georgia volunteers, de missus say she cain't promise to protect us'ns. She say we has to go and to take two mules wif us'ns and run to de Yankee army."

Near Bridgeport, the home guard stole their mules and sent them running. They went into hiding, had stayed with several freed slaves before deciding on journeying to Huntsville, occupied now by the Federals. When the Union army had been defeated at Chickamauga the previous week, they settled into this cave area with other freed slaves who came and went in the past few days.

"Will you go on to Huntsville now?" Nat asked.

"S'pose we might jes' do dat."

"I might just come with you."

Maggie started. "Comin' wif us? Mean yo' be leavin' dem so'jers? Leavin' dat white frien' o' y'all?"

"Can't help them much now."

"Whachoo mean yo' cain't he'p dem now?"

Nat heard the accusing tone of Maggie's voice, became defensive. "Why do *you* need to know?" he asked.

"It seem to me, Nat, dat yo' be runnin' out on de men what he'ped you de mos'. Dat white boy, Marcus, he'ped you survive and gets yo' in de Army to hide, and have to hide hisself 'cause of yo' action. And yo' say dey all need vittles to eat and powder for dey guns. Yo' say dat dey depend on yo' wagons. 'N now dat dey take yo' wagon and set it afire, you gwan take yo'self and dem two hosses and skedaddle? Is dat wha' I jes' heered from yo' lips, Nat?"

Nat stood speechless, kicked at a rock, sent it swirling into the stream, a spray of water spreading along the bank. He picked up the dropped gladius, slipped it into the sheath strapped on his leg.

"You wouldn't understand, Maggie."

"Oh, I unda'stan' well 'nough. Yo' wants to get dat treasure and dose two fine hosses of Massa Ashbie's and get safe to Emma up Nort' and drop yo' frien' jes' 'cause dem Rebel so'jers chase you a bit! Am dat de Nat Ashbie I wanted so much dem years ago?"

Nat looked up and glared, "I ain't no Nat Ashbie, Maggie. I'm just plain Nat."

"No, yo' ain't. Yo' actin' like yo' still belong Massa Ashbie." Her voice trembled, the passionate words were insistent. "When yo' gwan *act* free? When yo' gwan he'p dat white boy what he'ped yo'? Seems to me he done give yo' a chance to live. Yo' gwan return dat kindness?"

Nat looked about. They stared at him, all of them expectant, Everett, Maggie, the five other strangers, now free but still on the run like himself.

"He can take care of himself," Nat answered.

"Mebbe he need yo' to take keer o' him more'n yo' even knows."

Nat thought on Marcus, thought on the times he helped him through the sicknesses at Camp Buckingham, thought on Marcus' despair when the sutler showed up in Nashville, the one who was still out there somewhere, still looking for him and for Marcus. He kicked another rock into the stream. Silence followed, broken only by the gurgling stream, crickets beginning to warm up for their nightly serenade. No one spoke. The decision hung in the air with the night's hush. His words silently returned to him. *And I'll always care for you, Marcus.*

Everett finally spoke softly. "Yo' know what needs doin', Nat."

Nat stared at the stream, thought on his choices.

One of the other men stood up. "Anyways, yo' ain't comin' wif us, boy. Yo' wearin' a uniform. Dat gwan 'trac too much attention, like bringin' flies on a carcass."

Maggie looked at the man, smiled. "No. He not comin'. He know what he need do." The silence was deafening. Finally she clutched him on the shoulders, kissed his cheek, pointed. "Chattanooga be dat way."

Nat walked to the horses, untethered them, climbed on Queenie's back, holding Daniel's rope.

"Emma be proud o' you, Nat."

"That way?" he pointed.

"Dat way, Nat," she nodded.

+ + + + +

Nat had ridden for three days, trading from Queenie's back to Daniel's, resting each of his horses in turn, followed off-road paths quietly through the forested areas, riding at a gallop when the cover opened to farmland. He traveled in the shadow of Raccoon Mountain, passing Anderson's Crossroads, the burned out shells of 800 blackened wagons, the maggot infested rotting carcasses of executed mules. The cavalry was still out there somewhere, but he saw no living soldiers or horses. His two horses grazed on grasses whenever he could give them a long break. But he hadn't eaten in three days, and lived on the water he could get from the streams he passed. Nat felt the effects, the dizziness that came and went, the gnawing in the pit of his stomach. Finally passing a cornfield that had been untouched, he feasted on what he could hold without saddlebags, nearly sickening himself from overeating. Plenty here for the federals if they had troops enough to come out and get it and still defend against Rebel cavalry.

The long way around to the north of Chattanooga had been left open, as if to encourage the federals to ride back into the trap of starvation set for them in Chattanooga. One bridge remained, and Nat saw it was heavily guarded by Union pickets. Best ride around to make a direct frontal assault on the defenses. Better chance of being let in there. He didn't want to surprise anyone with a slippery trigger in the dark, so no time to waste. He dismounted, led both horses along the banks of the Tennessee, keeping low near the water. The picket lines had thrown up crude fence-rail defenses and he approached the line. An older sergeant saw him, called him to a halt.

"It's just me, Sergeant. It's Nat. You know – the blacksmith."

"Don't know you 't all, boy. But I do know them hosses you got with ya'."

"Oh, yessir. This is Queenie and Dan'l. Glad you know 'em. Where's the 65th? I'm lookin' for Marcus Armstrong."

"Scattered about in here, I imagine. But since I don't know you, reckon you just have to wait til I get authority to let you in."

"You might want to hurry up. Them Rebs up on the mountain have been eyeballin' me all the way along here, and they may wanna' send a cannonball over here just for spite." He pointed up to batteries along the ridge of Lookout Mountain, continued, "Reckon we might have to send it back to 'em then. Or maybe he will," and he pointed to a familiar face in the battery of the 6th Ohio. "Ain't that so, Adam?"

"Nat!" he yelled. "Where've you been and what happened to the wagons?"

Armed with the intelligence of the supply train destruction, Nat told the entire story of its demise. The sergeant of the guard immediately took him to Colonel Harker where he told him of Wheeler's cavalry raid and that no supplies got through. The report finished, Adam accompanied Nat to Marcus, working at a large house being used as a hospital. Marcus listened in awe of Nat's escape from the cavalry, of finding his long-lost Maggie, and his subsequent return to be encircled with the rest in Chattanooga.

"Nat! You were free and clear. Why you back here? You'll be starving along with us in this hell hole!"

"Aw, Marcus, you know even Hell needs a good blacksmith. Besides, you haven't taught me enough writing yet."

Marcus shook his head, couldn't help but laugh at him. "That's really stupid of you, you know that?"

"Den we best be gittin' to studyin' afo' de war am over an' I still be stupid."

Chapter Thirty
Missionary Ridge, Chattanooga, Tennessee

The month of October had dragged on, and the wretchedness and squalor of the living conditions took its toll. The 65th had reinforced the defenses of their assigned portion of the city. They used wood from any fence, and shed or small barn to create walls inside the perimeter. The walls might not stop a Minié ball and definitely not an artillery shell, but they would allow the daily business of walking the city streets to continue, out of eyesight and thus out of the temptation of a Reb sharpshooter to try his luck.

Occasional shells were lobbed in the vicinity of the front lines, the federal troops answering with their own artillery, all doing little more than annoying each other. Ammunition dwindled slowly, food much quicker. Men searched everywhere for any stores that the citizens had spirited away. They began to forage among the horses' food, taking any bits of parched corn that dropped into the dirt to wash off and use in any form. Then the mules began to die off, the horses too. The army was ordered onto half rations, soon to half of that. A depressing gloom hung over the city like a gray pall. Some of the wounded from Chickamauga had been sent out on wagons and ambulances to Bridgeport, dodging the prying Rebel cavalry. Marcus had helped the wounded George Washington Harlan from Columbiana County into a federal ambulance. He had been wounded in the forearm near the Dyer Field at Chickamauga and had been given a furlough to go home to Ohio and recover.

"When you get back to Ohio, let father know I am well. He will let my sister know. Give my regards to Tump Haines if you see him."

"I will. And take care of yourself, Marcus. I'll see you when I return."

The wagon train left, taking the circuitous sixty-mile route around Moccasin Bend and back toward Bridgeport and Stevenson. Men could get out, through a treacherous journey, but at least the wounded that could evacuate wouldn't face the hunger of the city. Daily Marcus transported men who had starved to death to the growing graveyard.

"It isn't how I expected it to be here, Nat." he said, loading the body into his ambulance. "They don't even have the wood for a coffin for these men. These blankets are his final shroud."

"How did you 'spect it to go, Marcus?"

"I want to save these men, these young boys too, and I can't."

"I guess we can't save 'em all, Marcus, but we can save some of 'em. And anyway, isn't that the best we can do?"

"Not for me. I need to do more!"

"Why?"

"To do something worthwhile."

"No one will know, Marcus."

"I will know."

"You're doing something for me, Marcus. I don't know where I would've gone, what I would've done without your teaching me. Thanks to you, I can read. Thanks to you, I don't sound much like one o' them ol' field hands. Thanks to you – and to your sister, Emma is safe and we can have a new life – when this is all over. You can have one too. No need for an Underground Railroad now that we are all set free. That job is done. But," he said, indicating the groups of blacks huddled around their tents and campfires, "all of these freemen here will need help settling after the war. They will all need teaching. Maybe your teaching, Marcus."

"I thought you didn't like my teaching. Didn't like my – what was it you said once? Trying to make you 'white'?"

"They will never be white. But at least when the war is over they can survive in a white world with the right teaching. That's something you is – are – good at. It's true that I have changed myself. But it was you who showed me how."

"When the war is over – " Marcus repeated absently, his voice trailing off.

"What?"

"Here. I have something for us to read." And he dug through some papers in a wooden box by his ambulance.

"Will there be big words? I will need help."

Marcus continued to sort through the papers, selecting one well-worn sheet. "Let's start with this."

And the coughing and moaning from inside the hospital faded away as Nat and Marcus were absorbed by the lesson, Marcus reading in duet with Nat.

+ + + + +

November 23, 1863

Weeks passed, the army barely subsisting on the meager rations, until U.S. Grant broke through the Confederate blockade and established what the news reported as "the cracker line," a supply line that first brought in the crackers – the hardtack biscuits – to snatch the Army from the jaws of certain death. Colonel Brown of the 64th Ohio Volunteers from Camp Buckingham led the supply wagons in to loud cheers from the men. Food had finally arrived, and with it, the much anticipated armies of the Mississippi under General Joseph Hooker and William T. Sherman. It didn't take long for a plan to formulate for breaking out of the stalemate. On October 27, General Thomas launched a surprise attack at Brown's Ferry, driving the Confederate Army away from the river and opening up the entire western bank for the supplies to enter.

The following night, Marcus and Nat sat near the 6th Ohio artillery batteries with Adam and listened to the distant echoes of battle as the federal troops repulsed the rebels to the west near Wauhatchie. The battle for Chattanooga finally would move forward, and Grant's plan for exploiting the inferior Confederate numbers began immediately. The men daily had faced the artillery from the towering Lookout Mountain to their front and from the guns of Missionary Ridge and Orchard Knob to their left. Those two imposing defenses were soon targeted for attack.

Marcus's duties kept him busy with burial details and assisting the doctors in caring for the sick and wounded. Nat worked his blacksmith trade, shoed the horses that had looked more like skeletal phantoms with each passing week. Several of the freed slaves who flocked into Chattanooga had set up their own village within the city, isolating themselves from the prejudice that still pervaded everyday living. Many wanted to join up with the soldiers to help in the fight. But Nat was ashamed to see some who when given the chance to finally shoulder a musket shied away from the duty.

A roar of cannon from Lookout Mountain erupted again. Another annoyance. Nat saw the explosions land on the shore near Moccasin Bend. The fire and smoke carried into the air wood fragments and burning cloth, waving like a fiery flag of surrender. There would be casualties. He ran through the mud of a side street, passing shuttered shop windows to the hospital, met Marcus pulling up on his suspenders, buttoning his shirt. They sprinted toward the picket lines.

"That's Adam's battery over there!" he cried.

Nat ran aside him, sloshing in the muddy wagon tracks, slipping, catching each other, a dead even race for the scene. Adam stood leaning on the sponge ramrod, dazed.

"Adam!" Marcus screamed.

"Marcus. It was the damnedest shot I ever saw! Off the mountain up yonder," he said nodding toward rocky face of Lookout Mountain.

"But you're OK?" Nat said.

"I felt much better before this, but at least my gun is still good," he said, indicating his Parrott rifle.

They didn't need to look far, the flaming wreckage of a suttler's wagon crackled as the men tried to douse it with water from the river. Two soldiers and a civilian lay twisted to the side. A bloody felt hat with a torn rabbit fur lay close by. Marcus and Nat bent over the figure, his skin half torn from his face his side teeth exposed from a stripped upper lip. He looked weakly at the two.

"Thet you didn't ex'ect t' see thee," he mumbled.

Nat looked down at the pathetic scene. "Thought you got away on that horse."

He gagged, a stream of blood flowing from his mouth. "I did. Shoulda' ke't ridin'. Sorry I didn'." He looked at Marcus. "You Ar'strong?" he choked.

Marcus nodded.

"He a good voy, for a nig...." His eyes fixed on Marcus and his face went limp.

+ + + + +

November 24, 1863

The army stirred awake with a pungent coffee aroma breezing through the rows of tents. Since the supply line had finally opened, and the food had first arrived, the soldiers' main staple of precious coffee had fulfilled its duty to lift their spirits, and their patriotism. It was a wonder to witness how the troops' outlooks changed with just a cup of morning

272

boldness. They could lick the entire Reb army with just two more cups of morning fortification. This morning had a feel to it. Marcus couldn't put a finger on it, but he sensed it when he awoke to the aroma rushing between the rows like an unstoppable wave. It was the first day since he had retreated to the banks of the Tennessee within the confines of the Army's fortification that he felt expectant of great achievements. Whether it was the quickened sense of smell or a sixth sense of something else in the air that stirred him, he felt positive that soon he might get his chance to show his gallantry. The entire army was astir now and the men went about their duties: brushing their uniforms, cleaning boots, wiping down the morning dew from their muskets – all this while fortifying their anxieties with cups of black liquid courage. It was a grand show, and Marcus noted how the officers were unusually demanding about their soldiers' appearance. A demonstration of their might now began to form. No one knew the truth, but the rumors immediately hopped from man to man faster than bedbugs.

"I heered Bragg retreated an' we're gonna chase after him!" A thorough scrutiny of the enemy positions on Missionary Ridge shot down that theory before it could sprout wings.

"Naw, you don't know what you're talkin' about. Bragg's gonna attack us, and we're gonna give 'em hell all the way along the Tennessee!" Once again, a careful study of the enemy fortifications blew that rumor into tiny fragments.

"But we drove 'em off that Orchard Knob up there. Why wouldn't they jes' pack up an' skedaddle?"

"Mebbe they aren't as smart as we thought."

"Hey Marcus, can you find out the truth for us? What's the captain say over with the 6th battery?"

"Adam's been packed up for a while. I expect we will know soon enough anyway."

Marcus buttoned his uniform, tried to look passable for standing inspection. He walked toward where Lieutenant Joseph Sonnanstine and Corporal Thomas Johnston were engaged in animated conversation, interrupted, "Sir, begging your pardon, but are we going to take the fight to them today?"

"Indeed we are, Private," was the gleeful reply. "Hear those guns? The fight has begun. Look your best. We want to put on a good show for them."

"But I drive an ambulance, sir," Marcus said.

"Then look your best in your ambulance. We will need you today."

Marcus searched for Nat and his blacksmith wagon near the center of the town. He jogged past the walls of boards that formed the interior perimeter to screen movements from rebel sharpshooters. Here men moved freely for the past two months in relative security, protected from prying eyes. Toward the back of the town, nestled up against the Tennessee River the supply wagons sat empty. The teamsters were no longer needed to drive them. Many of the escaped and newly emancipated slaves who, like Nat, had joined to help the cause were now permitted to shoulder a musket and join the fight. At first, all who entered the camp had voiced their willingness to "kill Rebs," but now that the official permission came from President Lincoln, most of them appeared content to remain in the rear as cooks, orderlies, and mule drivers. Clearly the wagons were going nowhere. Marcus found Nat awake by his blacksmith's forge, no fire kindled, but he sat sharpening the edge of his knife blade with a file.

"Going hunting, Nat?"

"Mornin', Marcus. I just might."

"I believe we are all out of rats. Pickings are mighty slim."

He gestured with the long blade toward the low ridge in the distance. "Oh, there are plenty of rats to go around."

"Nat, you don't mean to say you're joining the fight out there!"

"I mean exac'ly that. If I don't join with these soldiers, then I'm no better 'n these no 'counts that slipped into the city for the victuals. I have to fight, Marcus."

"You don't have a rifle! And you can't believe you're going to attack the Rebs with that homemade blade of yours now, do you?"

"I'll have me a rifle soon. This is just for when I get close enough to give 'em a hug."

Marcus shook his head, trying to understand. Nat was willing to jump into the battle as an untrained soldier. "Nat, you haven't fired the rifle more than a couple of times. You've never stood in line of battle. You don't know how to advance on them!"

"I'll learn."

"Learning on the line is no way to learn!"

"Marcus, none of these soldiers had fired a shot at an enemy until their first battle. Oh, they all stood together and trained. I watched them. Lordy, how I watched them! Time and again I stood at my forge a safe distance away from the fighting, and I listened and watched them train. And I itched for it to be my turn! Now, it's my turn."

"What about Emma?"

"What about her?"

"Nat! Think! Of all you've gone through, of all you've worked for, of all I've gone through to get you schooled – all of this will come to nothing, if you get yourself killed out there," he said, gesturing to the distant ridge.

The report of cannon exploded in the distance far off to their right. Then another exploded, and another. The sound of battle echoed across the city and soldiers scrambled to the

275

front lines preparing to attack. Marcus and Nat rushed to the breastworks that ringed the city, watched the cannon trade fire from Mission Ridge to the valley that led to Tunnel Hill.

"It's Sherman's boys!" One captain yelled to the men gathering. "They're attacking Bragg's right flank!"

"Without us?" a young private said, clutching his rifle in one hand, his ramrod in the other.

"Without us, it looks like," said a glum freckle-faced, red-haired boy, leaning on his musket. About fifteen, Marcus judged. Too young to be ready to die, he thought.

"Just be glad you're not in that mix-up out there," he said.

"Why?"

"Because I don't want to come out with a litter and pick up the likes of you! Understand?" Nat heard the anger in Marcus' voice, studied him. He had rarely seen him so agitated.

"I thought you lived to do that duty, Marcus. He's just one more for you to save on the battlefield."

Marcus' face flashed in a rage, turned on Nat, "Not him! Understand?" He pointed emphatically almost in the youth's face. "Not him!"

The cannonading continued its deafening roar, and the men cheered in seeing the smoke from federal troops assaulting Tunnel Hill. It was a grand show, the men remarked. The unit flags advanced slowly toward the Confederate positions. Then they were lost from sight by the hills, the gray-blue musket smoke, the charcoal gray clouds from the cannons. Then they appeared again, only to disappear again. The situation gradually became uncertain to the men and the cheering and huzzahs began to fade away. The firing from the summit intensified. The men formed in columns, the drums beating, regimental bands blaring brass bravery into the air, and they moved out and into the valley of death before the rifle pits where entrenched Confederates waited to rain down .58 caliber death. Far down the valley, the battle had begun with General Hooker's divisions attacking the Confederate left flank. But the center lay untouched, waiting for General Wood and General Sheridan's divisions to move into line of battle. The men had stepped out smartly from the defenses of Chattanooga, moving south along the Rossville Road and spreading into line of battle. The artillery rounds fell among them, and Marcus noted where clouds of smoke and patches of earth were tossed into the air, some bearing the bodies of boys in blue, some ominous harbingers of the day's wages. And yet they moved on.

Marcus pulled his ambulance far behind the line of troops, waited with half a dozen others for the carnage that would soon need them. From behind him, the Union artillery opened a deafening roar. The pall of smoke now began to settle on the valley and the orange-white flashes from Missionary Ridge answered, the argument to end only when the enemy guns could be silenced. The small squad of blue uniforms bearing the flag of the 65th Regiment now wheeled left. Nat had fallen in line with Company F and walked with the red-haired young boy in the third rank as its four ranks turned for the assault. Marcus began to shake uncontrollably. With a collective shout, the army rushed toward the defenders' rifle pits. Explosions tossed men and limbs like cord-wood among the debris of clods of earth and splinters of wood fencing, and bark-stripped trees. Marcus saw puffs of smoke from cannon and rifle fire all along the center of the Confederate positions. Then the firing dwindled as the rebel sharpshooters began to draw back, some dropping their muskets, others shouldering them and fleeing back toward the safety of the ridge. The Federal soldiers cheered and rushed on. A ghastly white flash landed in F Company's ranks, and Marcus lost sight of Nat. Instinctively he jumped from the

277

ambulance, rushed to the back and grabbed the handles of the litter.

"Armstrong!" one orderly yelled. "Where in hell do you think you're going?"

"To my duty!" he called.

"Not yet. We'll have time enough when they get up that ridge!"

"My friend has fallen!" he yelled, tucking the folded litter across his chest and rushing toward the battle.

The orderly slammed the reins of his horse aside and jumped from his ambulance. "Damn, Armstrong!" He grabbed his litter, folded it and began to jog after him. Marcus reached a group of wounded soldiers, scanned over them for recognition, and then rushed past them toward where Nat had disappeared. In a small depression in the ground Nat sat rubbing his head, ruffling the dirt from his hair.

"You gave me a fright!" he said, half smiling.

"Me too," Nat said, and looked at the freckle-faced youth lying beside him, a gash in his thigh.

"Be still," he said. "We'll help you."

The boy nodded and clutched Nat's sleeve.

Marcus unfolded the litter, locked the cross braces and lay it beside the youth. Together they half rolled him onto the litter. Marcus stripped off the soldier's belt and quickly made a tourniquet on his thigh.

"Now! Lift!" Marcus shouted, and with Nat at the feet, Marcus at the head, they lifted the soldier and litter to begin the long rush back across the battlefield to the waiting ambulances.

Then a deafening explosion sounded. Nat felt the litter drop behind him and in that instant he was hurled face-first into the earth. His ears rang and all other sound blocked out. And in that moment of utter silence Nat raised himself to his hands and knees, struggling to inhale. He collapsed to the ground again, punching the breath from his lungs once more. He coughed heavily and spat out the dust from his mouth, and his senses returned. The musket fire, the cannon roaring, the distant screams of men in victory and in agony crescendoed to bathe the valley in noise. Then the realization struck him like a bullet. He turned to see Marcus on his back, his legs bent up under his back in a contorted posture. A wound at the side of his neck gushed blood on the ground, a shard of metal protruding from it. Nat screamed in horror, grasped at the shard and pulled it from the wound, blood flowing freely. Marcus felt nothing. The youth on the stretcher lay moaning, grasping the tourniquet on his thigh. Two boots appeared beside Marcus's head, and Nat looked up at the orderly, tearfully clutching his litter.

"Help me?" Nat asked in a painful cry.

Together they lifted the youth and carried him back to the ambulance, sliding him onto the back. Nat turned back to the battlefield. "I need you to help me get these others," the orderly called.

"Not just yet," Nat yelled angrily. He jogged to Marcus's body, clutched him under the arms and hefted him up like a field-hand's cotton-filled bag, then in one motion muscled him onto his shoulder, clutching at the knees. He stumbled under the load and the littered field, tripping on discarded canteens, haversacks, muskets, cartridge boxes, clumps of rock and soil, placed Marcus gently on his back in the ambulance and lay beside him, exhausted, stroking his hair and weeping. The orderly reluctantly turned horse and wagon, drove on, leaving behind the cheers of victory, the cacophony of battle, the long line of blue charging up the face of Missionary Ridge to drive Braxton Bragg's army finally and for all time from the field.

Chapter Thirty-One
Near Bridgeport, Alabama

Nat solemnly finished readying the wagon, had finished harnessing the horse which soldiers noted he had strangely taken to calling "Dan'l." He swept the wagon clean, picked out a spider he found hiding beneath a loosened board. He had thought about merely pressing his heel on it, decided to toss it into the grass. He wanted his wagon clean. Adam blinked away the mist from his eyes, joined Surgeon Todd, and stood at the side of the open coffin.

"We're ready," Nat said quietly.

"Are you sure you don't want anyone else? I can arrange furloughs for anyone else you name," said Kyle.

"Thank you, but Adam and I will be all right as we are."

The private lifted a wooden lid from the stack, just one more of the hundreds he had already moved. He carried it indifferently to the coffin and dropped it on the side walls, positioned it and picked his hammer and a handful of nails from his haversack.

"Just a moment," Nat said. "Help me."

Adam took one side and they reverently lifted the cover, placed it on the ground. Nat reached in his haversack, drew out a worn, often rolled and unrolled length of yellow ribbon. Surgeon Todd looked at Adam for meaning. Adam merely shrugged his shoulders. The three watched as Nat reached in, placed Marcus' hands over each other, stared for a moment at the quiet, peaceful face, the neck wound covered by his buttoned up uniform. He bent over and placed the end of the ribbon in Marcus's wet grasp then draped the rest over the clasped hands. He laid his hand on Marcus's heart, whispered inaudibly to the right ear, and softly patted the chest of his coat. He rose to his feet, his cheeks wet, his eyes reddened and nodded his head to the private.

"Now," he said.

Adam and Nat rested the lid on the coffin, squared the edges to an even fit, holding it firmly in place. The private struck the first nail, and Nat instinctively shuddered. The hammering continued around the edge until the lid was secure. The four men lifted the coffin, slid it onto the wagon, the horse reflexively lurching forward.

Nat spoke gently. "Easy, there Dan'l."

Lt. Anderson stepped toward the men, holding rolled documents. "Here are your furlough papers men. The train will leave for Nashville in less than one hour. When your business is finished in Ohio, report to the commanding officer, Camp Buckingham and he will have your orders to rejoin the regiment. Godspeed."

Adam and Nat stood at attention, saluted the lieutenant, climbed onto the wagon. Nat grasped the reins, shook them lightly, "Git up there, Dan'l." The horse and wagon lurched forward.

Lt. Anderson looked at Surgeon Todd. "Dan'l?"

"I dunno. He says he knows the horse will answer to Dan'l."

"But why Dan'l?"

Kyle shook his head vaguely. "The teamsters all say just trust him when he works with the horses."

Daniel plodded deliberately down the road from the Battery Hill fortifications as if he too was absorbed in this solemn occasion. Lost in his thoughts, Nat held the reins loosely, guiding him on past the stacks of arms, the crates of supplies now awaiting the ferries from the Tennessee River landing.

Adam's voice stirred him. "Any chance of returning to that farm and giving it a more thorough search?"

"Oh, there's more than a chance, I suppose. But I have this duty first."

"I mean after...."

"I know what you mean, Adam. When I get this boy back to his family, then I'll see about getting back on that farm. I expect the regiment – or another – will be camped all around this area, so it won't be hard to take a small trip of visitation."

"Settling scores, eh?"

"No. I'm done with that. Just need to get what's mine."

"For that girl of yours?"

"For both of us. Marcus's sister says she is still safe in Columbus and won't need any more hiding. She is working as their paid house servant so she is above suspicion. But I need the silver and gold to start up again."

"Marcus said you want to go back to live in Alabama. "

"Did."

"Not now?"

"No point in it now. I reckon to make my home In Columbus, start up my trade there after the war."

Adam looked at him, a sly smirk, "And marry that girl of yours?"

Nat smiled sheepishly, "If she still wants me."

"That will be a great day when we finally have peace. We can get home, wed, start families."

The smile faded. "Yeh, only 'ceptin' this boy."

"Except this boy," Adam echoed.

Nat reached into his haversack, drew out a book, and from it a folded sheet of paper. He stared at it, squinted trying to focus on the words as the wagon bumped on the road, read it aloud:

But when the birds of morning sing,
And all the wars are over,
Our laurels at your feet we'll fling,
And then we'll play the lover.
We all will say 'tis time to wed,
As gayly drums shall rattle,

Before our conquering column's head,
When marching home from battle.
Adam spoke softly, "Amen."

"Marcus had this with him. Taught me to read it when we were holed up in Chattanooga."

"He write it?"

"He said General Lytle did."

"Good words, Nat."

"Marcus thought so too."

Adam was quiet, thoughtful as they drove on. He brushed away a tear. "He always wanted to achieve great things, Nat. As long as I knew him, he wanted to do great things."

"He did, Adam. He saved me."

The wagon meandered on toward the depot. Everywhere soldiers gathered: the wounded, the unblemished, the fallen waiting in sealed coffins for their final journey to their Northern interment. The vanquished gathered too. Under guard they lay or sat about, dejected and exhausted, their spirited bravado displayed after Shiloh now drowned by the blue tide that had flooded over them at Missionary Ridge. It was a different kind of battle. Shiloh had been a stalemate, the ground abandoned only after prudence dictated their tactical withdrawal. This time they were whipped. The federals had overwhelmed all resistance and drove them into a full retreat toward Atlanta. The war for them was ended, paroles would not be forthcoming. Their internment in Yankee prisons awaited and they had gathered gloomily about the railroad station in a hastily assembled stockade of fence posts, fence rails, and armed guards.

Adam and Nat drove by, looking over the weary Rebel soldiers. Few of them bothered to look up to acknowledge them. But one soldier stood, advanced in quick strides to the fence rail as if to leap it, barred by the point of a guard's bayonet aimed at his chest. He looked deep into Nat's eyes in recognition. Jonah Kenton, Nat thought and nearly spoke the name aloud. What a consolation to know that the man with the whip at last could punish no one else. He couldn't hide the look of joy.

"What you starin' at, Boy?" the Rebel called out, stirring others to gather at the fence.

"Starin' at the likes of you!" Adam shouted back.

"Not you," Kenton yelled. "I mean that black sonofabitch drivin' that horse!"

"Hey! He's a Union soldier and you can – "

"Adam," Nat interrupted, pulling him back by the sleeve. "I can handle this." Nat stood up, dropped the reins across Adam's legs, drew out his gladius from the sheath on his back, vaulted down from the wagon seat. He glared at Kenton, now surrounded by a half dozen more Confederate soldiers.

"I know you! You're that runaway. You're from John Ashbie's farm over by Huntsville. Yeh, you're John Ashbie's boy!" he sneered. "You're Nat Ashbie! Hey, boys! That's Nat Ashbie! Wearin' a Billy Yank uniform, no less!"

Nat walked menacingly toward the men, his fist tightening its grip on the knife alongside his right leg. Two federal guards extended their muskets to cross bayonets in front of Kenton and the other captives, blocking Nat from advancing further into them. Nat stopped, his neck muscles straining, every muscle tensing. A hush fell over the group, a storm cloud about to burst. But Nat's face became placid, composed, the anger fading. He calmly returned the deep searching stare back into Jonah Kenton's eyes, still gripped the knife. He considered the face, the smirk that he most surely wore as he whipped Samuel nearly to death. His fingers fidgeted with the handle, repeatedly squeezing his grip. He thought of the times Jonah Kenton had flogged men and women and children on the surrounding farms, the fear he had instilled in every slave in the district. But while his heart raced as he studied him, on the face of his enemy suddenly flashed the image of Marcus, the first white boy who had completely earned his trust, the white boy who had taught him how to be free, the white boy he was now charged with carrying home. He saw Marcus' sensitive face smiling at him on this face of hatred, and a peaceful calm spread over him. His hand relaxed. He quietly slid the gladius back in the sheath slung across his back. Kenton and the others sneered in smug satisfaction. Nat folded his arms across his chest, raised up his tall frame and looked over all of the prisoners, fixed his stare on Kenton.

"I have no idea who you are talking about, Johnny Reb," he said. "I don't know any John Ashbie, I don't know any Huntsville, and I surely don't know any Nat Ashbie. I hail from Columbus, Ohio, Johnny Reb. The name is Nathaniel Armstrong." And he turned about and walked purposefully to the wagon, climbed up, gave the reins a shake and called, "Git up there, Dan'l."

Adam clapped him on the back and broke into a wide tearful grin which Nathaniel mirrored. The wagon rolled past the stockade, leaving the fading taunts of the rebels behind. The men pulled up to the station platform where a detail of soldiers worked, loading dozens of coffins into a freight car. The engine's pistons hissed a loud spray of steam, the conical smokestack belched out a large volume of black smoke.

"C'mon, Nathaniel," Adam called as this final coffin was loaded onto the freight car.

Nat turned to a black soldier, a stable hand by his looks, handed him the reins. "His name is Dan'l," he said softly. "Take good care of him." He patted Daniel on the neck, stroked his face, then climbed onto a box and into the freight car.

"Hurry up, Nathaniel," Adam called again.

"You go on ahead and get your seat, Adam. I think I want to ride with him for a bit."

Adam took a last look at the curious spectacle of Nathaniel, his head bowed, his arms spread across the coffin, kneeling before it in the open freight car. Adam climbed onto the next passenger car's steps, held the handrails, leaned out for a better view. And from the trailing car the sound of a solo voice singing a hymn soon died away, muffled beneath the engine's bellowing, the mighty shush-shush-shushing of the pistons, the creaking of each car and the metallic cra-a-ack of each car's coupler jerking into motion. The train pulled from the station. Gathered speed. The treasured cargo, rolling through the Alabama valleys. And a long iron ribbon pointed the way toward Nashville and home.